GPLG

W9-DJQ-376

JUN - - 2018

BURIED SECRETS

This Large Print Book carries the
Seal of Approval of N.A.V.H.

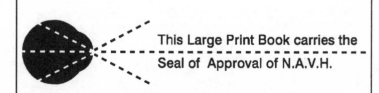

This Large Print Book carries the
Seal of Approval of N.A.V.H.

BURIED SECRETS

BARBARA CAMERON

THORNDIKE PRESS
A part of Gale, a Cengage Company

Farmington Hills, Mich • San Francisco • New York • Waterville, Maine
Meriden, Conn • Mason, Ohio • Chicago

GALE
A Cengage Company

Copyright © 2018 by Barbara Cameron.
Scripture quotations are from the King James Version of the Bible.
Thorndike Press, a part of Gale, a Cengage Company.

ALL RIGHTS RESERVED
This is a work of fiction. Names, characters, places, and incidents are products of the author's imagination or are used fictitiously. Any similarity to actual people, organizations, and/or events is purely coincidental.
Thorndike Press® Large Print Christian Fiction.
The text of this Large Print edition is unabridged.
Other aspects of the book may vary from the original edition.
Set in 16 pt. Plantin.

LIBRARY OF CONGRESS CIP DATA ON FILE.
CATALOGUING IN PUBLICATION FOR THIS BOOK
IS AVAILABLE FROM THE LIBRARY OF CONGRESS

ISBN-13: 978-1-4328-4896-5 (hardcover)

Published in 2018 by arrangement with Gilead Publishing

Printed in Mexico
1 2 3 4 5 6 7 22 21 20 19 18

For
Deb
&
Kasey

For
Deb
&
Kasey

ONE

Home.

She was finally home.

Rose felt her heart stir when the buggy turned the bend in the road and the old farmhouse came into view. The big trees that surrounded the house were shedding their leaves of gold, russet, and scarlet. A brisk fall breeze sent them dancing across the lawn.

She took a deep sigh and glanced at her *schweschder* as they pulled into the drive. "It's so *gut* to be home. I missed it. I missed you."

Lillian smiled and hugged her. "I missed you too. Well," she said briskly, "you haven't seen the inside yet. It needs a lot of work. There just hasn't been time to keep up the place since *Daed* died."

"Of course not. You had enough on your hands taking care of him at the end," Rose told her. "I was sorry I couldn't be here."

"You were dealing with Sam's illness, then the farm in Ohio."

Rose sighed. "So much to handle for both of us." She gazed at the farmhouse. "I don't mind work." She needed it, needed to keep busy to keep the awful thoughts at bay. Her *mann* was gone and never coming back. She was going to have to find a way to live without him and raise their *sohn,* Daniel.

"Mamm!"

She turned her rapt gaze from the house and smiled at the towheaded miracle that was her *sohn.*

"Ya?"

"Home?"

"Home," she said.

"I'm *hungerich*!"

Rose laughed as she climbed down and helped him out of the buggy. "Let's go explore. Then we can see if there's anything in there to eat. Knowing *Aenti* Lillian, there'll be something delicious for us."

"Me *hungerich* too!" John cried from the back seat.

Lillian helped her own *sohn* out. "We'll find the potty for you too."

The two little boys raced off toward the house on sturdy legs.

"I can't believe they're four already. Time passes so quickly."

Rose watched her *schweschder* gently shake the shoulder of her five-year-old *dochder*. "Time to wake up, *kind*. We're going to look at *Aenti* Rose's house."

Annie woke with a frown and a pout. "She always wakes up grumpy," Lillian said in an aside to Rose. "Then she's her usual sweet self the rest of the day."

"Daniel wakes up happy," Rose told her. "Sometimes I hear him singing in his bed in the morning."

"John is much the same."

Annie climbed out and ran up the walkway to the farmhouse. The boys had found some pieces of board on the porch and were stacking them like blocks. She joined them and began telling them how they should do things, just like a big *schweschder* did.

Lillian retrieved a wicker basket from the buggy, and then she and Rose linked arms and strode up the walkway.

"*Danki* for persuading me to come home," Rose said with a heart-felt sigh.

"You're *wilkumm*." Lillian smiled "You know me."

"*Ya*, you love to organize things. People. Especially me."

Lillian stuck her tongue out at her and laughed. "True. It's what I do best."

They climbed the steps to the porch. The

9

paint on the boards on the porch was peeling, and two of the front windows were boarded up.

"Amos didn't have a chance to take care of this before you let us know you were coming. We worked on the inside first."

"You both did so much while I was gone. It's fine. It just needs a little more love."

"A lot of love," Lillian said.

"You said you had a man lined up to help me?"

"I do. I can't wait for the two of you to meet."

Something in her tone had Rose glancing at her *schweschder,* but Lillian was shooing the *kinner* inside.

"A lot of love," Lillian repeated. "Let's go explore. Upstairs first, then we'll work our way down and to the kitchen for lunch. *All-recht?*"

Rose nodded. "We'll see our new bedrooms, Daniel."

Her *schweschder* had sent her letters and had written about what needed to be done. Still, it was a bit of a shock when they went inside and Rose got a good look for herself. They each took the hand of one of the boys and climbed the stairs to the bedrooms. Annie trailed behind them.

First stop was the master bedroom. An

old bed sat near the large windows.

"We rented it out briefly to a family while they did some repairs to their house after a fire. They left a few things," Lillian said. "I figured you could get rid of them after yours got here on the moving truck and you decided what you wanted to keep or not keep."

"*Gut* idea." Rose walked over to the window that overlooked the backyard. A huge oak tree carried a swing that moved in the wind. The kitchen garden, neglected for the years the property had sat vacant, looked forlorn. Rose couldn't wait until she could plant it in the spring. She'd brought seeds from her Ohio garden.

Fields stretched out on all sides. The thought of what was involved in planting them overwhelmed Rose, even though she'd been a partner to Sam on their farm in Ohio and had grown up here on a farm in Paradise. But she reminded herself that some days everything felt overwhelming. The widow's support group she'd attended back in Millersburg had taught her it was a common emotion.

She turned to Daniel. "Let's go see your bedroom."

There were four bedrooms to choose from, but she wanted him near, so they

11

walked into the one closest to the master. Daniel squealed and began running in circles. He was such a happy, easily pleased *kind*. Knowing him, he'd have been happy if she'd shown him a closet and handed him a blanket and pillow.

"Look, Daniel, a big-boy bed," she told him, gesturing at the twin bed. "No *boppli* crib. And we'll paint the walls blue. You love blue."

"Blue," he agreed, his eyes shining. *"Mamm?"*

Lillian glanced down at her *sohn.* *"Ya?"*

"I'm *hungerich.* "

"Me too!" Daniel chimed in.

"Me too!" Annie told her.

"I brought sandwiches and potato chips," Lillian said. "Let's go downstairs and eat."

There was a big wooden table with chairs around it in the kitchen. Lillian began pulling food from the basket as Rose ran her hand over the worn surface of the table. "Our old family table's still here. So many meals were served on this."

"See if the refrigerator is running. The gas company told me they'd have everything turned on today," Lillian told her.

Rose opened the refrigerator to a blast of cold air. *"Ya,* it's all ready for some food."

"One less worry." Lillian looked at Rose

12

and bit her lip. "I just want you to be comfortable and happy here. I'm so glad you're back. I didn't like the thought of selling it when it's been in our family for generations." She pulled out a package of paper plates. "It's a small farm. I know you can manage it with the help of Luke Miller, Abraham's cousin. He'll be coming over to talk to you about it in the next day or so. He's from Ohio, too, you know. You're *schur* you've never met him?"

"So you've told me a couple dozen times. And no, I didn't know him. Millersburg was a big place."

"Well, you'll meet him soon and figure it all out. Luke came to help Abraham after a buggy accident and wants to stay in the area, so this works out perfectly."

Rose admired Lillian's optimism. Hers seemed to fluctuate so much since Sam died.

Lillian handed her a jug of lemonade and a package of paper cups, and Rose poured the lemonade into the cups as Lillian set out the paper plates, putting sandwiches on each, then a handful of potato chips. Before they could call the *kinner* they ran into the room and scrambled up onto the benches around the table. Daniel reached for a potato chip, then caught himself and set it back onto the plate as the blessing for the meal was said.

The *kinner* fell onto the sandwiches and chips. Rose picked up a half sandwich and began eating, aware of her *schweschder*'s eagle eye watching her. Lillian had always enjoyed being the oldest. It didn't seem to matter that she was older by only fifteen minutes. Lillian had always worried over her like a *mudder.*

"They're going to live close to us now?" Annie asked her *mudder.*

"Ya. Won't that be *wunderbaar?*"

Annie took a bite of her sandwich and stared with wide eyes at the two boys sitting at the table across from her. *"Ya,"* she said slowly. *"Wunderbaar."*

A loud rap sounded on the front door. They heard it open. "Anyone home?" a male voice called.

"Luke! Come on back to the kitchen!" Lillian called.

A tall man strode into the kitchen and grinned at them. He swept off his black felt hat, revealing thick blond hair. His face was strong and handsome, and he had the deepest blue eyes.

"Luke Miller, this is my *schweschder,* Rose Troyer. Rose, this is Luke."

He stared at her with the expression she

14

knew so well.

Luke realized he was staring. "Sorry, I didn't know you were twins," he said slowly, looking from one to the other. They looked so much alike, although Rose seemed a pale shadow of her *schweschder* — thinner, less vibrant.

"I guess I never thought you didn't know," Lillian said with a chuckle as she leaned over to wipe her *sohn*'s chin with a paper napkin. "Have you had lunch? We have plenty."

"I haven't," he said. "I was driving past and saw your buggy, so I thought I'd stop." He sat next to Annie and accepted a plate with a sandwich and a pile of chips. "My parents had benches at the table," he told them. "That way we had room for all of us. I have five *schweschders* and four *bruders.*" He looked across the table at Daniel. "Hi, there."

"This is my *sohn,* Daniel," Rose said, giving the boy a fond smile. "He's four and a half."

Luke studied him. He seemed shy and avoided his gaze. "It'll be fun to play with your cousins here, *ya?*"

Daniel nodded but stayed silent, his eyes on his plate.

"Daniel's not usually shy," Rose told him. "It's just that everything's a little new for him."

"Have you been outside to play on the swing in the backyard yet?" Luke asked him.

"There's a swing?" He looked at his *mudder.*

"*Ya,* my *dat* hung it for us when I was a *kind.* I saw it's still back there."

"Can I go see it?"

He watched as Rose checked her *sohn*'s plate. He'd cleaned it. "Of course."

Lillian nodded before John could even ask, and the boys scrambled into their coats and hats and were out the door before Luke could blink. Boys hadn't changed much since he'd been one.

Annie sat there calmly munching on her sandwich.

Luke studied Rose. She was quieter, more reserved than Lillian. He wondered if she was always like that or if it was because she was a widow. Her looks were softer too — more rounded. She wore the dress and *kapp* of the Ohio community she'd lived in. The deep blue of the dress fabric brought out the blue of her eyes and seemed to heighten her pale complexion.

"When is the moving van due?" Luke asked her.

"Tomorrow afternoon."

"I'll stop by and help."

"*Gut.* Can't have enough help." Lillian stood. "I'm going to check on the boys. Annie, come along with me."

Annie nodded, daintily wiped her mouth with a napkin, then turned to him. "See you later, Luke."

They shrugged into their coats and bonnets and went out the kitchen door.

Luke turned back to Rose. "So, you're back to live here."

She nodded. "The farm's been in our family for generations."

"Why was it allowed to fall into disrepair?"

She stiffened, and he wondered if he'd touched a nerve.

"My *mann* had family in Ohio." She began clearing the table. Her movements seemed slow, mechanical. "Lillian's *mann* already had a farm here in Paradise, and they couldn't care for both."

"Lillian called me when you wrote that you wanted to come back. She asked if I could help you with it."

Rose threw the paper plates and cups into a plastic garbage bag, set it by the back door, and then washed her hands. "And you're *schur* you want to work on a farm that isn't yours?"

17

"*Ya.* I like it here in Paradise."

She sat at the table, folded her hands, and looked at him directly. "And how long will you do this? What if you find a place of your own?"

"The prices here are making that difficult. Lancaster County is so much more expensive than my county back in Ohio."

"You're not inheriting your family's farm in Ohio?"

Luke shook his head. "My *bruder,* Wayne, will."

"What if we don't agree on what we should do here?" she asked, looking directly at him. "Are you *schur* you can work for a woman?"

"I wouldn't be here if I didn't think so." He met her unflinching gaze.

"My *mann* and I worked on the farm in Ohio together, and I made a lot of the decisions at the end when he was ill. I'm a farmer's daughter and a farmer's wife. I know what to do here, but I'll need help with the heavy manual labor."

"Do you usually look for problems before they arise?" he asked her.

Her gaze fell, and she traced a pattern in the wood on the table. "I didn't use to," she said with a sigh. She looked at him again. "Daniel and I need this to work."

There was a wealth of meaning in her words. "I know. Me too." He leaned back in his chair. "So, have you thought about what crops you want to plant in the spring?"

"*Nee,* not yet."

"That's fine. We have plenty of time to plan before spring."

A branch knocked against the kitchen window. Rose jumped.

"I'll go take care of that for you now," he said. "Don't want it breaking the window if there's a big wind."

"You sure you have time right now?"

"Of course. I'm helping Abraham out until I start here. And building some furniture for a store in town." He rose and pulled on his coat and hat.

"*Danki.*"

Luke opened the back door letting in a gust of wind before he quickly closed it again. It didn't take long to find a handsaw in the barn. He found himself glancing in the window as he cut the branch. Rose sat at the table looking lonely. She must have sensed he was watching her, for she raised her gaze, and he saw a haunted look in her eyes before she glanced away.

What was it like to lose a mate? Lillian had told him that Rose had been married for six years. He'd been lucky. The only

19

people he'd lost had been his elderly *gros-seldres.*

And he'd never even been in love with a woman.

He tossed aside the branch and stored the handsaw back in the barn. When he returned to the house, Lillian was herding the *kinner* in the back door and helping them shed their outdoor things. Luke watched Rose bend to help her *sohn* take off his mittens. She cradled his cheeks in her hands.

"Oh, your cheeks are so cold!"

"Hot chocolate?"

She glanced at Lillian. "I haven't shopped yet, Daniel."

"Maybe you should look in the cupboards," Lillian suggested.

Rose opened one near the sink. "*Ach,* look at this!" she cried and pulled out a box of hot chocolate mix. Next to it sat mugs all lined up, brand new from the look of them.

Lillian grinned. "I got a few supplies until you could get to the store."

"*Aenti* Lillian thinks of everything," Rose told the *kinner.* "Who wants hot chocolate?"

"Me!" they chorused.

"Me!" Luke said.

"Hot chocolate for everyone." She found a pan in a cupboard and filled it with water. After she set it on the range to boil, she

20

turned. "Everyone wash up and have a seat."

Luke waited his turn and then joined the others at the table. Hot chocolate had been one of his favorite drinks as a *kind.*

"Luke? Do you want marshmallows?" Rose held up the bag of mini marshmallows. "Lillian thinks of everything."

"I'm coming to see that. *Ya,* marshmallows, please."

Soon, Rose poured hot water into the mugs and stirred in the hot-chocolate mix, then added marshmallows to all the mugs. Lillian helped pass the mugs around, urging the *kinner* to let the drink cool.

Luke took a sip, then realized the *kinner* were watching him. "Still a little too hot," he said and got an approving nod from Lillian. He blew on his drink. The *kinner* followed suit, and soon marshmallows were topping — then spilling over — the mugs and laughter filled the room. It was a scene that reminded him of his childhood back in Ohio.

He wrapped his hands around the mug, warming them, and watched Rose talking quietly with her *sohn.* When he took a careful sip of his drink and ended up with a marshmallow mustache, it brought a smile to her lips, and the haunted look vanished.

He wondered what it would be like to

work with this woman to bring this farm back to life.

He wondered if being back in her home would bring Rose back to life.

TWO

The moving van arrived the next morning, and organized chaos quickly reigned.

Rose was grateful for Lillian as they supervised the unloading of the furniture and boxes from the Ohio home. Her *schweschder* had recruited family and friends. Soon it was like she'd never left as she received hugs and good wishes, and people streamed in and out of the house helping her unload. And as beds and tables and boxes of dishes and pots and pans were brought in, Rose felt herself being studied by Luke.

He and Ben, one of her childhood friends, carried in the sofa and positioned it along one wall as Rose requested. End tables were brought in and oil lamps set atop them. As Rose stood there, she pursed her lips and realized the space looked empty without the chair that had been such a part of her last living room. Specifically, Sam's recliner.

23

He'd loved sitting in it in the evening and reading the *Budget* or a favorite book after a long, hard day. At the end, it had been the most comfortable place for him, and he'd spent many nights sleeping in it.

Well, Sam was gone, so having a recliner made no sense. She'd never liked sitting in one and seeing it had just made her feel sad, so she'd sold it back in Ohio. Now it was time to discover what *she* liked, what made a house a home for her and her *sohn.*

She stood in the middle of the living room and looked around. This had been her family home, and now it was hers to care for, to bring back to life.

Lillian walked in carrying a box. "This is the last." She stopped and looked around. "There's no more furniture on the truck."

"Nee."

Lillian frowned. "Something's missing." Then her frown cleared. "You didn't have any living-room chairs?"

Rose took a deep breath. "Sam had a recliner. I sold it."

Lillian set the box down and crossed the room to hug her. "I should have realized. I remembered when we visited how he loved that chair."

"I had to sell it. Some things reminded me too much of him . . . of those last sad days. I kept many things for Daniel and me, but I just couldn't keep that chair."

"I understand."

Luke walked in. "The movers are ready to leave."

"Ask them to wait just a minute, please," Rose said.

She went into the kitchen for her purse and withdrew the check she'd made out along with a generous tip for the driver and his assistant. She put both in a tote bag along with a thermos of coffee and a dozen of the cinnamon rolls Lillian had brought. The men were grateful and wished her luck with her new home. She watched the truck with the bright-red cardinals painted on its side lumber down the drive and then head on down the main road.

It felt like her last tie with Ohio.

Gradually, friends left, giving her hugs and telling her they were glad to have her back. Still, she stayed on the porch, feeling adrift, too tired to move.

"Let me know when you want to talk about the farm."

Rose turned and saw Luke standing there studying her. "I will. Maybe next week?"

He nodded.

"*Danki* for the help."

"You're *wilkumm.* Try to get some rest."

She heard the front door open, and Lillian appeared at her side. She slid her arm around Rose as they watched Luke's buggy going down the road. "*Kumm* inside. It's chilly out here."

Rose let her *schweschder* lead her inside to the kitchen and into a seat at the big table.

"I'll make us some tea." Lillian opened a box labeled *Pots and Pans* and found a teakettle. She filled it and set it on the stove. "We can have tea or hot chocolate."

"Tea's fine, *danki.*"

"I got peppermint. Your favorite this time of year."

"*Danki.*"

"Rose?"

"Hmm?"

"You did bring your bed, right?"

She smiled and nodded. "Like I said, Sam spent a lot of nights in the recliner those last months before he died." She sighed and rubbed her arms. "It's so quiet without Daniel here."

"Amos is bringing him home. You know it was best not to have him underfoot while we unloaded the truck."

"I know. It's just not easy to have him out of sight." She accepted the mug of hot water and dunked a tea bag into it.

26

"I know. But he's fine. Probably having a *wunderbaar* time playing with his cousins."

"It'll be *gut* to be around family again. I missed you. And I never got to be friends with Sam's *mudder* the way I'd hoped. It never really felt like my home there. So why do I miss it?"

"You miss Sam. He was your home."

Tears filled her eyes. "You always understand me."

Lillian reached across and patted her hand.

The front door opened, then slammed shut. "*Mamm!* I'm home!" Rose blinked back the tears and smiled. All was right with the world again.

Daniel ran into the kitchen wearing a chocolate mustache.

"Did *Onkel* Amos give you hot chocolate?" Lillian asked him.

He nodded vigorously. "How did you know?"

She merely laughed, wiped his mouth with a paper napkin, and showed him the evidence.

He grinned. "*Onkel* Amos says, are you ready to come home?"

"Tell him just a few more minutes."

He ran out the door, slamming it again.

"Boys," Lillian said as she rose to put her

cup in the sink. "I brought a couple of casseroles today. They're in the freezer. I figured you'd be tired getting settled the first week."

Rose pulled herself up and hugged her *schweschder.* "I don't know where you get all your energy."

Lillian stood back and studied her with serious eyes. "Yours will come back."

"I hope so."

She walked Lillian to the front door, then called for Daniel and took him upstairs to play.

"My room," he said happily.

She smiled. *"Ya."* She left him and went into her own room. Lillian had found the box of linens and made up the bed, topping it with Rose's quilt. She sat, telling herself she could do so for only a moment, and then found herself sinking down onto the mattress. How *gut* it felt to rest. She lay there watching the dust motes that drifted in the light from the bedroom window. She was only twenty-eight but at that moment felt like an old woman.

She had a new life to begin here in Paradise. But right now she felt so unutterably tired. She could hear Daniel playing in his room. What would she have done if she hadn't had him to take care of after Sam

28

died? What did women who didn't have *kinner* do after their *mann* died?

Daniel came rushing in and cupped her cheeks with his pudgy hands. "*Mamm!* I love my room!"

"I'm glad. Why don't you lie down on your new bed and take a nap?"

"No nap. Story."

"First a nap. Then a story. Then supper."

He tilted his head and considered it. "*Allrecht.*"

She smiled. He was such an easy *kind.*

Off he went. She could hear the clatter of him playing with toys for a few minutes and then there was quiet.

She slept.

Supper at the Millers always made Luke feel right at home.

Kinner chattered a mile a minute, passed big bowls and platters — even the littlest ones — and fell on food like a pack of hungry wolves.

Luke had lived with his cousin Abraham and his *fraa,* Lovina, ever since the family was injured in a buggy accident last year. He'd done what family did and come to help them with their farm while Abraham's broken arm healed and Lovina slowly recovered from the emotional toil of seeing not only her *mann* hurt but her *kinner* bruised and scared from their buggy being forced off the road by a teenaged *Englisch* driver.

He'd thought about returning to Ohio after Abraham's arm healed, but something about Paradise and the Amish community here had kept him. For a time he'd thought it was because of Miriam, a woman he'd been attracted to. But they had realized they weren't meant for each other. Soon after, Miriam had married the *Englischer* Mark Byler, who she'd loved for many years. Luke had honestly been happy for her. Now the two of them lived on the farm Mark's *grossdaadi* had wanted him to have.

Luke had begun looking for property here. The Troyer farm sat neglected and sad, and he'd been told to ask Lillian about it, only to find that her *schweschder* was moving back here and would be taking it over. He'd been disappointed but Lillian had mentioned that Rose was a widow and would need help. Since he didn't have anything else lined up and didn't want to return to Ohio, he figured it wouldn't hurt to talk to Rose about it. For all he knew she could decide running a farm without a *mann* was too much for her even with hired help.

He hadn't expected her to look like a pale shadow of her *schweschder.*

He hadn't expected to find himself drawn to her.

It wasn't just a matter of protectiveness. Her air of fragility inspired that, of course, but she had a delicate beauty that intrigued him.

"You're awfully quiet tonight, Luke," Lovina remarked. "Tired from helping with the move?"

He shook his head. "We had a lot of help. I was just thinking."

"That's why there was smoke coming out of his ears," Abraham joked.

"Luke has smoke in his ears?" one of the *kinner* cried.

"It's just an expression," Lovina told him, casting a rueful look at her *mann.*

"You didn't tell me she and Lillian were *zwillingbopplin.*"

"Oh. I guess it's because we're all so used to them," she said. "Sometimes I forget you didn't grow up here."

"It's *gut* for her to be back. Family should be together," Abraham said.

"What about Rose's *mann*'s family?"

"His parents died not long after they were married." Lovina's response was tinged with sadness.

"I see."

"She and Lillian were always so close. One

31

knew what the other was thinking. Eli, I saw you elbow your *schweschder.* Behave."

"Sorry."

Lovina rose and fetched pumpkin pie and vanilla ice cream. Luke swore he could hear a pin drop as everyone dug into the creamy, still-warm pie with the spicy scents of cinnamon, nutmeg, and cloves and the cold vanilla ice cream. It was a *gut* time for Rose to come back, he decided as he ate. She'd have the winter to get settled and plan for the spring planting. He'd go over seed catalogs with her, see what repairs were needed on the barn, go to auctions to purchase livestock. He wondered if she had a buggy to get around.

Maybe it was time to make a list. Before he could do that, however, he needed to finish his pie and coffee and join Abraham in the barn for evening chores.

"So, what did you think of Rose?" Abraham asked him as they fed the stock.

"We didn't get to talk much," he said as he offered quartered apples to the horses. "We're going to talk next week when she's settled."

"The farm's sat empty for a few years, as you know," Abraham told him. "You'll have your work cut out for you."

"I was thinking of starting a list."

Abraham nodded. "That's a *gut* start. She grew up on the farm, so she'll know a lot."

"Maybe she won't take my suggestions."

"Maybe. Not a *gut* idea to look for problems before they crop up."

"True."

Abraham glanced around the barn. "Well, time to be done for the day."

They walked out, closed the barn doors, and headed for the house. The kitchen was empty when they went inside, scrubbed clean. He could hear the patter of little feet overhead as Lovina got the *kinner* into bed.

"More coffee?" Abraham shed his jacket and hat and hung them on pegs by the back door.

"Love some." Luke hung up his outdoor things as well and accepted the mug of coffee. He sat at the table and was grateful for the warmth of the kitchen after the walk from the barn to the house.

This was the best part of the day. When the day's work was done, when those you loved were all tucked safely in the house. It made him think about the future and a time when he'd have a *fraa*, a family, a home. He truly believed God had set aside a woman to be his *fraa*, but so far he hadn't met her.

His thoughts went to Rose. He couldn't imagine how she felt losing her *mann* at so young an age, having to raise their son by herself. Starting over. Still, a woman as lovely as she would surely find another *mann* after she grieved. He wondered if she'd dated any men here before she'd met her *mann.* Maybe they'd be making her acquaintance again. He wanted to ask Abraham, but couldn't figure out how without being too obvious.

"I feel like another piece of pie," Abraham said, breaking into his thoughts. "What about you?"

"There's some left?"

Abraham grinned. *"Ya."*

Lovina came into the kitchen as he was scooping ice cream onto the two plates of pie. She put her hands on her hips and stared at him.

"Do all women do the look?" Luke asked Abraham.

"Hmm? The look?" He put the lid back onto the ice-cream container.

Lovina cleared her throat. He glanced up, saw her for the first time, and immediately looked guilty. "Luke wanted pie."

"Hey! It was your idea!" he protested.

"Don't worry, I know whose idea it was," she told him with a grin.

"Want a piece?"

"There were only two pieces left," Abraham confessed.

"You can have mine," Luke told her, hoping she'd refuse. Her pumpkin pie was the best he'd ever eaten.

"Such a gentleman. Unlike my *mann*." She looked pointedly at Abraham.

"He jumped ahead of me. I'd give you my pie, love of my life."

She reached for it and laughed when his face fell. "You can have it," she said, pushing it back toward him. "I just wanted to see if you'd really give it up." She poured herself a cup of coffee and brought the mug and a cookie to the table.

"Luke was telling me he and Rose are going to meet next week to talk about the farm."

Luke set his fork on his empty plate. "Are the two of you *schur* you don't mind me staying here a while longer?"

"Of course not," they said in unison.

"I don't know how long I might work for her."

Abraham shrugged. "Only God knows His plan for you."

"Or her."

"What?" Luke stared at Lovina.

"We don't know what God's plan is for Rose," she said simply, looking thoughtful. She took a bite of cookie. "I think it will be interesting to see, don't you?"

He thought about that as he climbed the stairs to the room he'd lived in since he came here. The oldest boy had given up the room to him without a grumble and the whole family had made him feel a part of them. But as he lay in the narrow bed waiting for sleep he found himself wondering how long he'd be a single man in search of his mate.

THREE

Rose woke to a darkened room and a warm little body tucked against her. She smiled. As much as Daniel had loved his new big-boy bed, he'd still crawled in to nap with her.

She lay there, absorbing the peace and quiet and the comfort. He was a typical boy — never still — so she cherished times like this when she could snuggle with him and he wouldn't immediately dash off for some adventure.

What a perfect little boy he was, a blond angel with cheeks that were losing the chubbiness he'd had as a *boppli.* People always said the years passed quickly when you had a *kind.* She hadn't believed them — until now. It was hard to believe he'd be five in January.

Too soon he stirred, opened his eyes, and gave her a sleepy smile. "Hi."

"Hi, yourself. I thought you were going to

take a nap in your bed."

He grinned. "Story now?"

"Schur."

He scrambled off the bed, ran down the hall to his room, then returned with his favorite book. Rose reached over and turned on the battery-operated lamp on her bedside table. Then she propped herself up on her pillow, held out her arms, and cradled him as he opened the book and began to "read" to her.

Times like this she wondered if he missed his *dat.* Sam had read to him so often, especially at the end when he couldn't do much but sit in his recliner. She'd often found the two of them enjoying a story after she finished doing the dishes. Sometimes the two had fallen asleep and she'd sat on the sofa and just watched them. Such a bittersweet memory.

"The end," he said as he closed the book. *"Mamm,* I'm *hungerich."*

She tickled his tummy. "You're always *hungerich."*

He giggled and slid from the bed. "Cookie?"

"Supper," she said, getting up. She smoothed the wrinkles from the skirt of her dress, slipped into her shoes, and followed him downstairs.

Lillian, bless her, had left one of the casseroles she'd brought in the refrigerator when she tucked the others in the freezer. Rose turned on the oven and set it inside.

"Cookie?" Daniel again asked hopefully.

"Apple," she said, choosing one from the wooden bowl on the table.

"Apple." He held out his hand. "Please."

He sat at the table, kicking his legs as he ate the fruit. She fixed herself a cup of tea and sat with him as they waited for the casserole to bake. Soon the delicious aroma of chicken and noodles filled the kitchen and warmed the room.

Daniel ate two helpings of the casserole and still had room for a cookie. Rose found she was hungry after the long day working to unpack and get them settled. She cleared the table and gave Daniel some paper and crayons to occupy himself while she washed the dishes and put the leftovers in the refrigerator. They'd have them for supper tomorrow night.

Finished, she sat, took a piece of paper and a crayon, and began making a list of things she needed to do. Daniel glanced over. "Draw a picture, *Mamm.*"

She laughed. "*Nee, Mamm* needs to work. Daniel."

He held up the picture he'd been coloring. Tears rushed to her eyes when she saw the three figures that were roughly drawn but clearly a man, woman, and child.

"*Daed*," he said, pointing to the man. "You. And Daniel." He grinned at her.

"It's beautiful. Let's put it on the refrigerator."

They posted it there with the help of some alphabet magnets, and then Daniel insisted on putting up Rose's list.

"Time for a bath."

He needed no urging. Sometimes she thought it was his favorite time of the day. He scrambled up the stairs and began tearing his clothes off while she filled the tub. She sat beside it and found her thoughts wandering as he splashed and played with his bath toys. She'd always wanted to be a *fraa* and a *mudder*. She and Sam had tried so hard. At the time Daniel came along, they'd been married for more than two years, and she'd begun to despair that they'd never have a *boppli*. Meanwhile, her *schweschder* and her *mann* had been blessed with *kinner*.

She sighed. Now she was blessed with a *kind* but no *mann*. Who would have ever thought her life would turn out like this.

Daniel splashed and brought her back to the present.

40

"Look at your hands!" she exclaimed. "You're turning into a little prune."

"Prune?" Perplexed, he stared at her.

She grasped his hand and showed him how wrinkled it was but he didn't seem to understand. So she rinsed him off, pulled the plug, and together they watched the water swirl down the drain. She wrapped him in a big bath towel, dried his hair, and helped him pull on warm pajamas.

Then it was time for another evening ritual. He chose his favorite books, and they read them together until his eyelids drooped. Rose knew she let him stretch out this time and silently chided herself. After he went to sleep the house always seemed too quiet, too lonely. But she couldn't expect a *kind* to meet her emotional needs.

"Sweet dreams," she told him, bending to kiss his forehead.

"Sweet *dweams*," he said, giving her an angelic smile.

"See you in the morning."

But he didn't repeat her words. He was already asleep.

She tucked the quilt she'd made him around his little body, turned off the lamp on his night table, and tiptoed out of the room.

There was more to be done — more boxes

that could be unpacked, something else to clean. Busy with caring for her own home and family, Lillian hadn't been able to do more than make the kitchen, living room, and two bedrooms habitable. But Rose knew she wouldn't be able to do everything in a few days — even a few weeks. So she pulled her list from the refrigerator and sat at the table to work on it some more. She needed so much: a horse and buggy, seed for the spring crops, and horses for plowing. Chickens. What state was the coop in where they'd raised chickens when she'd grown up here, she wondered. Feeding the chickens and gathering eggs had been her favorite chore growing up. Well, that and taking care of the kitchen garden.

She smiled at the memory of those chickens. Lillian hadn't liked them, and they must have sensed it, because a couple of the hens had seemed to chase her bad-temperedly.

Stock and seed, and who knew what repairs would be needed on the barn . . . She had money from the sale of the farm in Ohio, but she'd have to be careful. The wage she'd be paying Luke was fair, but it was an expense that wasn't a part of a farm's budget since there was usually a *mann* running it. On the other hand, she didn't have a mortgage on the farm.

She rubbed her temple. A headache was starting up just at the thought of it all. She sighed. Worry wouldn't accomplish anything. Hadn't she learned that? Worrying over Sam's health hadn't kept him from getting worse, hadn't kept him from dying. She had to keep giving up her worries, her concerns — *allrecht,* her fears — to God.

The list went back on the refrigerator next to Daniel's sweet drawing of the family they'd been. She climbed the stairs to her solitary bed.

The farmhouse looked very different when Luke visited for a meeting with Rose a week later. There wasn't a box in sight. A quilt lay draped over the back of the sofa, a pottery jar filled with pussy willows sat on the table near it, and there was a scatter of toys spilling out of an old wooden chest near the fireplace.

It looked like a home not a work in progress.

"I thought we could have some coffee and meet in the kitchen," she told him, leading the way.

The kitchen looked even more lived in. A big soup pot sat on the back of the stove and whatever was simmering in it smelled incredible. Coffee was brewing in the battered percolator, and a plate of fresh-baked cookies sat next to two mugs. He sat at the table and watched her move gracefully, stirring whatever it was in the pot with a big wooden spoon, checking the percolator.

"The coffee will be ready in a few minutes."

She put the cookies before him, and he took one. "How did you know oatmeal-raisin is my favorite?" he asked, biting into one that was truly excellent.

"A little bird told me," she said with a smile.

Lovina had probably told her. She and her *kinner* baked them often for him.

"Where's Daniel?"

"Napping. Otherwise you'd be fighting him for the cookies."

He chuckled. "So he knows a good cookie, eh?"

"He bargains for them all day."

Luke glanced over at the refrigerator as she opened it. An alphabet magnet held a picture of a family, obviously drawn by a child. Beside it was a to-do list written in a purple crayon — by an adult hand.

He frowned. It was going to take a lot more work on his part if she thought getting the farm back to being profitable was as simple as a crayon-scrawled list.

She closed the refrigerator with a snap and set the carton of cream down on the table. Going to the drawer, she pulled out a spiral notebook and placed it on the table. Then she poured the coffee, gave Luke his mug, and sat.

Opening the notebook, she pulled out a list and handed it to him. "This is a list of what I think we should start with. Seed order, stock, repairs."

Stunned, he stared at her. "Uh, *ya,* this is a *gut* start."

"I grew up on this farm, and I helped my *mann* with the one in Ohio," she reminded him.

"I know that." He poured cream into his coffee and added a teaspoon of sugar to give himself time to think. "I wasn't underestimating you."

"Nee?"

Luke felt color rush into his face. "Well, maybe I did."

Her expression said there was no maybe about it. "My *schweschder* felt that we could work together," she said quietly. "Lillian is seldom wrong."

He took a deep breath. He wanted the job so he could stay in the area and find a farm of his own. "We *can* work together," he told

45

her. "Let's start again." Picking up her list, he scanned it. "First thing we should go over is what crops you want to plant. What's worked for the farm?"

They talked for an hour over several cups of coffee and most of the plate of cookies before Daniel appeared rubbing his eyes.

"Hi," he said to Luke.

"Hi."

Daniel then looked at his *mudder* and gave her a winning smile. "Cookie?"

"See what I mean?" she told Luke.

"See what?" her *sohn* asked with his mouth full.

"Nothing." She pulled out a chair and he climbed up into it. "Want some milk?" He nodded and she rose to get it for him.

"*Gut* cookie, ya?" Luke asked Daniel.

The boy nodded enthusiastically. "*Mamm* makes *gut* cookies."

Luke felt a little guilty he'd eaten so many. But he doubted Rose would have allowed the boy more. It was too near suppertime, and *gut mudders* didn't let their *sohns* spoil their supper.

He might not be as hungry for supper himself, now that he'd eaten so many cookies, but he'd manage somehow. Lovina fed her family well.

And it certainly smelled as if Rose did too.

"Well, we got a lot done," he said with an eye to the clock. "There's an auction next week. We could look over plow horses. There's no hurry for those, though. I'd like to look at the barn again, talk to you about necessary repairs."

"*Mamm?*" Daniel spoke up. "I'm *hungerich.*"

He saw her glance at the kitchen clock. "I need to feed him supper."

"I can give it a look, and we can talk again."

"That would be *gut.*"

There was no invitation to supper. Luke hadn't expected one. This would be a business relationship, with him working for her. Lillian had assured him she'd spoken to the bishop about it, but he knew single women and men weren't supposed to be alone together. He wanted to make sure he didn't do anything to harm her reputation in the community.

Luke stood and ruffled Daniel's hair. Such a cute *kind.* He wondered if he missed his *dat.* "*Danki* for the coffee and cookies. I'll see you both at church on Sunday."

He donned his jacket and hat and headed out to the barn. The structure had looked pretty sturdy when Lillian showed him around, but a more in-depth look showed some wood rot and other damage. He pulled a notepad and pencil from his pocket and began jotting things down. The repairs were something he could take care of himself. He'd start with making *schur* one or two stalls were clean and not exposed to the weather. He could make them ready before they got a buggy horse.

An old buggy sat in one corner of the barn. It wasn't in *gut* shape, and he didn't know much about repairing one. The best thing he could do was find out who did buggy repair in the area and get an estimate. It would take a bite out of Rose's budget if she had to buy a new one.

He stopped, found himself wondering why Rose hadn't brought her horse and buggy from Ohio. He'd have to ask her the next time he saw her. Abraham was finishing up chores in the barn when Luke got back to the house.

"How did your meeting go?"

"Just fine." He didn't think his cousin needed to know about his misstep with Rose.

"I grew up with the twins. That Lillian loves to organize everything. Rose'll be easier to work for."

"Hope you're right."

Abraham clapped him on the shoulder.

"Might feel different working for a woman instead of a man, but seems to me you're working for the same purpose. Bringing back the farm," he added when Luke looked at him questioningly. "It's been hard to see it sitting there, but Lillian and her *mann* couldn't manage two farms. There was some talk of selling it for a while. Anyway, it's suppertime."

Lovina was putting supper on the table when they walked into the house. The kitchen was warm and filled with delicious aromas. Luke took off his jacket and hat and washed up. He wondered what Rose and her *sohn* were having for supper. Whatever was in the big soup pot on the back of the stove had smelled heavenly.

"How did your meeting go with Rose?" Lovina asked with a smile.

"It went well. We got a lot done." He took his seat at the table.

"She was a friend of mine before she married and moved away. I'm glad she's back, although I'm sad about why." She sighed. "But it's not for us to question God's plan for ourselves or others."

She walked over to the stairs that led to the bedrooms. "Supper!" she called, then returned to the stove to finish dishing up.

The *kinner* came to the table eager to eat.

Luke had once heard an *Englischer* complain that her child was a picky eater. He didn't think he'd ever seen one in his community.

Talk turned to the coming holidays.

"I'm glad Rose will be here with family," Lovina said as she helped one of her *kinner* cut up his pot roast. "I can't imagine how hard it was for her to face them by herself last year after her *mann* died."

"She's been widowed for, what, a year now?"

Lovina nodded. "A little more than." She turned to Abraham. "I wonder if Naiman will ask her out. They dated for a long time before Sam came to visit his *aenti* and asked Rose to marry him."

"Likely she won't be a widow long," Abraham commented. "She's a *gut* woman, and now she has a farm. And you know the bishop likes to match up singles. He feels it makes for a more stable community, men and women of age married."

That had been true in his own community as well, Luke remembered. As he helped himself to a portion of pot roast and potatoes and carrots, he found himself frowning at the idea of Rose being with another man. *Schur,* part of the reason was because he wanted to be the one who helped her with

50

the farm. But he had to admit that part of the reason was because there was something about Rose that he liked very much.

FOUR

Rose was pouring herself a cup of coffee
when the kitchen door opened and Lillian
stuck her head inside.

"Grab your jacket and come outside. I
have a surprise for you."

She set her mug down. "What?"

Lillian grinned. "It's a surprise. C'mon!"
She stepped inside, grabbed the jacket, and
tossed it at Rose. Curious, Rose pulled it on
and followed her *schweschder.*

Two steps from the door she stopped and
gaped at the horse tied to the back of the
buggy. "Star? You brought Star over for a
visit?"

"I brought Star over to give her back to
you."

Rose descended the porch steps slowly. "I
gave her to you when I moved to Ohio with
Sam. She couldn't go with us because she
wasn't well."

"Well, Amos and I talked about it, and we

think she belongs with you now."

"Oh, girl, I missed you so." She wrapped her arms around the horse's neck. She'd been afraid to visit her at Lillian's since she'd been back. "Are you *schur*?" she asked Lillian.

"Ya."

"Star, wait until Daisy gets here. It'll be like old times." She looked at Lillian. "She's being driven down from Ohio next week."

The barn door opened. Luke stepped out and walked over to them. *"Guder mariye."*

"Guder mariye. I wasn't expecting you."

"Lillian told me she was bringing Star over. I'd noticed some of the stalls needed repairing, so I thought I'd take care of it. Wanted to make sure there was straw and hay too."

"That's very nice of you. *Danki.*"

"Hello, Star. It's nice to meet you." He rubbed a hand over her flank. "Let me put her in the barn to stay warm while I work. Keep me company."

Rose nodded. "Bet it'll seem like home again to her."

"Oh, here." He pulled a scrap of paper from his jacket pocket. "This is the company that did *gut* work on Abraham and Lovina's buggy when it was damaged last year. You

53

might want to call them about repairing yours."

"*Danki.*" She looked at her *schweschder.* "Are you coming in for some coffee?"

Lillian shook her head. "I have to get back home." She glanced over at the kitchen door. "Look who's up." Daniel stood at the door dressed in his pajamas. "How about you let me take him home and you can get some things done?"

"You don't have enough *kinner* to run after?" Rose asked her ruefully.

"I don't have boxes to unpack like you."

"*Gut* point. Let me get him dressed."

"Put his jacket on him and he can borrow some of John's clothes."

"He hasn't had breakfast yet."

"I think I can find him something to eat," Lillian said with a grin. "Come on, *Mamm.* He can have fun with his cousins for the morning."

"*Allrecht.*"

Minutes later she stood in the drive watching her *sohn* waving happily as they drove off. Silly of her, but she was already missing him.

She walked over to the barn and went inside. Luke looked up from one of the stalls. "I thought I'd say hello to Star." She walked over to the horse and hugged her again.

"You said she wasn't feeling well, so you had to leave her behind when you moved?"

She nodded. "Star was going through a difficult pregnancy, and the vet didn't feel she would do well to be moved. Besides, she'd belonged to my family, and Lillian loved her too." She patted Star and walked over to sit on a bale of hay. "You've gotten a lot done already."

"Didn't take long." He tested the stall door and adjusted it. "I think I should go up on the roof and check it before the weather gets too bad."

"*Gut* idea. Let's hope it doesn't need any repair." She sighed. "But I guess that would be unrealistic. This old barn's been standing for a long time. Who knows how long it's been since anyone checked the roof. It's *schur* been a long time since my *dat* did. He died several years ago and was in no shape to go up there himself for a long time." She frowned. "It might not be safe —"

"Don't worry, I'll be careful," he said quickly. "I won't go up unless there's someone else with me. That ladder over there doesn't look like it's in *gut* shape anyway, so I'll have to borrow one from

Abraham."

Luke picked up a bale of hay with seemingly little effort, carried it to the stall, and filled the hay rack. When he'd finished, he looked at Star. "Well, pretty lady, let's see what you think of your new home."

He called a horse a pretty lady. Rose thought about the last time she'd been called pretty. Sam had just been so ill for so long, and such things were unimportant when he'd been fighting for his life.

"You *allrecht*?"

She looked up. "Hmm? *Ya,* I was just thinking of something."

"It must have been difficult to leave Ohio. Even if it meant coming back here to family."

His understanding surprised her.

"It was. But I didn't want to stay at the farm after Sam died. It didn't feel like home after he was gone. And he had a relative who wanted to buy it, keep it in the family." She glanced around. "This is home, even if it isn't going to be easy to bring the place back to life. What about you? Lillian told me you came here to help your cousin."

"My *bruder* inherited the family farm in Ohio and I was helping him. Then we heard that Abraham was hurt in the buggy accident, so I came here to help him."

"Do you miss it? Ohio?"

He shrugged. "Sometimes. But I really like it here. And it's not far if I want to visit."

Rose watched him work for a while before she finally got up. She had tasks of her own in the house. "Come inside when you're ready for a cup of coffee."

"I will, *danki.*"

Inside, she lined some more shelves in her kitchen cabinets, filled them with dishes and glasses, and was ready for a break when Luke came in.

"Coffee smells *gut,*" he said as he shed his jacket and hat. "Something else too."

"Split pea and ham soup. I keep a pot of soup cooking most days in the fall and winter."

"My *mudder* did that. Warmed a body up real well. A bowl of soup is a *gut* meal when it's cold."

She poured them mugs of coffee and set out a plate of pumpkin bread she'd baked. "How much do I owe you for the supplies for the barn?"

He pulled a receipt from his jacket and handed it to her before he sat. "If you have some time I thought we could talk about your budget for the horse auction."

"*Schur.*" She pulled her notebook from the kitchen drawer and joined him at the table.

"It helped to get Star back from Lillian. I can deduct that expense."

"Every little bit helps," he agreed and helped himself to a slice of the pumpkin bread. "If you want I could call that buggy repair company and get an estimate."

She nodded. "The phone's hooked up in the shanty." She crossed off the amount she'd estimated for a buggy horse from the page in her notebook designated for stock.

He finished his coffee and donned his jacket and hat. "I'll make the call and then I thought I'd work a couple more hours inside the barn."

"If you don't need to help Abraham, that would be *wunderbaar*. Oh, and Luke? Come inside at noon for lunch."

He nodded and left.

The hours flew by as she worked on her task list and tidied up around the house, and before she knew it Luke had returned for the midday meal. They were sitting at the table eating soup and bread when she heard a knock on the front door. She went to answer it.

"Hello, Rose."

"Well, Naiman, I haven't seen you in so long."

He grinned. "Heard you were back and thought I'd come say hello."

"Come in. We're just finishing lunch."

" 'We'?" He took off his hat as he stepped inside. "I heard you were back. I'm sorry about Sam."

Rose shut the door. "*Danki.* You know Luke. He's here helping me with the farm. Come into the kitchen for some coffee."

Luke looked up as Rose stepped into the kitchen. He knew Naiman — Sarah King was his *schweschder.* He was tall, with dark-brown hair, and wore his Sunday-best shirt and pants. Luke narrowed his eyes as the man looked at him and his smile faded. "That didn't take long," Luke muttered, remembering what Lovina had said about him.

"Excuse me?" Naiman stared at him. His gaze wasn't particularly friendly.

"Nothing."

"Naiman? Have you had lunch?"

He looked regretful. *"Ya."*

"Can I get you some coffee?"

"Danki."

The two men eyed each other while Rose poured coffee for Naiman and they took a seat at the table.

"I came by to welcome you back to Paradise," Naiman said as he stirred sugar into his coffee.

"So, you're back for *gut*?"

"That's right."

Naiman turned to Luke. "I hear you're helping Rose with the farm?"

"That's right."

Luke dragged out eating the last of his soup. No way was he leaving the table while this man was here. He glanced at Rose, but she didn't seem aware of the tension between him and Naiman.

"It's *gut* to be near family and friends," Naiman said. He blew on his coffee. "Remember when we were in *schul* together? You and Lillian and me? Those were fun days, right?"

She nodded. "Except for when you were pulling my braids."

"Just teasing you," he said with a grin. "That's what guys do in *schul*. Right, Luke?"

"I never did."

Naiman shrugged and sipped his coffee. "Well, I just came to offer my help."

"We're doing fine," Luke told him. "Don't need any help." Then, aware he'd sounded abrupt, he added, *"Danki."*

Rose glanced at Luke, then Naiman. "*Ya, danki,* Naiman, but we don't need any help at the moment. Luke is doing some work on the barn today."

Luke spooned up the last of his soup. He let the spoon clatter in his bowl, and it caught Rose's attention.

"Would you like some more?" She gave him a warm smile.

"Ya, danki." He'd already had one big bowl and two slices of bread. Hopefully Naiman would leave before he had to eat much more. Tasty as the soup and bread were, even his stomach had limits.

Rose took his bowl to the stove, ladled more soup into it, then set it on the table before him. "Sure you don't want some, Naiman?"

"I'm fine, *danki.* Maybe next time."

Luke wanted to roll his eyes. He ate his soup. Naiman drank his coffee. And Rose chatted easily, still unaware of any tension.

"So, you decided to stay on in the area for a while," Naiman said politely, eyeing him. "You're not planning to go back to Ohio?"

Luke looked at him directly. "I'm here to stay."

They stared at each other for a long moment. Naiman was being very polite but Luke saw the coldness in his eyes and knew the man disliked him.

"Well, I have to get going," Naiman said finally, giving Luke a glowering look. "Have some work to do."

"It was nice to see you again," Rose told him, rising to walk him to the front door. "Say hello to your family."

Luke listened hard but couldn't hear the man's response. He did hear the door close and ate the rest of his soup quickly.

Rose walked back into the room. "So, you never pulled a girl's hair?"

He laughed at the unexpected question. "Never at *schul.* I won't say I never pulled the hair of one of my *schweschders* at home." He sighed. "Lunch was delicious. *Danki.*"

"Glad you enjoyed it. *Schur* you don't want more?"

Luke gave her a wary look. *"Nee, danki."* Was it his imagination, or was there a sparkle of mischief in those normally quiet blue-gray eyes? "Well, I'm going out to the barn to work some more."

Back outside, he got to work in one of the stalls, wondering if the visit by this Naiman guy was just the first he'd be seeing. After all, Rose was an attractive young widow with a farm. He hammered a nail into a board with a little more force than necessary. She was too nice a woman to be pursued by someone for what she owned instead of what — *who* — she was.

Well, it wasn't his business. What could he

do about it anyway?

He heard the sound of buggy wheels on the gravel drive. When he opened the barn door, he was relieved to see it was Lillian. She got out and helped Daniel down. The boy spotted him and ran toward him.

"Luke! I had fun at *Aenti* Lillian's house! Whatcha doin'?"

"Fixing the stalls so we can get some horses."

"How's Star adjusting?" Lillian asked as she walked toward him.

"Well. Come see."

"Can I see? Can I see?" Daniel bounced in his sneakers.

"Schur." He held the door open for them and led them to where Star stood happily munching on hay.

"Pretty horsie," Daniel told him. "Can I get on?"

"For a minute." Luke lifted him, opened the stall, and set him on Star's back. He held him firmly and Daniel gently patted the horse's mane.

The barn door opened. Luke turned his head and saw Rose step inside. Her hand flew to her throat.

"Mein Gott! What's he doing up there?"

"It's *allrecht,*" he assured her. "I'm holding him."

"Get him down," she whispered in a strangled voice. "Please. Now. Right now."

"Time to get down," he told Daniel, lifting him into his arms. He walked out of the stall and put the boy in Rose's arms. "Here, see, he's *allrecht.* Nothing bad happened."

She clutched Daniel to her and raised terrified eyes to him. "He could have been hurt."

"I wouldn't have let him fall." He kept his voice low and soothing, as if she were a frightened mare. "Don't frighten the boy."

She started to speak but instead turned on her heel and rushed from the barn.

"I'm sorry. Maybe I shouldn't have done that," he said to Lillian.

"It's fine," Lillian told him. "I'm *schur* she's just overreacting because of Sam. I should have thought of that when he asked."

"Sam? Was he killed by a horse?"

She shook her head. "But she lost him too early. She feels Daniel's all she has left."

"I see." He felt stupid. Really stupid. "I'll go apologize."

"Give her a little time. Rose never stays upset for long."

Luke picked up a nail. "Hope you're right. I was hoping to work here for longer than a day."

She laughed. "You will." Her gaze went to

the other side of the barn. "Wonder how much it'll cost to repair the buggy."

"Don't know. Guy's coming out to give an estimate tomorrow. Then Rose will have to decide if it's worth repairing or if she should get a new one."

Lillian frowned. "Oh. You think it might not be worth repairing?"

"The more I look at it, the more I wonder." He pounded in the nail with the hammer. "No use worrying before we find out."

She sat on a bale of hay and sighed. "Don't put the cart before the horse?"

He chuckled. "Something like that."

"I just hope it's not going to be more expensive to get the place in order than we thought."

Luke stopped working and met her gaze. "It'll work out. It was right to get her to move back here and be near her family. You know it was."

Lillian stood. "I do. I'm more *schur* of that every day." She patted Star's head. "I'm going to say goodbye to Rose and Daniel and then head home. See you at church on Sunday."

"See you."

He finished his work. When he was done, he decided, he'd apologize to Rose. Lillian had said she didn't stay upset for long. He *schur* hoped she was right.

FIVE

Rose looked up as Lillian walked into the kitchen. "You think I overreacted."

Lillian reached down to hug her. "*Nee,* I understand. You lost Sam and you were afraid Daniel could fall and hurt himself."

She sniffed. "Luke must think I'm over-protective."

"Doesn't matter. You're entitled. For a while."

"A while?"

"If you're still afraid to let Daniel up on a horse in a couple of years, I'll think you're overprotective."

"I lost the love of my life," Rose burst out and the tears began to flow. "Sometimes it feels like it happened yesterday. I just can't lose someone I love again." She put her face in her hands.

Lillian sat and touched her hand. "I'm not going to tell you not to worry. That's like trying to, I don't know, tell the wind not to blow. But trust God, Rose. He loves you. He really does."

"I'm trying." She dug into her apron pocket, found a tissue, and wiped her eyes. "You're the only one I can tell that I felt He took Sam from me. That He was punishing me." She took a deep breath. "Sometimes I've felt like if one more person says it was God's will I'm going to scream." She sighed. "Oh, I know I will get through this. I don't want to keep questioning God and being afraid of something happening."

She rose and put the kettle on. As she waited for the water to boil, she saw a flash of red at the window. A cardinal sat on the windowsill and peered inside with bright eyes. It tilted its head and appeared to study her.

"What is it?"

"We're being watched."

"Watched?"

"Look out the window."

But when Lillian rose and walked over, the bird flew away. "Probably looking for some food."

"Probably." The kettle shrieked. She turned off the flame and poured mugs of hot water.

Lillian sat back down at the table and handed her a tea bag from the bowl there.

68

"Here, you always feel better when you have a cup of peppermint tea."

Rose managed a watery chuckle. "*Ya.* Peppermint tea fixes everything." She steeped the tea, then sighed. "Naiman stopped by."

"Really? Why?"

"He said he just wanted to offer condolences and welcome me back. Funny thing: Luke was here, eating lunch after working in the barn. I don't think the two men like each other. There seemed to be this . . . tension between them."

"Hmm. I wouldn't have expected them to have a problem with each other."

Rose shrugged. "Maybe it was my imagination."

The kitchen door opened and Luke poked his head in. "Everything *allrecht*?"

Lillian stood and put her cup in the sink. "I have to get back home." She pulled on her coat and was out the door before Rose could say anything.

Luke looked at her. "I want to apologize."

"It was my fault. I overreacted."

"It's understandable. I won't do it again."

"Do you want some coffee?"

"I can get it, *danki.*" He poured himself some coffee and sat at the table. "Where's Daniel?"

"Upstairs supposedly taking a nap." Almost at that moment they heard little feet running around above their heads. "As you can hear, Daniel always does what he's been told."

He grinned. "I remember I always did."

She nodded sagely. "I'm *schur.*"

Bedsprings creaked. Rose got up and walked to the stairs. "Daniel, you stop jumping on that bed and take your nap!"

The bedsprings stopped. "I will, *Mamm.*"

She sat again and sipped her tea. "You got a lot done today."

"I'll come over tomorrow with a ladder and check out the roof."

"And bring someone," she reminded him.

"And bring someone. And we'll get everything done. One day at a time."

Her gaze went past him as she caught a glimpse of scarlet at the window. He turned to see what she was looking at. "That bird's been hanging around the yard all day," he told her.

"Lillian said it's probably hungry. Maybe I'll get some birdseed next time I'm in town, put up a feeder for the winter."

A loud *thunk* sounded from overhead.

"Excuse me," she said and rushed up the stairs.

She found Daniel sound asleep in his bed.

The noise had apparently come from one of his books that had fallen from the bed. A dozen others lay around him on top of his quilt. Breathing easier, she picked up the books, carefully removing one from under his cheek, and set them in his bookcase. Then she covered him with the spare quilt folded at the bottom of the bed.

She ran her hand over the quilt made of scraps of material she'd sewn from shirts and pants for Sam. She'd wept so many tears as she'd sewn it. Bitter tears, angry tears, hopeless tears. Sometimes she'd wanted to give up the effort. But she'd persevered because she wanted Daniel to have something of his *dat.*

Luke looked up when she walked back into the kitchen. "What happened?"

"He's finally asleep. The noise was one of his books falling off his bed."

"I took far worse to my bed."

She held up a hand. "Please, don't tell me. I'm not looking forward to some of what I hear boys do."

He chuckled. "Just part of growing up. I had *schweschders,* and they weren't always the sweet, innocent little girls they pretended to be in front of our parents."

"I guess there are two sides to every story — or siblings."

71

"What was it like to grow up as a twin?"

Rose smiled. "Very special. I had a friend before I was even born. We had our own language no one else understood. And she knows what I'm thinking almost before I do." Now it was her turn to chuckle. "Sometimes that's good, sometimes that's bad."

"Did you ever pretend to be the other one?"

"I'll never tell."

He glanced at the kitchen clock. "Well, I'm going to head on home. I'll be back tomorrow with a ladder."

"And a helper," she reminded him.

"And a helper. *Danki* for the coffee. And lunch."

She watched him pull on his jacket and don his black felt hat. "Luke?"

He turned. *"Ya?"*

"Danki for being kind to Daniel today. I panicked and shouldn't have."

"I told you, it's understandable."

"Well, maybe. But you're not a man who would let him be harmed. And he loved it. Maybe we can let him spend some time with Star and ease me into him getting riding lessons."

"I'm so sorry that I caused you fear," he said slowly. "Lillian said you had a forgiving heart," he said. "She was right."

And with that he was gone.

Rose and Daniel were in the backyard the next day when Luke and Abraham arrived. She waved at them from where she stood near the swing hanging from the oak tree.

"Luke!" Daniel cried and ran over to him to throw his arms around his knees. "Hi!"

"Hello," he said, surprised and touched by the show of affection. "How are you?"

"*Gut! Mamm* said she'd push me on the swing! Will you push me?"

"Luke's here to look at the roof on the house and the barn," Rose told him, coming to stand by him.

"I have a few minutes to push you," Luke said. "Hop on!"

"It's kind of you," she began.

"It's the least I can do." He glanced over at Abraham. "Keep him off the roof for me, will you?"

She nodded and walked over to where Abraham was setting the ladder against the barn. He watched as his cousin stopped when Rose neared him.

"Can I go on the horse again?"

Luke looked back at Daniel. "Sorry, not today. And I want you to promise you won't go out to the barn without your mom or me. Promise?"

Daniel's lower lip thrust out. "But I wanna sit on Star."

"And you will. Just not today. I have to make sure Star's house is nice and safe for her, *allrecht*? We don't want her to have it rain or snow on her head, do we?"

"Nee."

Luke bit back a grin. The kid made it sound so sad. "Hold on. I'll give you a good push and then I have to go work with Abraham. I'll send your *mudder* back."

"I'm here now," she said. "I can push him so you can get started."

"Look, *Mamm,* the red bird is back." Daniel pointed at the cardinal perched in a nearby tree.

"I see."

"I brought some birdseed," Luke told her. "It's in the buggy."

"Oh, that was nice. There's a bird feeder in the barn."

Daniel slipped off the swing. "Can we get it and see Star?"

Rose grabbed his hand. "You have to promise me you won't go into the barn *ever* without me. Promise?"

He nodded solemnly. "I promise."

She glanced at Luke. "It might be a *gut* idea to put a lock higher than you-know-who on the barn door."

74

"Agreed. I'll get on that right after I look at the roof."

He met Abraham at the ladder. "*Allrecht,* I'm going up."

"Be careful!" Rose called over.

Luke exchanged an eye roll with Abraham. No one needed to tell him to be careful. Amish men had been climbing ladders and working like this since they were boys. "Women," he said under his breath, and his cousin nodded.

He climbed the ladder and stepped carefully on the roof, then walked around slowly looking for loose shingles and soft spots. Ten minutes later he descended the ladder. He hated giving Rose bad news but bad news was what he had. He sighed as he got to the bottom of the ladder.

"Not *gut*?" Abraham asked him.

"*Nee.* Needs a new roof." Luke glanced over at Rose.

"Well, can't be helped. It's an old roof." Abraham lifted the ladder. "You coming back with me or staying?"

"I'm staying to work. I'll walk home. *Danki* for the help."

Abraham shrugged. "All I did was stand here."

"Rose told me I couldn't go up on the ladder if someone wasn't here with me."

75

"Got to listen to our women."

"She's not —" He stopped as Abraham grinned.

"Whatever you say. See you at supper." He walked off to put the ladder in the buggy.

Luke wandered over to where Rose was hanging a filled bird feeder on the low branch of a tree. Daniel stood watching her. He grinned when he saw Luke.

"We're gonna feed the red bird," Daniel said excitedly.

"Cardinal," Rose told him.

"Card-nal," he said with a nod, making the word two syllables instead of three.

"So, how much do you think it'll cost to fix the barn roof?" she asked him.

"I have to call about supplies," he told her. "I'll use the phone in the shanty again, if that's okay? I don't have a cell phone." She nodded. "*Gut.* I'll make some calls. We can get started on it this weekend if you want. Abraham will ask some of the men to help me."

"*Kumm,* Daniel, let's go sit on the back porch and see if the birds will come to the feeder."

Luke went into the phone shanty and looked up roofing-supply companies. Soon he'd connected with several businesses and had an estimate drawn up. When he returned to the back porch, Daniel was sitting, rapt, watching a cardinal feasting at the feeder.

"I have an estimate for you," he said as he climbed the steps and sat in a rocker next to Rose. He handed her the slip of paper he'd written it on and saw her wince.

"Well," she said with a sigh. "It could be worse."

"True. Will you be *allrecht*?"

She nodded. "At least the house didn't need roof repair."

"True. Well, I'm going to do some more work in the barn unless you want me to do something else first."

"*Nee,* it'll be important to have those stalls done before Daisy comes." She turned to Daniel. "Let's go inside and make some Christmas presents."

"Chris-mas." He jumped to his feet and raced to the back door.

"We got a late start with the move," she told Luke. "I'll start a pot of coffee. Just come inside whenever you're ready for a cup." She rose and handed him the slip of paper with the estimate. "Of course, if you see any presents being made, you're sworn to secrecy."

Luke traced an *X* over his heart and grinned. "I won't tell a soul."

Later, as he walked home, he thought about the events of the past two days. An innocent desire to give a little boy some fun had frightened his *mudder* to death. Not a good way to impress the woman he was going to be working for. He was grateful that Rose had forgiven him as Lillian said she would. But he was certainly going to be careful not to make such a mistake again. So much depended on this job. He wanted to stay here in Lancaster County and he wanted to help this woman he felt drawn to.

Something fluttered to his right. A cardinal flew beside him, then rose to perch on a branch of the tree ahead. It sat there watching him. He'd seen a cardinal flitting around Rose's farm most of the past two days. Well, it might not be the same bird — cardinals were common in Pennsylvania, after all. Ohio, too, for that matter.

A chill filled the air, but he found it invigorating, and he was warm enough in his jacket. Soon, it would be a cold walk, but he'd never let the weather bother him.

Farms around here weren't much different from those back in Ohio. With the harvest over, fields lay fallow. The winter gave the farmers time to work at making furniture in their barns or elsewhere in town. There was time to repair equipment and plan for the spring planting.

He had a lot to do repairing the barn, helping Rose reestablish the farm.

The farm he'd wanted to buy. He sighed. He'd so hoped to buy it . . . yet if Rose hadn't returned he'd never have met her.

He turned up the drive to Abraham and Lovina's farm. Abraham was just leaving the barn and lifted a hand in greeting. They walked to the back door together and went inside.

"Get cleaned up. Supper's on the table in five minutes," Lovina told them.

Abraham sniffed the air. "Baked stuffed pork chops? With apple stuffing?"

"You've always got a *gut* nose for your favorite," she said with a grin. "Bet you've already figured out what's for dessert."

"Rice pudding."

"Thinks he's so smart," she told Luke as he waited for his turn to wash his hands. "Did you have a *gut* day at Rose's? You didn't come home for lunch."

"Rose fed me." Fortunately, Naiman hadn't paid a visit again.

"How's Daniel? Settling in *allrecht*?" Abraham finished washing his hands at the sink, then dried them on a dish towel.

"Just fine. Nice little boy." Luke took his turn at the sink and accepted the towel from

Abraham. "We're going to have to do some work on the barn roof soon."

"Always a *gut* idea to check it out before we get a heavy snow," Lovina commented.

"That's what I said," Abraham told her.

Lovina called the *kinner* to supper and adult conversation ceased as the usual merry chaos of the evening family meal ensued.

Another night spending time with family. Family that wasn't his own *fraa* and *kinner*. Luke held back a sigh.

SIX

Rose stood at the window watching the men working on the roof and sighed. She'd had so many other ideas of where she'd wanted to spend that money rather than on shingles and wood and such . . . How much more she'd rather buy some paint for the outside and inside of the house. Some wood for Luke to build some furniture and . . . Oh, and just keep the money in savings in the bank. She wanted something for an emergency. When she'd had a *mann,* there'd been no need for hired help like Luke, but now she had to be careful with her money.

Thank goodness the men in the community had come to help Luke with the roof and saved her the cost of labor. Now all she had to do was provide them with a hot lunch. And that was easy since the women of the community were coming to help her.

Not quite a barn raising but almost . . .

"I'm here!" Lillian called as she came in

the kitchen door carrying a big basket. "I brought three big chicken pot pies."

"*Wunderbaar.*" The kitchen timer dinged so Rose grabbed potholders and pulled a pan of apple crisp from the oven and set it on the back of the stove.

Soon the kitchen was full of women and more delicious scents, along with warm sentiments such as "*Wilkumm* home!" and "I'm sorry I wasn't able to help you move in."

"Do we have enough coffee?" someone asked.

"Fannie Mae said she was bringing coffee," answered another. "She's just running a little late."

"Fannie Mae always runs late."

"Truer words were never spoken."

Laughter and chatter filled the air as the big wooden table was set and dishes of food placed in the center.

"It feels like the place is coming back to life," Lillian said, and her eyes filled.

Rose hugged her. "It does."

"Our parents would be so happy."

Rose thought about how this was the first time she was welcoming old friends and new into her home for a workday and a meal. And it *was* her home now — not her parents'. She and Daniel were the family living here.

"Call the men in," she told Lillian. "Let's eat while it's hot."

A blessing was said, bowls and platters of food were passed around, and talk and laughter filled a room that had been too quiet since she'd moved in.

Fannie Mae arrived with the coffee and her usual breathless story of why she was late. She'd done this since way back in their *schul* days, Rose remembered. It was never Fannie Mae's fault that she was late. The alarm hadn't gone off, she'd say. Or she'd run late doing morning chores. Always something. Before Rose had left for Ohio Fannie Mae had rushed up as the packing of the moving truck was nearly done and proclaimed that traffic was awful. It was, of course, always a little worse when she was on the road in her buggy.

"Someone came to the door just as I was leaving and I had trouble getting away," she explained today.

Rose wondered who it could have been. So many of their friends sat around the table now, eating and chatting. She shrugged and took one of the containers of coffee from Fannie Mae and invited her to take a seat.

"We got a lot done already," Luke told

her as she passed him a bowl. "We should be finished before the end of the day."

"*Gut* thing," Abraham said. "We're due for some early snow later this week."

Snow. It brought back a memory of Sam — the first time they'd met he'd been visiting a relative here and attended a church service. Rose had slipped descending the porch steps of the home where the service had been hosted. She'd landed ignominiously at the bottom of them, emerging with a face full of snow.

A man had appeared before her. She brushed at the snow and stared up at him. Sam something. She couldn't remember his last name. He'd held out his hand and helped her up, and their gazes had locked. His eyes were so dark, so intense. Then he'd smiled that wonderful, sweet smile of his and told her that she had sparkles on her eyelashes.

"Sparkles?" She'd laughed at that and brushed her fingers over her eyelashes. She might have landed with her face in the snow, but it should have melted off quickly as red as her face felt. Could a *maedel* have been clumsier?

"Are you *allrecht*?"

She'd nodded, a little dazzled by the way the sunlight behind him made a nimbus of his dark-blond hair.

"You're *schur*?"

"Just a little cold," she'd admitted, shivering.

"Maybe a cup of coffee would warm you up."

Sam was flirting with her, she had realized. She decided she liked it.

"Maybe."

So he'd gone to get the buggy he'd come in. Later Rose found out that Sam had asked his relative if he could get a ride home with someone else so he could take her out.

They'd been inseparable from that day on. She married him and followed him like the biblical Ruth to Ohio. And she'd still be with him if only —

Luke was talking to her. She turned to him. "Sorry, what?"

"Did I tell you that the buggy should be ready for delivery tomorrow?"

"Buggy?"

"Your buggy. Did I tell you that it'll be ready for delivery tomorrow?"

"Nee, you didn't. That's *gut.*"

He smiled. "Where did you go just now?"

"Go?"

"You've been sitting there staring at your plate but not eating," he said quietly.

Rose glanced around, but everyone was

eating or chatting and wasn't looking in her direction.

She shrugged. "Just thinking."

"If you're worried about the cost, I was assured that the repair was below the estimate."

"I'm glad to hear it. Every penny saved is a penny earned."

"Just what my *dat* used to say."

"Mine did too. I guess that's where I got it."

"Good advice, *ya*?" He glanced out the window. "I'm glad we're getting the roof taken care of before it snows."

"Me too."

With the meal soon over, the men returned to work and the women cleaned up the kitchen and left. Rose sat in the silent house with a cup of tea. It felt so *gut* to be getting her home ready for the coming winter. Sam had been all about preparation for the coming season. Looking forward to the future. A *gut* farmer had to look ahead.

Now she was truly looking ahead to a life without Sam. The thought didn't provoke instant tears as it had for so long. But she still didn't look forward to the coming winter. It wasn't the cold weather. She was used to that. But winter was a slower time between the almost frantic fall harvest and the so-busy spring planting. She couldn't help being apprehensive about having too much time to think of this new life she was living without Sam. It had been very hard over the last year, but now she was in a new home with new challenges.

When, oh, when would she stop feeling so alone, so unprepared for a future without her *mann*? Suddenly feeling chilled, she pulled her shawl more closely around her shoulders and sipped the tea, seeking its warmth. Thinking of seasons always made her remember Ecclesiastes. To everything there was a season, a time for every purpose under the heavens. She'd had time to weep, to mourn. Soon it would be time to plant.

When would it be time to heal, to feel peace?

She closed her eyes and prayed. "Thy will be done," she whispered. Then again, "Thy will be done." Already she felt stronger. "Thy will be done."

Warmth filled her. Peace descended. She prayed it would endure this season and more.

Luke stood up on the roof and surveyed the new surface.

The men had labored long and hard that day and the work was *gut.* It, like the building, would last a long time and keep stock and property safe and protected from the weather.

A sense of satisfaction filled him as he looked at the shingles, then the fields surrounding it below. Until he remembered he had been only a worker, not the owner, of this structure or this land.

"Are you coming down any time soon?" Abraham called from below.

With a sigh he climbed down the ladder and found his cousin standing there at its base.

"Didn't think you were ever coming down."

"Just giving it one last look."

They carried the ladder over to Abraham's buggy. Luke watched his cousin climb in and then give him a questioning look. "Aren't you coming?"

"I think I'll see if Rose needs anything else. You go on. I'll walk home."

"Suit yourself. It's getting chilly."

Luke shrugged. "I'll be fine."

"Don't be late for supper."

He gave his cousin a disbelieving look. "When am I ever late for a meal?"

Abraham chuckled. "Never known you to be."

"See you later."

He headed to the house and, when he opened the door into the kitchen, surprised Rose sitting at the table. Her hands flew to her face, and she wiped at it quickly.

"I thought you'd gone home."

He looked away, uncertain if he should acknowledge her tears. Did a man ever get comfortable with a woman's tears — especially a young widow's?

"I wanted to make *schur* you didn't need anything." He stood awkwardly by the door, shutting it only when she shivered and drew her shawl closer and he realized he was letting in cold air.

"I'm fine. *Danki* for the hard work today."

"You're *wilkumm.*"

"Is Abraham still here?"

"*Nee.* I told him to go on."

"Have a cup of coffee before you go. It'll be a cold walk home."

Luke started to tell her that he'd get the coffee, but she was already on her feet hurrying to the stove so he took off his jacket and hat and hung them on a nearby peg.

She set the mug of coffee before him and added a small plate of cookies. When she sat again he noticed she sipped at her mug of tea but didn't indulge in any cookies. Luke ate three and wondered if he'd be considered a pig if he had four.

89

"You worked hard today. Eat all of them if you want."

He grinned. "You read my mind."

"Easy to do when it comes to men and food."

He munched on another cookie. "Awfully quiet in here."

She tilted her head. "Won't be in another minute or two. Daniel doesn't nap long these days."

A board creaked in the ceiling overhead and then he heard feet rushing down the stairs. Daniel burst into the room, his blond hair standing on end and looking like a newborn chick's. He dragged a small quilt in one hand.

"Luke!" Daniel cried.

"Daniel!"

The boy's gaze slid over to the plate of cookies, then traveled up to his *mudder.* "One," she said. "And you eat it at the table."

He climbed up into a chair and studied the plate. With unerring accuracy he chose the biggest one and bit in. He grinned at Luke, showing a missing front tooth and scattering crumbs.

"Eat with your mouth closed," his *mudder* said sternly. She rose to fetch milk and poured it into a plastic cup.

Luke had heard the same admonition countless times as a boy. Did all *mudders* say the same thing? Or was it they said it to boys only?

He found himself wondering idly why she and her *mann* had had only one *kind*. Many Amish couples had more than one in the amount of time he knew they'd been married.

Rose picked up the quilt Daniel had dropped in his pursuit of the cookie, folded it, and placed it on the back of a chair. Luke studied it. The pieces of material worked into the design looked like they'd been cut from fabric often used for men's shirts. It struck him that she'd probably made it from fabric she'd used for Sam's shirts. He knew a thrifty Amish woman used every inch of fabric, but it was a sweet thing to do for her *sohn* as well.

Daniel finished his cookie. "*Mamm?* Can we have beanie weenies for supper?"

"Again?"

He nodded vigorously. His big blue eyes shone.

She sighed and gave Luke a rueful glance. "He'd eat them every night if I let him."

Luke grinned. "Me too. And 'spizgetti' was always a favorite of mine as a boy. Still is."

91

"Spizgetti's *gut,*" Daniel agreed. "We could have spizgetti. Luke could eat supper with us. Please, *Mamm?*"

Luke watched Rose blush. "Luke has to go home," she told him.

"But I could come another night," he said boldly.

"Ya!" Daniel yelled.

"Daniel. Use your inside voice."

"Ya!" he said an octave lower.

Luke finished his coffee and stood. "Then I'll see you both tomorrow and plan on staying for supper."

" 'Bye, Luke!"

The boy was just the cutest. "Goodbye, Daniel. Goodbye, Rose."

When he opened the door and stepped outside Luke discovered the temperature had gone down quite a bit since earlier that afternoon. Still, he wasn't sorry he'd turned down a ride home with Abraham. He'd enjoyed spending time with Rose and her *sohn.*

He heard a buggy behind him as he walked along the road. It slowed and then stopped. "Hello, there, Luke!" Turning, he saw Vernon, the bishop. "Climb in. I'll give you a lift."

"Allrecht, danki."

"How'd the roofing go today?"

"Gut."

"Sorry I wasn't able to help."

"It was no problem. Many men showed up. And women, of course. They fed us well. You missed some fine food. Rose made a delicious apple crisp."

"Speaking of Rose . . ."

Luke felt his stomach lurch. *"Ya?"*

"While some things are different from one Amish community to another, there's one thing that remains the same: single men must be conscious of a single woman's reputation."

Where was he going with this? "Of course."

"Abraham vouched for you, said you're a *gut* and honorable man."

He nodded.

"Rose is a *gut* Amish woman, widowed at a young age. Has a young *sohn.*" Vernon turned and looked at him for a long moment. "They need a *gut* man to look after them. Take care of the farm." He returned his gaze to the road.

"I'm helping her with the farm."

"She needs a *mann.* Daniel needs a *dat.*"

"Are you suggesting I should ask her to marry me?" He knew the Amish community liked the stability of having those of marriageable age married.

Vernon turned again and met his gaze. "Luke Miller, are you a smart man as well as a *gut* and honorable man?"

"I like to think I am."

"Then I wouldn't think you'd need anyone to suggest it."

Luke tried not to chuckle.

Vernon pulled the buggy up in front of Abraham's house.

"*Danki* for the ride."

"You'll think about what I said?"

"*Ya,* I will." He stepped out of the buggy and Vernon drove on.

A flash of red caught Luke's attention. A cardinal flew up and landed on the fence. It sat there, eyeing him with bright black eyes. Luke frowned. He'd been seeing an awful lot of cardinals lately.

The bird cocked its head. It looked familiar somehow. Was it the same one he'd seen around Rose's farm so much?

Luke chuckled and shook his head. A familiar-looking cardinal? He must be more tired than he thought. It had been a very long day today. Time to eat some supper, help with chores, and get some sleep.

SEVEN

The days grew colder, the nights longer. Winter was coming.

As she prepared her home for the coming cold weather, Rose thought of how no one prepared for the season more than the Amish. There were shelves of vegetables and fruit preserved and stored. Firewood was cut and stacked. Cold weather clothing was brought out of storage and mended.

Rose loved winter when the hard work of summer harvesting and canning and preserving was done.

And the fall weddings were nearly over. Rose had loved attending the wedding of Mark and Miriam. She and Miriam had been friends before Rose moved to Ohio with Sam and had wondered if the two of them would ever become more than friends. Miriam had spent a lot of time with Mark, the *Englischer* who'd visited his grandfather's farm in the summer, but Mark had become a big-city attorney. Who knew he'd give that up, become Amish, and marry Miriam?

Now as she sat at the final wedding of the season, she breathed a sigh of relief. It was the last time this year that she'd have to witness two joined in love before God and have to look happy for the couple. She *was* happy for them. It wasn't in her nature to envy the happiness of others. But it was difficult to hear the sacred words and not remember standing before the minister and marrying Sam.

And so hard to remember that just two years after they were married he'd started getting sick — so very sick.

Lillian slipped her hand in hers and squeezed it in sympathy. Rose squeezed back and smiled at her. As she did she saw that Sarah King was watching with damp eyes. It must be hard for her, too, she thought. Sarah was a fellow widow who had lost her *mann* two years before in a farming accident. Their gazes met, and unspoken understanding passed between them. Only a widow understood the pain of another.

The pain had lessened, but would it ever be completely gone?

Lillian squeezed her hand again and Rose realized that the wedding was over.

"Are you *allrecht*?" Lillian whispered.

"Fine." Rose smiled at her. "It's not just the wedding. It's the time of year."

"I know. Want me to come by this afternoon? The boys can play."

Rose nodded. "That would be nice. I'm going to go talk to Sarah before we eat. Save us seats in case I can persuade her to stay."

"I will."

She caught Sarah's eye and they moved toward each other. "It's *gut* to see you," she told Sarah.

"You too."

"I've been so busy getting settled again. But Lillian insisted I have the quilting circle at my house this week. Will you come?"

"I don't know."

Rose hesitated, then stepped forward and put her hand on Sarah's. "I avoided seeing people for a long time after Sam died. It sounds terrible, but I got so tired of people saying they understood how I felt. How could they? They haven't lost their *mann.*"

Sarah stared at her, surprised. "That's what I want to tell them! I know they mean well but . . ."

"But it hurts more when they say it."

"And the bishop —" Sarah stopped, glanced around. "He stopped by for a visit, and we talked. I said I was trying to get over

97

the pain and he said, 'Don't try. Do.' How I wish it was that easy." She frowned. "Then he asked me if I had thought of marrying again. That my *mann* would want that. I don't want to even think of that. I don't care how long it's been. I still hurt so much."

Rose nodded. "I know." She sighed. The bishop in her Ohio community had done the same thing. So far the bishop here hadn't. "Come visit me next week even if you don't come to the quilting circle. I'd love to talk with you more."

"I'll . . ."

"Try?" Rose said, and Sarah laughed ruefully.

"I will."

"*Gut.* And stay for the reception for a while."

"You knew I was going to slip away, didn't you?" Sarah said.

"I did. And I confess I wanted to slip away as well. Come sit here at the table with Lillian and me."

"*Allrecht.* For a while."

The reception was a boisterous affair, full of laughter and fellowship and *kinner* running around. It started with the midday meal — a sumptuous one with tables laden with baked chicken and *roasht,* so many vegetables and relishes and pies and baked goods. Following an afternoon filled with congratulations for the newly married couple sitting at the *eck* — the corner of the wedding table — games would be played and another meal eaten. There was wedding cake, a simply decorated one the bride's family had made as it had most of the food served here in their home today.

Everyone in the Amish community had come to enjoy.

Sarah stayed for two hours with Rose and Lillian before slipping away. Rose walked her out to her buggy, and they hugged.

"I'm glad I stayed," she told Rose as she climbed in and picked up the reins. "See you next week," she said before Rose could remind her.

"Next week."

Rose stood there on the porch for a few minutes watching as the buggy rolled down the drive. It would be the first time the quilting circle had met at her house. Lillian had been pushing her to have it there since she'd moved back, but she'd resisted, saying she hadn't gotten the house into shape yet.

She heard the door open behind her and turned. Luke walked out.

"You coming back in? It's cold out here."

Nodding, she pulled her shawl closer

99

around her shoulders. "Just seeing a friend off."

"Why is she leaving so early?"

"Weddings are hard for widows," she said simply. "She stayed as long as she could." She moved toward the door.

"Are you going home too?"

"*Nee,* I'm fine." As she reached the door and glanced back at him, she saw his look of concern. "Really, I'm fine."

"*Allrecht,* if you say so." He hesitated. "Rose, I'm curious about something. You know, there are some differences in customs here. Some things are different in Ohio. I need some help understanding something."

She stopped, raised her brow. "What don't you understand?"

"Why is there so much celery on the tables? Raw celery, creamed celery . . . Every time I turn around I see celery."

Rose couldn't help it. She laughed and shook her head. "That's your question?"

"*Ya.*"

"It's a Lancaster County thing. It's always been this way. I don't know that anyone really knows why at this point. But it wouldn't be a wedding around here without celery. Sometimes you can get a hint that a family expects a wedding when you see a lot of celery planted in their kitchen gardens."

She stared at him. "Any more questions?"

"Can't think of any at the moment. I'll let you know."

Her lips quirked. "You do that." With a last smile, she went inside.

Luke knew he'd asked a silly question. He'd intended to and he didn't regret it. He'd made her smile. She'd looked so pensive during the wedding ceremony.

His own *mudder* had once said that watching weddings often made a woman think about her own ceremony . . . what the day had meant to her. He figured that's why she'd looked thoughtful, at times sad. The only time she'd smiled was when someone had talked to her and then she'd summoned a small upward curve of her lips. The smile had quickly faded the moment the person who'd spoken had looked away.

He hadn't needed Rose to say weddings were hard for widows. He'd figured they were. Probably they were just as hard for the women who considered themselves old *maedels.*

As he cleaned his plate for the second time that day Luke decided he liked weddings just fine. Who didn't love a day off? And *gut* food in abundance? It gave him a chance to meet more people in the community as well. There were even a few *Englisch* guests the bride and groom knew. He was getting a real taste of the community while sampling yet another delicacy from the dessert table.

"Enjoying the desserts, eh?"

Luke turned at the sound of a familiar voice and came face-to-face with Vernon, the bishop who'd given him a ride home from Rose's several weeks back. He'd been grateful for the ride but vividly remembered how the man had used the time to encourage him to court Rose.

"What Amish man doesn't love a *gut* dessert?"

"I recommend my *fraa's* apple dumplings."

"Had one. You're a lucky man, Vernon."

"Rose bakes a fine spice cake."

"I've had that too."

"Have you thought about our conversation?"

Luke glanced around. Rose stood at the far side of the room chatting with another woman. *"Ya."* He forked up a bite of the cake on his plate. "I'm doing some research on what crops to plant come spring," he said, hoping to change the direction of the conversation.

Vernon studied him then nodded. "Planning is always a *gut* thing." His glance slid over to Rose before returning to Luke. "I think I'll go get a cup of coffee."

Luke continued to eat his cake and considered what Vernon had said. The man had *not* been subtle when he'd said what he had about planning, and Luke had caught his message. Well, he did have a plan in mind when it came to Rose, and he didn't need Vernon to be telling him what to do.

Apparently the bishop here tried to guide single men and women into marriage much like the bishop in Ohio. But Luke hadn't felt that any of the *maedels* back in Ohio were the one set aside for him by God. He was glad he'd come to help his cousin here in Lancaster County and met Rose. After weeks of working for her, he'd realized he felt she was the woman for him.

It didn't matter what he thought, though. Rose wasn't over the death of her *mann*. That much was very obvious. He'd come upon her crying more than once and it didn't take a genius to see that she was still grieving. When she thought she wasn't being watched, her eyes were haunted. Her shoulders hunched as if she carried the weight of the world, and her attention was . . . somewhere else.

She reminded him of a little bird with her delicate bones and way of darting around taking care of her *sohn*. Ate like one too. He'd watched her just pick at her food and eat next to nothing. Why, her *sohn* ate more than she did. How did a body — even a tiny one — get along on so much nervous energy and so little food?

Yet despite her fragility at times, she could summon strength when she needed it. Like taking on the task of bringing the family farm back to life. He supposed being here in the home where she'd grown up gave her comfort but it *schur* was taking a lot of time, effort, and money.

He wondered what she'd think if she knew he prayed for her each night before he slept.

"Luke!"

He turned and looked down. Two boys stood grinning up at him, their faces smeared with frosting. He frowned, perplexed. They were as alike as two peas in a pod — blond hair, big blue eyes, same height. Peering closer, however, he saw one had a missing tooth in front and recognized the familiar gleam of mischief.

"Daniel?"

"This is John," he said, slinging his arm companionably around the shoulders of the other boy. "He's my cousin."

"I see. Having fun?"

John nodded vigorously.

"Did you have cake?" Luke asked Daniel politely, despite the fact that his face was smeared with the evidence.

"Only a little piece." Daniel gave him a sly look. "Can you get us some more? John likes cake."

"Daniel, there you are!" Rose hurried up to them. "I've been looking all over for you. And John, your *mudder* is looking for you too."

John ran off. Rose grabbed a napkin from a nearby table and knelt to wipe frosting off her *sohn*'s face. "Did you enjoy the cake? You have most of it on your face."

Luke bit back a grin as Daniel looked at him, then his *mudder*. "It was *wunderbaar, Mamm*. Can I have some more?"

"Later, maybe." She stood and looked at Luke. "Are you enjoying the cake?"

"Very much. I hope I'm not wearing it."

She smiled. "*Nee*. Perhaps one day soon Daniel won't wear his food either."

Daniel just giggled. "*Mamm*, they're playing a game!"

"Go. But stay inside, you hear me?" She shook her head as he raced off. "Why do little boys think we don't know where they've been?"

"Grass stains on the knees clued you in, eh?"

She laughed then stopped and touched her fingers to her lips. "What?"

"What what?"

"You're staring at me."

He shrugged. "It's just today's the first day I've seen you genuinely laughing."

"That can't be true." She frowned. "That makes me sound humorless."

"Nee," he said. "You're not. Life's been pretty serious for you. But you're back here where your family and your friends can help."

She looked at him for so long he wondered if he'd overstepped. *"Ya,"* she said finally. "You're right. I'm glad I can count you as one of those friends, Luke Miller."

Daniel came running up and grabbed her hand. *"Mamm!* I'm *hungerich!* Can I have some cake? *Aenti* Lillian said she'd get me a piece if you say it's *allrecht.* Can I?"

"May I?" she said automatically, not taking her eyes from Luke.

"You want cake too?" he asked hopefully.

She tore her gaze from Luke and frowned at her *sohn.*

"May I?" he asked, giggling, clearly not chastened.

Luke watched her continue to give him a

stern look.

"Sorry, *Mamm. May* I?" He gave her an angelic look that would have made the hardest heart melt.

"*Ya,* but one piece. And no more today. Understood?"

He nodded and was off before she could say another word.

"I know what you're thinking," she muttered. "I shouldn't let him get away with it."

Luke grinned. "Who could resist that face?"

She sighed and smiled. "Daniel's a *gut* boy. But it wouldn't do to let him think he can always get what he wants." Her smile faded. "That wouldn't be life, would it?"

He was glad when someone stopped to say hello to her. How could he have answered such a question?

EIGHT

Lillian came early to help prepare for the quilting circle. She brought John and Annie.

"Annie stayed home from *schul* today. Her stomach is bothering her."

"I'm sorry, Annie."

"*Danki, Aenti* Rose."

"Where's Daniel?" John wanted to know.

"Upstairs." She barely got the word out before he was racing up the stairs.

"So much energy," Lillian said with a sigh as she settled into a chair at the kitchen table. "Annie, you can lie down in the spare bedroom if you want."

She nodded. "I brought my books to study."

"*Gut.*"

"I asked Sarah to come, but I'm not sure she will." Rose set the teakettle on the stove then reached up into the highest cupboard and took down a plastic container. It worried her that Lillian was looking tired and a little pale.

"What's that?"

She grinned. "I baked cookies. Hid them from Daniel."

Lillian laughed. "I have to hide them from the biggest *kind* at home — my *mann*."

Rose opened the container and began arranging cookies on a plate. "If there are any left you should take some home to Amos. I know he likes snickerdoodles."

"He likes any cookie either of us bakes. I'm not *schur* who loves cookies more — men or *kinner*."

Rose chuckled and lifted the plate. Lillian nipped one from it as she passed her. "Mmm. *Gut*." She finished the cookie in two bites and then followed Rose to choose another. "I'm so *hungerich* lately."

Rose nearly bobbled the plate. She stared at Lillian. "Are you . . . ?"

"Am I what?"

Rose felt a lump form in her throat. "Oh, my," she said. Setting down the plate, she hugged her *schweschder*. "You're going to have a *boppli*."

"I'm not —" Lillian began. She stepped back from Rose's arms. "I don't know for certain yet. I was going to wait another couple of days to do the home test."

Rose just grinned. "*Zwillingbopplin* know these things."

"*Ya.*"

"Maybe you'll have *zwillingbopplin* —"

The kitchen door opened, letting in a gust of cold air. "*Guder mariye!*"

"Sarah! *Gut* to see you!"

She quickly shut the door and then set a foil-covered plate on the kitchen table. "I brought some cinnamon rolls."

"That's *wunderbaar.*" The teakettle whistled, so Rose turned to take it from the burner. "How about a cup of tea?"

"That would be *gut.* It's getting cold out there." Sarah pulled off her jacket and bonnet. "I'll go put my things in the front room."

"I'm glad she came," Lillian said after Sarah left the room.

"Me too. It'll do her *gut* to be with other women." Rose filled three mugs with boiling water and set them on the table. "I haven't had much time to get together outside of church. And there's been little time to quilt with all the moving and getting settled here."

She touched the quilt Daniel had left on his chair when he came down for breakfast. "This is the last one I made. I sewed it for Daniel for Christmas. That was a year ago."

She sighed. "I had to wash it after I finished it. I think it had as many tears in it as stitches." Her fingers traced the pieces of fabric she'd cut from shirts from Sam and Daniel.

Sarah came back into the room. She sat at the table and dunked a tea bag in her mug. "I got here a little too early, I guess."

"I'm glad you did." Rose gave her an encouraging smile and pushed the plate of cookies toward her. "It gives us a chance to catch up."

"There's nothing much to tell." Sarah sipped her tea. "*Mamm* moved in with me. Into the *dawdi haus*. She said she was tired of living alone since *Daed* died a couple of years ago. But I think she wants to watch out for me."

"Sounds like Lillian here."

"I don't think I have to watch out for you," Lillian protested. "It's just nice having you close."

"*Ya.*" Rose smiled at her and then turned to Sarah. "You didn't bring your *sohn.*"

"He woke up with a tummy ache and *Mamm* thought it might be best if he stayed home with her. Give me a little time of my own too," she said.

"Every *mudder* needs that."

Said the woman who was carrying yet

111

another *boppli,* Rose mused.

"Seems a little quiet up there," Lillian said as she gazed up at the ceiling.

"I'll go check on them."

To her relief, Rose found the boys sitting on Daniel's bed chattering a mile a minute. In the guest room, Annie had settled down on the rag rug and was coloring in coloring books she'd brought. Rose made sure they were all settled and knew the rules, then went downstairs and found her living room filled with women who were getting set up to work on a quilt that would be donated to raise funds at the next mud sale. As they stitched the women chatted about what the next quilt — to be donated to an auction for Haiti — would be.

It felt *gut* to sit in the company of other women in the home her *eldres* had built and where she and Lillian had grown up. Sitting before a fire, piecing together a quilt, was tradition, continuity, and went a long way toward healing her hurting heart.

She heard a buggy pull into the driveway and got up to see who the latecomer was. Luke got out, lifted several pieces of wood, and carried them into the barn.

"Who was it?" Lillian asked her when she returned to her seat and picked up her needle.

"Luke. He's going to be building some furniture in the barn this winter. There wasn't enough room in his cousin's barn so I said he could do it here. Especially when he said he could make a few things for me."

"He's a *gut* worker." Fannie Mae checked her stitches and nodded in satisfaction.

"Very nice man," Mary Troyer said as she threaded a needle.

"It's *gut* he was here to help you out when you moved home," Anna Zook added sagely.

All eyes turned to stare at Rose. She saw Lillian was struggling not to laugh.

"I think I'll make more tea," Rose said. "Lillian, can you help me?"

"You think that's funny, do you?" she asked her *schweschder* when they got to the kitchen.

"They mean well," Lillian told her. Then she burst out laughing. "I wish you could see your face. What if it froze like that?"

Rose rolled her eyes. "That's something *Mamm* would say."

"I know. I'm becoming our *mudder.*"

"You've always acted like you're my *mudder.* You're only fifteen minutes older."

Lillian hugged her. "You'll always be my *boppli.* My *boppli schweschder.*"

"*Boppli*? Are you having another *boppli, Mamm*?"

They turned and saw that Annie had walked into the kitchen.

"I was telling your *Aenti* Rose she's my *boppli*," Lillian told her.

"Your *mudder* was being silly," Rose said.

"The boys said to go away when I went into Daniel's room to talk to them. Can I sew?"

"*Schur.* How about some hot chocolate first? If your stomach is feeling better?"

Annie nodded. "With marshmallows?"

"With extra marshmallows." Rose pulled a bag from a cupboard. "And mean boys don't get any until they apologize."

"*Danki, Aenti* Rose!" Annie settled into a chair at the table.

"Girls are so much easier to raise than boys," Lillian whispered to Rose.

Luke set the load of wood down in the barn and headed back to the buggy for the last pieces. As he moved, a flash of red came at him, a cardinal nearly plowing in his face. He slammed to a stop, waving his arms, and it turned and flew back outside.

"Pesky bird," he muttered. As he left the barn he looked up, and the bird zoomed over his head, chirping madly, nearly knocking his hat off. He followed its flight to —

Daniel was hanging out of his second-story bedroom window. "Hi! Luke!" He waved his arms enthusiastically.

Luke had always thought the expression "My heart stopped" was just that — a dramatic expression. But in that moment he felt his heart stop, then start again. "Daniel! Get back inside! Now!"

The boy stopped waving and turned. And then slipped. His body tipped forward and Luke saw terror flash over his face. "Luke!" he croaked.

"Hang on!" He raced toward the house. If the boy fell could he catch him?

"Rose!" he yelled, hoping she'd hear him. "Rose!"

He stood under the window and hated the helpless feeling that swept over him. "Grab the window, Daniel!"

Did he imagine that he heard another child's voice? No, there it was again.

"I gotcha, Daniel!"

The kitchen door opened, distracting Luke. Rose appeared, wiping her hands on a dish towel. "Did you call me?"

"Run upstairs!" he shouted. "Daniel's falling out the window."

She dropped the towel and disappeared. Luke focused on the little boy hanging out the window above.

"Please, God, don't let him fall." He

began praying, harder than he ever had for anything.

What felt like hours — but must have been seconds — later, Rose appeared in the window. She grasped her *sohn* and yanked him inside. Luke began breathing again as he saw her clutching Daniel. He saw another *kind* standing near the window now, the blond boy Daniel had said was his cousin.

Then Rose was setting Daniel down, reaching to close the window with a snap. The three of them disappeared. Luke rushed inside and saw Rose descending the stairs.

"Danki," she said, her voice shaky. "I have never been so scared." She raised a corner of her apron and wiped at her eyes.

"Me either." He touched her arm. "I would have caught him." Or hoped to, he thought, but he didn't want to say it. She looked scared enough.

"When I got up there, John was holding onto his legs. I thought they were both going to go through the window."

He wasn't going to tell Rose just how scared he'd been when he looked up and saw Daniel hanging out the window. That wouldn't do anyone any good. But his heart was still beating so fast. He remembered Rose's reaction to Daniel being on the horse that day and began to understand her fear now. Her wanting to protect her *sohn.* "Do you want me to put some bars across the window?"

She bit her lip. "That might be a *gut* idea. I don't think he'll be opening it again anytime soon, but that might relieve my mind."

He realized he was still touching her arm. He dropped his hand. "I'll do a temporary fix until I can go into town tomorrow and get some bars."

"I'll make you some coffee." She turned and looked over her shoulder. "*Nee,* Daniel, you're in time-out for an hour." She turned back and smiled at Luke. "Just come on in and go upstairs after you get your tools."

He got his toolbox out of the buggy and did as she'd told him to. As he worked on nailing the window shut, he remembered some of the stunts he'd pulled when he was a boy. It was probably best if he didn't tell Rose any of them. Maybe Daniel would be less of a challenge than he'd been. On the other hand, he'd only known the boy a short time, and this was the second time he'd scared his *mudder* . . . although to be fair the other time it had been his fault putting Daniel on the horse. He gave the window a shove, and it didn't budge.

Satisfied, he picked up his toolbox and went downstairs. The two boys sat at the kitchen table, clearly sulking. Daniel looked up at him, and his expression cleared. "*Mamm* said I need to 'pologize for scaring everyone."

Luke nodded. "She's right."

The boy hung his head for a moment then looked up at him, his expression sober. "I 'pologize."

"You were lucky your cousin was there." His gaze shifted to the other boy.

"I held onto him so hard," John told him earnestly.

"That was *gut* thinking."

Rose walked in.

"*Mamm,* I 'pologized."

"I'm glad to hear it."

"Luke's staying for supper tonight, right?"

She looked startled. "If he still wants to."

He grinned. "I do."

Rose walked over to the refrigerator, took a package from the freezer, and set it on the kitchen counter.

"Are we still in time-out?" Daniel asked her.

She rolled her eyes, then pointed at the clock on the wall nearby. "Until the big hand and the little hand are on the twelve." She pushed the coloring books and crayons in the middle of the table toward them. "Now you can have some fun with these or you can come sew with us in the other room."

With a collective, enormous sigh the boys dragged the books closer and began thumbing through the pages.

"I'll be out in the barn if you need me."

"Wait, I promised you a cup of coffee." She walked over to a cupboard, pulled out a thermos, and filled it with coffee. Turning, she handed it to him.

"That's more than a cup."

She grabbed a paper towel, wrapped a cinnamon roll in it, and handed it to him. "It's the least I can do." She cast a meaningful glance at her *sohn.*

"Well, I'm getting supper too. I'd consider it a fair trade."

"Spizgetti," Daniel spoke up.

Luke nodded. "Spizgetti." He headed out to the barn with his coffee and cinnamon roll.

The next time he came inside, hours later, the kitchen smelled amazing. Rich, spicy spaghetti. Baking bread. He breathed it in as he walked to the sink and washed his hands. There were no boys at the table. No coloring books and crayons. Instead, there were three place settings.

119

The timer on the stove went off. Rose hurried in and saw him. "Oh, you're here. Ready for supper?"

"I'm not too early?"

"*Nee.* Perfect timing." She turned the timer off, grabbed potholders, and pulled a pan of garlic bread from the oven.

"So, no more time-out?"

She shook her head and gave him a rueful smile as she set the pan down on the stove. "That was supposedly the longest hour he ever lived."

She turned and took a breath. Shook her head again. And then he watched, helpless, as her expression wobbled and tears began to run down her cheeks. "There's no way to tell a little boy that those seconds I spent racing upstairs not knowing if I'd see him alive again were the longest of *my* life."

"I can't know exactly what that felt like," he told her. "But those were very long seconds for me standing below too. I'm *gut* at catching a softball but I was so afraid I wouldn't be able to catch one little boy."

As her tears came harder, he worried that he'd made things worse. "I was much like Daniel when I was a boy. My *mudder* survived me. Most *mudders* do."

She put the potholders down, reached for his hands, and took them in her smaller ones. "You have big hands. And a big heart. If anyone could have caught him it would have been you."

He stared down at their joined hands, his heart so full of emotions he didn't know what to do with them. "God protected him. I prayed He'd keep him safe. And He did."

Her lips trembled. "*Ya*, He did. Thank God. I couldn't bear to lose him."

There was a thud overhead, then they heard footsteps race across the ceiling. "Someone's up from his nap," she said and dropped his hands.

By the time Daniel rushed into the room the two of them were on opposite sides of the kitchen. And Luke wondered what would have happened if they hadn't been interrupted by one little boy.

NINE

The spaghetti — or spizgetti, as Daniel called it — was a big hit. Daniel had two helpings, and Luke had three.

Luke had the grace to look a little embarrassed when he accepted the third helping. "It's really *gut*."

"Very *gut*," Daniel said, nodding.

Rose plucked a paper napkin from the holder on the table and wiped sauce from her *sohn*'s chin. He grinned at her and used his fork to twirl more spaghetti around it. She used to cut it but for the past year, he'd insisted on trying to eat it the same way she did. Much of the spaghetti slid back onto his plate, but he'd catch a strand or two and suck it into his mouth.

She sighed. *Sohns* and their table manners were a work in progress like the quilt she and the other women had worked on that day.

Rose passed Luke the basket of garlic

bread and he took a piece. She tried not to focus on his hands, so strong and big. Those hands that had almost had to catch this little boy slurping up spaghetti next to her.

"Don't think about it," he said quietly.

Startled, she stared at him. "What?"

"Don't think about it," he told her, tilting his head toward Daniel in a silent message. "It didn't happen."

She took a deep breath. "I know you're right. But I don't think I'll be sleeping much tonight."

"You'll survive it. My *mudder* did and she had four *sohns*. Why, the stories I could tell."

"Don't," she warned, tilting her head toward Daniel much as he had.

He grinned and bit into his garlic bread as he listened to Daniel chatter.

It felt so comfortable sitting here like this, the three of them. It was much like it had been when Sam was alive. At least before he'd gotten sick and made it to the family meals less and less. She wondered just how much of Daniel's fondness for Luke was because he needed that male influence. A boy needed a *dat*. Who knew if she'd ever be able to give him one?

She remembered how some of the women had talked about Luke at the quilting that afternoon and blushed at the memory. The last thing she needed was others matchmaking for her.

Then it struck her: Lillian had said nothing and yet weeks before, when she talked to her about hiring Luke, she'd been effusive in her praise of him.

Lillian was so *gut* at trying to run her life sometimes. Lovingly, of course, but still, she liked to think of herself as a *mudder* figure.

"You're awfully quiet."

She looked at Luke. "Hard to get a word in edgewise," she said as she wiped Daniel's chin again.

"You're not eating."

"I've had enough."

"Don't eat enough for a bird," he muttered.

"I always thought that was a strange expression. If you watch birds for any length of time you'll see they peck at things much of the day."

"Speaking of birds." He set his fork down and wiped his mouth with a napkin. "A cardinal flew into the barn just as I was coming out today. It was acting kinda crazy, flapping its wings and chirping at me. It made me look up, and that's when I saw —"

"Saw what?" Daniel wanted to know. A strand of spaghetti slipped from his fork to land on his plate.

"Saw that it was getting cloudy. It's going to rain tonight," Luke said quickly.

Rose stood and took her plate to the sink. "I didn't make dessert but there's some cake left from the quilting today."

"Cake!" Daniel said. His fork clattered to his plate.

"Finish your salad first," she said automatically.

His gaze went to Luke's plate.

"I always finish my salad. I like salad." Daniel dug his fork in the greens on his plate, then stuffed it into his mouth. "I like salad," he said.

"Don't talk with your mouth full."

"I used to hear that a lot," Luke told her as he rose and put his plate in the sink.

She put a slice of cake on a plate and served it, then poured them both a cup of coffee.

"Done!" Daniel held out his empty plate.

"I see." She cut him a piece of cake as well, and set it in front of him. Before she sat down she pushed his glass of milk closer.

She watched both of them wolf down the cake. Both looked over at the counter with hopeful expressions. Resigned, she rose and cut each of them another slice.

"Bottomless pit," she told Daniel.

He just giggled.

"She means me too," Luke told him.

"Luke's a bottomless pit!" Daniel chanted.

"Very funny. Now get done so you can have your bath and get into bed."

Daniel rolled his eyes and went back to his cake.

"So, did you get a lot done today?" she asked Luke, taking a sip of her coffee.

He nodded as he polished off his cake. "I'm making the dresser. You said that's what you needed first."

"You should work on something you can sell first. We talked about that."

"I'm fine for money. I can wait for the harvest."

She opened her mouth to argue with him and shut it when she saw Daniel watching them. "Drink your milk, then bath."

He sighed and lifted the glass. And drank so slowly she had to bite back a smile. Finally, he drained the last drop and set the glass down.

"I'm going to take him up for his bath," she told Luke. "Have more coffee if you like." She paused on her way out of the room. "And cake."

"Even I don't have room for more cake," he called after her. "I'll do the dishes."

"*Nee,* leave them. I'll do them later."

126

Upstairs, Rose filled the tub, undressed Daniel, and set him in the warm water.

"Boat, please."

She sat on the stool beside the tub and handed him the red plastic boat from the basket sitting nearby.

"Rubber ducky."

The rubber ducky was handed over. And the green bucket and the blue fish.

Daniel splashed and played and sang. It had taken forever to get him into the tub, and now it was taking forever to urge him out of it. Finally, she stood, washed and rinsed him, then lifted him from the tub to dry him. He ran naked to his bedroom and made a game of getting into pajamas.

"Story."

"One."

"Two."

"One."

It took two before he began to nod off. She slid the book from his fingers, set it on the table, and pulled the covers up to his chin. He stirred and smiled when she kissed him on the forehead. "Night-night, *Mamm.*"

"Sleep tight." She tiptoed away.

When she went downstairs, she found Luke still sitting at the table. The dishes she'd left in the sink had magically disappeared.

"You didn't have to do them."

Luke shrugged. "Seems like the least I could do after you fed me such a delicious supper. And two pieces of cake."

She smiled. "You didn't have another?"

"You might have had to roll me out to the buggy if I did."

"You're welcome to take home what's left."

"Danki."

"Sorry it took so long. There's no hurrying him up when you finally get him into the tub. Or into his bedtime book." With a sigh she sat at the table and smiled gratefully when he poured her coffee.

"I couldn't rush him," she told him as she poured in cream and stirred it. "Not after what could have happened today. Not after I know how quickly someone we love can leave us."

"So, tell me about Sam," he said quietly.

Rose stared at him. "Sometimes I forget you haven't lived here all your life."

"So, tell me about him."

She tilted her head and stared at him. "Why would you want to know?"

"He was important to you. And to Daniel."

"Poor Daniel. He only had his *dat* for a

128

few years."

"How did you meet?"

"Sam wasn't born here. He came to visit and we met when he attended church. I fell down the stairs in front of the home where we were having services that Sunday and looked up, and there he was." She laughed and shook her head. "He teased me later that I threw myself at his feet. He asked me out and it didn't take long for me to realize why I had never been interested in any other men in the community. He was such a *gut* man. A hard worker. Loved the land. Loved Daniel."

Then she frowned. "Lillian didn't like him at first. I think she figured out before I did that if Sam and I married we'd leave Paradise. And we did. A woman follows her *mann* after all."

"Schur."

"It wasn't easy for either of us. Lillian and I have always been so close. Twins are. Still, when I decided to marry Sam, she supported me in my decision and helped me pack to move to Ohio. She even came up to get us settled and visited several times with her *mann* and her *kinner*. And when Sam was struggling with the leukemia treatments, Amos brought her up to stay with me. She shouldn't have traveled."

She got up, paced to the window, stood there with her arms wrapped around herself as if she was cold. "It was too much for her. She delivered early, and then she couldn't go back home right away."

Turning, she looked at him, her eyes haunted. "She's sacrificed so much for me. More than I can ever repay."

"That's what family does."

She smiled. "That's true. And that's what you did. You came here to help your cousin and his family after they were hurt in the buggy accident."

Luke shrugged. "I'd been to Lancaster County with my family and Abraham and I got along well. And I liked it here. My *bruder* inherited the farm so I was free. It seemed time for a change."

"Well, it worked out for me. You were here when I needed help with the farm."

Perhaps it was time to tell her he had looked at the farm and wished it was available to buy.

Something fell above them.

"I need to check on Daniel." She rushed up the stairs.

Luke put the coffee cups in the sink and glanced at the clock. He should be going. But he was enjoying sitting here talking with her even if it was about the man she was

130

still grieving.

"One of his toys fell off his bed," she told him when she returned. "He insists on sleeping with every one he owns — and whatever book he was looking at before he fell asleep." She covered a yawn with her hand. "I'm sorry. It's been a long day."

Luke got his jacket and pulled it on. "*Danki* for inviting me to supper. I enjoyed it."

"And we enjoyed having you."

"See you in the morning."

Allrecht, maybe he should have told her about looking at the farm. But the woman was obviously tired. And he didn't quite know how to tell her.

Luke walked out to the barn and hitched up the buggy. And thought about what she'd said about Sam. He sounded like quite a man. But then he'd never known a widow to speak badly of the man she'd been married to — even if he hadn't been *gut* to her. It seemed any man became a paragon after he was gone.

Could another man measure up to that? He didn't know if he could, but he guessed he'd have to if he wanted her to be more than the woman he worked for. And it was becoming clear to him that he wanted that.

And after seeing for himself how Naiman

131

was interested in her he had to try for her or lose her. Maybe it wasn't humble to think so, but Luke felt he'd be better for her than Naiman. To his mind, something didn't ring true about the man. He knew Naiman was successful, that he owned his own farm. He could offer more, materially, than Luke could. But Luke felt Rose showed him more warmth than she had Naiman, and when Daniel had wandered into the room during his last visit Naiman hadn't said anything to him. Something told him Daniel wouldn't connect with Naiman the way he did with Luke.

His heart warmed. Who couldn't love a little boy who acted like he was a hero every time he saw him?

Guilt stabbed him. He'd been about to tell Rose he'd looked into buying the farm and had been relieved when she'd had to see to her *sohn.* What kind of man did that make him? He pondered that as he drove to Abraham's house.

Maybe there was no need to tell her. He hadn't spoken to anyone of looking at the farm with an eye to buy, except an *Englisch* realtor. Not even Abraham. Would Rose ever know?

He pulled into the drive, unhitched the buggy, and led the horse to its stall. He

132

spoke to it quietly as he watered it and gave a glance around to make sure all was well. And then he made his way to the house.

Abraham and Lovina sat in the kitchen talking. Luke greeted them and as he shed his jacket he thought of how similar the scene was to the one he'd just shared with Rose. It was the same kind of moment that was happening in many farmhouses in the Amish community right now. End of day. Chores done. *Kinner* in bed. Time for couples to talk and spend time together over a last cup of coffee.

She looked up. "Coffee's fresh. There's some pie left that we had for dessert."

"*Danki.* I'm full."

"So, you have a *gut* supper at Rose's?"

"*Ya.* I'm not *schur* who ate more — me or Daniel."

Abraham chuckled. "My *mudder* always said boys have hollow legs."

"Men too," Lovina said with a smile.

"True." Abraham pushed aside his dessert plate.

"I'm surprised there's pie left."

"You don't have it tonight, I can't guarantee it'll be here in the morning," Lovina told Luke. "Abraham's been known to sneak down in the middle of the night and have a snack."

"Hardly ever," he protested. "And a couple of times when you accused me you found out it was one of our *kinner.*"

She laughed. "True."

Luke glanced at the clock. "I think I'll turn in. See you both in the morning."

He climbed the stairs and went to his tiny bedroom. He felt more tired than he usually was this time of day and suspected it was because of the frantic fear he'd felt when he looked up and saw Daniel dangling from the windowsill.

As he lay in bed he said a prayer for Rose and her *sohn,* asking God to keep them safe.

TEN

The next morning, Rose sat sipping her coffee and watching dawn light filter through the kitchen window. Daniel would be up momentarily, an early riser like his *mudder.* So these minutes alone in the quiet were precious.

Even after more than a year, mornings were still hard. Too often she woke and found the other side of the bed empty. Daniel had crept into her bed for months after Sam died and she hadn't taken him back to his room. *Nee,* to be honest, it had helped alleviate the loneliness a bit. But finally she knew she had to get him to sleep in his own bed, and he'd learned to stay in it. She couldn't rely on the comfort of a small boy forever.

People so seldom talked about the person you'd lost. And as nice as it had been to have Luke ask about Sam last night, she couldn't read too much into it. Who knew how long he would want to stay in Paradise? She didn't know anything about his life back in Ohio. His only tie to this area was his cousin. While he'd promised to help her with the farm, nothing bound him to that promise. A man as hard-working as Luke could work for anyone. Could have his own farm if he wanted.

He could have any *maedel* too. She'd seen the looks he received from them at church.

Hadn't she even found herself giving him a second look more than once?

She told herself she shouldn't be surprised to find she liked Luke a lot and thought about him often. It would be too easy to look at Luke the same adoring way Daniel did and want to make him a part of the family by getting married.

A few minutes later Daniel came downstairs *hungerich* for breakfast and a little cranky — something he seldom was. She touched his forehead with her lips to check for fever the way her *mudder* had done when she was a *kind. Schur* enough he felt a little warm. So she fixed his favorite *dippy eggs* and gave him a large glass of orange juice which he promptly spilled.

Luke walked in on Daniel wailing over the mess and helped clean it up. "No more tears, big guy. *Mamm*'s not mad and everything's cleaned up. *Allrecht?*"

Daniel sniffed and nodded.

"I think he's got a bit of a temperature," she told Luke. "I'm thinking getting him to stay in bed might be a *gut* idea."

"No nap!" Daniel's lower lip jutted out.

She looked at Luke. "Just a normal day in the Troyer household. Spills and tantrums before 8:00 a.m. I can handle this better than a day like yesterday."

"I'm *schur*." He poured a cup of coffee. "Maybe later, after resting, Daniel and I could do something."

Daniel's expression cleared. "Do something?"

"*Ya*. We'll see how you feel then."

"*Allrecht*," he said reluctantly. Propping his head in one hand he began eating his eggs. Slowly.

"I'll be out in the barn working," Luke told Rose, and she nodded.

She sat at the table and ate her eggs and toast. Daniel finally finished eating, drank his juice without further spills, then climbed the stairs to his room with an aggrieved air — a boy going to his doom. She smiled, drained her coffee, then rose to clear the dishes.

Ordinary mornings. They were the best.

She filled the sink with warm water and

dish detergent and sang as she did the dishes. The day was gray and overcast but it didn't dampen her mood. Birds pecked at seeds in the feeder, a cardinal a bright spot of color among the other birds. As much as she didn't mind hard work, this time of staying indoors, with shorter days and easier chores, suited her just fine. For everything a season . . .

It was a *gut* day for soup. Into a big pot she tossed what was left of the ham from Sunday's supper, a package of split peas, onions, carrots, and some chicken broth she'd frozen.

After she tidied the kitchen, she tiptoed up the stairs to check on Daniel. She found him sound asleep, his cheek resting on one of his favorite books. She eased the book out and set it on the bookcase. When she touched her fingers to his forehead, it felt cool. Maybe he wasn't coming down with something after all.

Reassured, she left him and went into the room she'd once shared with her *schweschder*. She'd thought it would make a *gut* sewing room. She swept the room with her broom and then opened the closet and had to smile. There, on the pole where they'd hung their dresses, was the line she'd marked on the wood with a black pen. On the left, she'd written her name; on the right, Lillian's. She'd drawn it after a tiff when Lillian had taken up too much space in the closet and threatened to draw a line down the room.

Being a twin wasn't easy. They'd shared a womb, shared looks, shared a room. Sometimes sharing space had just become too much. Of course, in the way of *kinner,* when their *dat* had offered to move one of them into one of the unused bedrooms — the house had four but there had been no more siblings born — she and Lillian would have none of it.

Her grin faded. Her s*chweschder* had been her first friend — literally, while they had been in the womb. Her best friend. And her *schweschder* had shared so much with her, so many *gut* things.

Thinking about Lillian, she felt a keen regret that Daniel didn't have a *bruder* or *schweschder.* It was another of her losses.

She sighed. Most Amish families had many *kinner* but years had passed and she'd begun to wonder if she and Sam would ever have a *boppli.* Then he'd gotten sick, so very sick, and in the darkest hours when she thought he was going to die, she'd feared she'd be left all alone.

When Daniel had come along it had been

a miracle and he'd breathed new life into the house. They'd been thrilled, and Sam had reveled in being a *dat*. It had taken awhile and more treatments, but he'd finally recovered — a remission the doctors called it. No more long trips to the hospital for chemotherapy that drained him. No blood tests that had spirits soaring one day and plunging another.

And then, after two years of freedom, just when they'd begun to hope that that chapter in their lives was over, the cancer had come back and in what seemed like the blink of an eye, he was gone. She'd stood at his gravesite holding young Daniel on her hip as Sam's coffin was put into the ground.

Life had gone on because she had to take care of Daniel.

The sound of a door opening downstairs brought her back to the present. After a quick peek into Daniel's room she went downstairs and found Luke in the kitchen.

"So where's my pal?"

"Napping. Are you ready for some lunch?"

"*Schur.* If it's no trouble. I've told you that I don't expect you to feed me every day."

"It's the least I can do." She walked to the sink to wash her hands and then went to the refrigerator to pull out the makings for sandwiches. "You really don't have to do something with him when he wakes up, you know," she told him as she made him a ham-and-cheese sandwich.

"I don't mind. Daniel's a fun *kind.*" Luke washed his own hands and sat at the table.

She set the sandwich before him and went to a cupboard for a bag of potato chips. Sam had always liked them with his lunch sandwich and so she'd kept buying them.

She made herself half a sandwich and took it to the table. Luke hadn't touched his food.

"Did you want something else?"

"Nee." He hesitated. "I hope I wasn't being too personal asking about Sam last night."

"Nee, it's *allrecht.* Sometimes it helps to talk about him. When people don't it's like he didn't exist."

"I think sometimes people are afraid they'll say the wrong thing. So they don't say anything."

Nodding, she picked up her sandwich and bit in.

"Daniel looks so much like you. How is he like his *dat?*"

Rose swallowed and took a sip of her coffee. "His curiosity, I think. Oh, I forgot. I brought up a jar of pickles last night. They'd go *gut* with your sandwich."

"I'm fine," he said but she was already hurrying to get the jar. A movement on the stairs caught her eye. "Daniel! You're up!"

She picked him up and carried him to his chair and felt relief when Luke focused his attention on him. Questions about Sam were one thing. Questions about Daniel were another.

"Do something."

Luke looked at Daniel. "What?"

"You said nap and do something."

"I should warn you. He never forgets anything," Rose told him as she made Daniel a half sandwich and put it before him. She touched his forehead and found it cool. Thank goodness. They didn't need a cold. He tended to get them easily and hold on to them for weeks.

"I have an idea," Luke said. He handed Daniel one of his chips and mouthed *Buggy ride?* to her while the boy was distracted.

She bit her lip. "It's a little cool."

"We'll bundle him up. Maybe stop for something —" He hesitated and handed Daniel another chip. "— something warm on the way." He mouthed *Hot chocolate.*

She grinned and gave in. Soon it would be so cold that they wouldn't go out more than necessary. "I need a few things in town."

"Then a ride it is."

"Ride?" Daniel's eyes lit up.

Luke nodded. "*Ya,* we're going for a ride."

Daniel immediately slid from his chair. Rose grabbed his shirt sleeve. "After we eat, Daniel. After we eat."

He climbed back into his chair and resumed eating. But this time he didn't drag out the meal the way he had his breakfast. He chomped happily and finished his sandwich quickly then swung his chubby legs as he waited impatiently for them.

Rose exchanged a smile with Luke.

"Done?" Daniel demanded when she ate the last bite of her sandwich.

"Done." She picked up their plates. "Now, go potty and we'll get your jacket and hat on."

"Don't have to go now."

She merely gave him a look. He slipped from his chair and raced for the bathroom.

"Don't let him pressure you to hurry up," she told Luke.

He chuckled and pushed aside his empty plate. "I'm done. *Danki.*" He stood. "I'll go hitch up the buggy."

A few minutes later they were climbing in. "If we drive past a vegetable stand and they have pumpkins, keep going," she whispered quickly to Luke as Daniel clambered into the back seat. "I'll tell you why later."

"Allrecht."

They set off to town. Luke cast a glance at the back seat and saw Daniel staring wide-eyed at the passing scenery. He looked back at Rose. She looked thoughtful as she stared out the side window.

"I missed this place," she murmured so low he almost missed what she said. "I wanted to like Ohio since Sam did. But I missed my home here. I missed it so." She glanced at him. "Sometimes I feel guilty at being happy to be back."

"He wouldn't want that."

"Nee," she said and sighed.

"Well, we've made your young man happy. Where would you like to go first?"

Rose pulled a list from her purse. "I need some sewing supplies."

"Sounds like a girl activity."

She narrowed her eyes at him. "Men sew too. And I am a girl. Woman," she corrected.

He'd noticed. "I think Daniel and I need to visit the hardware store while you're shopping."

"Hardware? *Mamm,* what's hardware?"

"Just a store," she said, shooting Luke a

144

look that told him he should have done as he had earlier and asked her first before mentioning it in front of Daniel. "You don't have to watch him."

"It'll be fun. Give you an hour to yourself."

"I don't need one."

"All *mudders* do. My *mudder* used to say so."

"There's a lot of sharp things in such a store."

He glanced at her. "Not like your store? Needles and pins and such?"

She frowned. "You aren't going to try to tell me that there aren't far more dangerous things in a hardware store. Like hedge clippers and screwdrivers and —" She stopped, gave a quick glance into the back seat. "Little pitchers have big ears."

"We're gonna get pitchers?" Daniel asked, kicking the back of his *mudder*'s seat.

"Nee."

"Trust me. I'll take *gut* care of him." He stopped before the fabric store. "We'll be back in an hour. Have fun."

"Have fun, *Mamm!*"

Uncertain, she got out, then looked into the back seat. "You'll be careful?"

"We'll be fine," Luke assured her.

"Giddy up, horsie!" Daniel cried. "Go,

Luke! Hardware store!"

"We'll see you in an hour." He called to Daisy and the buggy moved forward. They left her standing on the sidewalk. When Luke glanced back, he saw her stand there for a long moment, and then she turned and went into the shop.

Not too far from where they'd left her, Luke parked behind the hardware store and barely managed to grab Daniel before he bolted out of the buggy by himself.

"Hardware store?" Daniel looked up at him with his big blue eyes.

Luke nodded. Daniel slipped his small hand into Luke's and Luke felt his heart squeeze a little.

They walked into the store and Luke saw it through the eyes of Rose. So many sharp things. So much danger.

The quilt shop would have been so much safer.

Luke gulped. An hour. All he had to do was keep one small boy alive and unharmed for an hour before returning him to his *mudder*.

Surely he could do that.

ELEVEN

She dreamed of Sam that night.

It was *wunderbaar* to be out in the fall sunshine riding to a Sunday service, Sam by her side, Daniel a rosy cheeked toddler chattering to his stuffed toys in the back seat. Leaves of gold and scarlet and russet rained down and carpeted the road in glorious autumn color. The air was chilly so everyone was bundled up.

Sam insisted on driving although he was clearly still feeling weak from the chemotherapy earlier that week.

"I can still drive," he told her. "After all, the horse does all the work. It doesn't take much to hold the reins and let Daisy take us where we want to go."

"Save your strength," she murmured. "Relax and let me take the reins."

"Want to be in charge, eh?" he teased, his gaze as warm as a summer sun.

Rose moved closer and slipped her arm

147

through his. "I want you to enjoy today and not get overtired. I want you with me forever, my *mann*."

"I want you with me forever as well, my *fraa*. God willing."

She nodded and fought back tears. "God willing."

Rose watched Sam carefully as he sat in the men's section in the warmth of the Hostettler home. He made it through the three-hour service and actually seemed to grow stronger as he sang the hymns he loved and prayed with his longtime friends and church members.

It was *gut* for him here, she saw, and was glad that she'd agreed to move here with him after their marriage.

But as soon as the service was over he swayed when he walked a few feet and they had to go home. His friends hitched the buggy up and helped him into it. And he didn't argue with Rose about driving but reclined in the back seat with Daniel on his lap.

They made one stop on the way home but he didn't get out. Daniel had spotted a roadside display of pumpkins and cried, "Punkin!" Rose hadn't wanted to stop but Daniel cried so excitedly that Sam had added his own chant of, "Punkin! Punkin!"

Rose had pulled over and gotten out, lifting

Daniel from Sam's arms and taking him to pick one out. When they returned to the buggy, Daniel carried a small one and held it out to Sam.

"*Dat*'s punkin!"

"Just what I wanted," Sam said and Rose saw he was touched.

"My punkin!" Daniel said, pointing to the one that Rose carried.

When they pulled up to their house a short time later, Rose worried that Sam — looking paler and more frail by the minute — wouldn't be able to make it inside by himself.

Two buggies pulled in behind them. Her heart sank. The last thing she felt like right now was company. But it was two of Sam's friends, and they looped his arms around their shoulders and cheerfully and gently got him inside and to bed in the downstairs bedroom they'd fixed up when he got sick.

She left Sam and Daniel in the bedroom and went to fix lunch since they hadn't been able to stay for the light meal after church service at the Hostettler home.

When she walked back in a short time later with a tray. She found Daniel snuggled up in Sam's arms, his own small arms still wrapped around his pumpkin. Daniel was absorbed in the magazine Sam was reading to him. *Nee,* not a magazine. A seed catalog. Sam kept a pile of them on the bedside table, beside his recliner in the living room . . . There were seed catalogs all over the house. But she never minded it. He was planning on spring planting and that hope kept him alive.

Sam grinned when he saw her staring at the catalog.

"He wanted me to read him a story," he explained as she set the tray down on the hospital tray table over his bed. "I'm telling him about the story of life. It all begins with a seed, right?"

"Punkin has seeds," Daniel said importantly. "And one day in the spring we'll put those seeds in the ground and grow more punkins, right, *Mamm*?"

"*Ya,* in spring my two farmers will be planting seeds," she agreed. "And there will be lots more punkins and all kinds of other things." She swallowed hard. "Now let's eat our lunch and have a nice nap, shall we?"

They sat on the bed eating sandwiches and the potato chips Sam always had to have with them. And crumbs got scattered and Daniel spilled some juice and it was the best meal Rose ever ate in her life.

Rose took the tray back to the kitchen and when she returned Sam was sound asleep with Daniel tucked under his arm. She reached down to lift Daniel, intending to put him in his

150

own bed for his nap, and then Sam opened his eyes and smiled at her. He held out his hand and she took it, slipped into bed with them, and they slept as the golden afternoon turned to dusk.

She stirred, woke, and found she lay alone in her bed.

There was no need to glance over at the bedside table to see stacks of seed catalogs no longer lay on it. She'd given them to one of Sam's Ohio friends before they moved. All of them except the one that Sam had turned into a story for Daniel. That one was packed with Daniel's books and came to Pennsylvania with him.

She didn't know how much Daniel remembered about Sam but he'd never lost his fascination with pumpkins and seeds.

Well, she supposed it was natural. After all, he was the *sohn* of a *mudder* who owned a farm as well as the *sohn* of a farmer. His obsession with them was a *gut* thing.

But last fall and again this year, Daniel carried a pumpkin everywhere he went as if it was a favored toy. A peek in his bedroom showed he had put his latest pumpkin on his bedside table.

With a rueful shake of her head, she started downstairs to fix breakfast. The kitchen was chilly but it took only a few minutes for it to warm up once she turned on the oven. She started the percolator, got out baking ingredients, and began measuring them. It was an unusual thing to be baking first thing in the morning but her dream had lingered after she'd woken.

A delicious scent filled the air as she sat down with her first cup of coffee for the day. She looked up after hearing the brief knock on the kitchen door. Luke walked in, sniffed the air, and looked at her hopefully.

"Smells like pumpkin."

"It was on my mind. I made pumpkin bread. It'll be out in a few minutes. Coffee's ready now if you want a cup."

"Don't mind if I do."

Rose glanced up as she heard a thud on the floor. "Someone's up." She rose and got eggs from the refrigerator. "Have you had breakfast?"

"*Nee*. Thought I'd get the first coat of stain on the dresser. You don't have to feed me."

"It's no trouble. I hope you like scrambled eggs."

"Love them."

"Luke!" Daniel rubbed his eyes as he walked into the room.

He turned. "Daniel!"

"Hey, I'm here too," she teased her *sohn*.

"Hi, *Mamm.*" He held up his arms so she could pick him up and he gave her a kiss.

She put him in his chair just as the timer went off. Turning, she pulled the loaf pan from the oven. "Pumpkin bread," she told Daniel.

"My punkin?" he cried, looking distressed.

"*Nee,* I didn't use your pumpkin. It's still up in your room."

She turned the loaf out onto a rack on the counter so it would cool, set a skillet on the stove, and dropped a lump of butter into it. A few minutes later, she was setting scrambled eggs and slices of pumpkin bread on the table.

Luke grinned at her. "This is lots better than the biscuits and couple hardboiled eggs I brought in a sack. I'll have that for lunch."

"I think we can do better than that. I make a pot of soup most days when it's this cold, remember."

They sat there eating and Rose's mind drifted back to the dream. Had she dreamed of that special afternoon with Sam and Daniel because she and Daniel had gone for the buggy ride with Luke the day before?

She watched Daniel grin at Luke and wondered if it was wrong to let her *sohn* become so attached to this man. Who knew how long he'd be here helping her with the farm? She felt a strong pull for the man herself but it was too soon to think of marrying again. And how could she give away her heart again? The pain of losing Sam had nearly killed her.

Did God set aside more than one man for a woman? She just didn't know.

Luke watched the fleeting expressions cross Rose's face as he ate. Something was troubling her. Sometimes he wished he could slip inside that mind and see what she was thinking. Then again, maybe it wasn't so hard when her glance went to Daniel, then to him, and she frowned.

Did she think the *kind* was getting too attached to him?

The truth was he was getting pretty attached to Daniel. Who wouldn't warm to a little boy who looked up at you as though you were something special?

Or a punkin. He grinned at Daniel. Spring planting was going to be fun. He'd make sure there was a special plot of land just for pumpkins.

He finished his breakfast, accepted a second cup of coffee, then told himself he needed to be getting to work. It was all too easy to sit here in the warm kitchen and feel he was in the most right place in his life.

Lost in his own thoughts, he was halfway to the door when he remembered he hadn't thanked Rose for breakfast. He glanced over at her and saw her gazing at him thoughtfully.

"What? Do I have something on my face?" he asked, brushing a hand over it, feeling like he looked like Daniel with crumbs all over his chin.

"Nee," she said and blushed as she stood to clear the table. "Don't forget you don't have to eat hardboiled eggs for lunch."

"I won't. And *danki* for breakfast. The punkin bread was *wunderbaar.*"

That brought a smile to her too-often sad face.

Luke went out to the barn, fed and watered Daisy, and then set about brushing a layer of stain on the dresser he'd built for Rose's bedroom. He hefted the bag of birdseed he and Daniel had picked up at the hardware store and walked around the yard filling the bird feeders. Almost immediately the male cardinal that had been hanging around the farm since Luke started working there flew up to inspect his work.

He'd never tell anyone he thought it was the same bird. But he knew that it was.

And if that bird hadn't caught his attention the day Daniel had nearly fallen out of his bedroom window, things might have turned out very differently.

He sent up a silent prayer of thanks to God for the special little winged creature.

A few chores later, he checked on the stain. It was already dry and looked even better than he'd thought it would. He hoped Rose would like it. While most Amish men made the furniture for their homes, it was the first he'd built for her. He didn't want it to be the last.

The barn door opened and a female figure walked in, silhouetted against the light. He smiled then realized it wasn't Rose but her *schweschder,* Lillian.

It was still a bit of a shock when he saw someone who looked so much like her. Still, although they were identical *zwillingbopplin,* he'd quickly discerned the differences between them. Rose was subdued, while Lillian seemed constantly in motion. Rose's features were softer, Lillian's sharper, with a more pointed chin. Both had slim builds but Rose was almost frail since she ate less than a bird.

"Nice work," Lillian said as she caught sight of the dresser. "Are you making it for sale?"

He shook his head. "Rose needs it for her bedroom."

She nodded. "She didn't bring all of her furniture from Ohio. Some of it belonged to Sam's family and she left it for them."

"I'm surprised they didn't try to talk her into staying."

"They might have," she said quietly. "But I was more persuasive."

Luke studied her. He bet she was.

"It's been *gut* for her to be back here," she told him. "I think she'll come out of her sadness here, being in her home again."

"I hope so." But she still seemed so sad to him.

"Rose sent me out to call you in for lunch."

Time had passed quickly. *"Danki."*

He opened the barn door and followed her outside. He stopped when she did.

"That reminds me. I owe you a *danki* for saving Daniel from harm the other day. Maybe even saving my own *sohn,* who was trying to hold on to him as he nearly fell out the bedroom window." She shivered. "Both boys could have been gone in the blink of an eye."

Luke shut the barn door. "No thanks needed. I would have hated to see either of them harmed." He frowned, remembering.

"Something made me look up as I walked out of here that day."

"Something?"

He hesitated. "There's this bird that's been hanging around the yard. It practically fluttered into my face."

"A bird?"

"Ya." He laughed sheepishly. "I know, you must think I'm *ab im kop.*"

Her expression became intense. "What kind of bird?"

"A cardinal."

She tapped a finger on her lips. "Interesting. Rose told me she's seen a cardinal visiting the yard a lot since she moved here. They're not uncommon this time of year. But some of us have seen them after a loved one passes. I did after *Mamm* and *Daed* passed. A pair of them visited my yard for months."

She looked over, and he followed her glance. A bright-red cardinal was perched on the ledge of the kitchen window, its tail feathers twitching as it stared into the room.

"Very interesting."

The back door opened and Rose appeared. "Are you two coming in for lunch or not?" she called.

"Ya, sorry!" Lillian answered.

As they walked toward the house the cardinal swiveled its head and watched them but didn't move from its perch.

Daniel joined Rose at the door. "C'mon, *Mamm,* I'm *hungerich!*"

Mamm? Luke squinted.

"When aren't you *hungerich,* John?" Lillian called back.

The closer they got, the more Luke could see it wasn't Daniel. Those cousins looked so much alike, for *schur.* More alike than any cousins he'd ever seen. Shaking his head, he followed Lillian into the house.

TWELVE

Rose peeked into Daniel's room. He was asleep. Finally.

How she wished she had the energy of a four-year-old. She quietly closed the door, went to her room, and got the box down from the top shelf of the closet. Climbing into bed, she set the box before her and opened the lid. She smiled. Her boy was growing so fast.

She pulled out the shirt she was sewing for him and stitched on the buttons. A new pair of pants was in order too. She'd bought a length of fabric for those and would cut them out tomorrow while he napped. If he napped.

Her task completed, she tucked everything back into the box and thought about her other surprise. A new sled was hidden on a high shelf in the barn. She couldn't wait to see what he thought of sliding down a snow-covered hill or skating across the ice of a frozen pond this winter.

It wasn't easy to think about another Christmas without Sam but she was determined to make this time of Christ's birth a wonder for Daniel. She wanted him to know about joy and peace and family.

So she'd do her best to hide the feelings of loss, of pain. And try to open her heart to the gift of life and joy and giving of self the season promised.

She climbed into bed, drew the quilt high up over her shoulders, and closed her eyes. Last night's dream lingered on the edge of her memory but she knew it wasn't wise to ask for another. Doing so just made it harder to let Sam go.

It was important to remember how blessed she was. She had a nice home, warm and sheltering. It creaked gently in the cold wind, but she was warm and tucked in bed. She also had a *sohn* just down the hall.

She couldn't wait to get out the manger Sam had made their first Christmas. When she'd brought it out of the box last year Daniel had been so delighted to put *Boppli* Jesus in his manger.

One child had changed her life. Now, as they approached the time of Christ's birth, she thought about how one child had changed the world forever.

Unbidden, her thoughts went back to the day when Daniel had nearly fallen out of his bedroom window. She would have been devastated. Had Sam been watching and wondering if Daniel would join him in his arms in heaven?

She was glad she still had Daniel. It was enough that she'd lost the *mann* she loved, the *eldres* who had raised her.

She drifted off to sleep feeling secure in His arms. There were no dreams of Sam that night. When she woke, she wasn't *schur* if she was happy or sad about that.

The next morning she was up early, feeding herself and Daniel, doing morning chores. Then she bundled them up and they went out into the backyard and the surrounding fields to find things to decorate the house for the season. They gathered fragrant evergreen boughs for the mantel in the living room and to form into a wreath for the front door. Daniel carried a bucket and filled it with pine cones and acorns.

Once they had enough, they dumped their bounty on the back porch and went inside to warm up with bowls of chili. Then she cleared the dishes, set them in the sink to wash later, and spread a plastic cloth over the table to protect it.

They carried in the things they'd gathered.

Daniel's eyes lit up when Rose set out the little bottles of glue and glitter she'd bought.

"You have to be careful with this," she cautioned and showed him how to squirt little dabs of glue on the pinecone and then sprinkle on glitter.

Of course he squirted on too much glue a few times and there was entirely too much glitter loaded on the "petals" of the cones. But patience won out and soon they had a collection of natural ornaments.

While they dried she gave him construction paper to make Christmas cards. She wrapped evergreen branches around a wire form to make a wreath.

Luke came in while they worked. "Picked up feed and some other supplies," he said as he walked in rubbing his hands together. "Cold out there."

"Chili's on the stove and coffee's fresh."

He paused by the table. "Well, look at the artists at work."

"Chris-mas is coming," Daniel told him. He picked up a pinecone with clumps of red glitter sparkling on it. "This one's for you."

"Wow!" he said, accepting it. "*Danki*. I love it."

Daniel went back to his cards, his little face scrunched up in concentration.

"Let me get you some chili," Rose said, setting down the wreath.

"*Nee,* keep doing what you're doing. I can get it." He washed up, then got a thick pottery bowl from the cupboard and ladled chili into it.

"Pretty," he said as he took a seat at the table.

"*Danki.*" She began wiring some of the sparkling pinecones onto the wreath. "I thought I'd set up a little stand out in front of the house. Lillian and I used to sell them this time of year. She decided she wanted to do some other crafts this year."

"*Gut* idea. I'll set up a table for you. When do you want to do it?"

"Saturday."

He nodded and began eating. "I have some leftover lumber. I could make up some birdhouses. Some for birds, some that are, you know, decorative."

"I like that idea. My *dat* made some of the ones in the backyard."

She glanced at Daniel. He'd gotten quiet and now she saw he was nodding a little as he sat there at the table.

"Time for a nap."

He straightened immediately. "Not tired."

Her little boy never admitted to being tired. Rose held out her arms. "Time for a

164

nap. You can read until you're tired."

Resigned, he let her lift him. She saw that despite keeping an eagle eye on him, he had silver glitter in his eyebrows. Sighing, she stopped at the sink, wet a dish towel, and got as much of the glue and glitter off his face as she could.

" 'Bye, Luke," Daniel mumbled as they left the room.

" 'Bye, Daniel."

When she came back downstairs Luke was serving himself a second bowl of chili. "Mmm. Best I've ever had."

"Danki."

"Don't tell my *mudder* I said that if you ever meet her."

She bit back a smile as she picked up a pinecone and wired it to attach it to the wreath. "I won't."

"Speaking of *mudders.*"

"Ya?"

"I got a letter from her yesterday. She wants me to come home for Christmas."

Luke watched Rose's fingers still on the wreath for a long moment and then she began working on it again.

"I'm *schur* she does. When will you leave?"

"I was going to tell her that I can't."

Rose raised her gaze. "Why would you do

that? You should be with family this time of year." She paused. "Did you go home last year? I remember Lillian telling me you came here to help Abraham after his accident."

"*Nee,* I didn't. He and his family needed me."

"But he and his family are doing well now. You could visit your family."

"I'm needed here."

"We can spare you to go home, Luke," she said quietly. "I want you to go if you want to. We never know how long our time with family might be."

"*Nee,*" he said. "But they wouldn't want you to be without my help."

"I can get help if I need it. Please don't let that stop you from going."

"I'll think about it."

"*Allrecht.*"

"I'll be going back out to work some more on the furniture. And start a birdhouse or two."

Luke glanced out the kitchen window as he walked to the back door. There was that cardinal looking in again, its black eyes so bright and inquisitive. He turned. "Rose?"

"Hmm?" She glanced up from her work, looking a little distracted.

"Never mind." He grabbed his jacket and

went out. The sky was overcast and the wind had a cold bite to it. The barn felt warm, though, the scents of hay and wood and horse familiar and comforting. He spent the afternoon cutting out a bedside table for Rose and then started on cutting a paper pattern for a birdhouse. He'd do the making, but leave the painting and decorating to Rose. He figured she'd do a better job of it than he could.

By the time he needed to head home he'd done a *gut* day's work. He cleaned up his work area, fed and watered Daisy and Star, and stuck his head in the back door to say goodbye to Rose.

"You'll think about what I said?"

He nodded. "See you tomorrow."

He thought about their conversation while walking home. As much as he wanted to see his family, he wanted to be here, with Rose and Daniel. *This* was coming to be home for him.

But it isn't home, his conscience reminded him. *They don't belong to you.*

He walked into Abraham and Lovina's and again felt he was in another man's space, another man's life. This was why he'd started looking for his own farm here. Staying with his cousin and his *fraa* and seeing them with their family had made his heart yearn for his own *fraa,* his own house. Rose, Daniel, the farm, and hopefully some more *kinner* in the future if God so willed.

The times he shared a meal with Rose and Daniel were so special. Now he sat at the table, prayed with his cousin's family, then helped himself to meatloaf and mashed potatoes and vegetables as they were passed to him. He stared at his full plate and sighed.

"Luke? Are you *allrecht?*"

"Hmm? What?" He looked up at Lovina.

"You're looking sad."

He shook his head. "Can't imagine why. I'm fine."

He was used to waiting. A *gut* farmer had to be. You waited for the right time to plant, the right time to harvest. Waited for your crops to sell and prices to rise.

Waited for the will of God.

So now he had to wait for Rose's grief to pass so she'd see him as the *mann* he wanted to be to her.

One of the *kinner* knocked over his glass of milk and Lovina occupied herself with mopping up the spill.

"Rose is making things to sell for Christmas," he said quickly when she turned her attention back to him. "You know, wreaths, decorations. I'll be helping her set up a table in front of the house on Saturday."

"She and her *schweschder* used to do that back when they were young. They sold a lot to the *Englisch* locals and tourists."

"I'm making some birdhouses for her to sell."

"Wooden trinket boxes sell well too," Abraham chimed in. "Don't take too long to make. *Englischers* like them to put small gifts, jewelry, that sort of thing into."

Luke raised his brows. Abraham seldom talked during the meal. "I hadn't thought of that."

Abraham nodded and went back to eating.

Luke had managed to make a number of birdhouses that afternoon. He figured he could make some of the trinket boxes in the next few days. Next year he'd get started earlier so they'd have more to sell.

Next year.

He knew it was dangerous to think like that. He didn't know for sure that he'd be here. It all was in the hands of God.

But hadn't he felt led to come here to help Abraham, then to the farmhouse? *Schur,* the farmhouse hadn't been for sale but then he'd found that the owner — Rose — needed someone to help her with it.

Then he'd discovered how much he was

attracted to her. Surely the next step was for her to see he was the man for her . . . the *mann,* the husband she needed, the *dat* she needed for Daniel and for the other *kinner* they'd have.

If only she wasn't still grieving for Sam. He'd seen a change in her from the grieving widow she'd been when she first arrived. But he could tell how much further she had to go. The only time joy lit her eyes, the only time she smiled, was when she gazed on her *sohn.*

He'd always loved *kinner* but there was something about that boy. He'd fallen for the *kind* almost as soon as he'd fallen for the woman.

Saturday dawned bright — and cold. Too cold for him to allow Rose and Daniel to sit in the wind out in front of the house. So Luke grabbed a piece of board and quickly painted a sign directing customers to the barn. There he pushed open the barn doors and set up a table consisting of a big piece of lumber over two sawhorses.

"We've never done it this way," Rose began when she saw what he'd done.

"It's just too cold for the two of you out there," he told her. "So let's start a new tradition. If it's warmer next Saturday we can always go back to doing this out front."

"You're right." She fussed with the placement of crafts on the table, then opened the plastic box she'd carried from the house.

"Cinnamon rolls," he said, leaning over to inhale the scent.

"They're for customers," she told him tartly.

He gave her his best disappointed look — the one that had always worked on his *mudder.*

"Well, I suppose you can have one."

He grabbed it before she could change her mind and bit in. "Mmm," he mumbled around a bite. "Heaven."

"I made a big thermos of coffee and one of hot chocolate. I just have to bring them out."

"I'll take care of that," he told her and headed for the kitchen.

When he returned Daniel was seated on a chair behind the make-shift table and busily gluing acorns on small, round wooden rings. Rose tied twine on the base ends of big pine cones and laid them on the table with a sign telling customers to spread a mixture of suet and seed or peanut butter for the winter birds.

"Couldn't people just do that themselves instead of buying pine cones from you?"

"Many people don't have them in their yards. Or have the time to go hunting for them."

"Oh."

"I love your trinket boxes," she told him. She'd given them a place of prominence on the table and that pleased him.

"We'll see if they sell."

He'd no sooner spoken than they heard a car pull into the drive. Several women got out and walked toward the barn, talking excitedly.

"I just love finding these sales on the back roads of the Amish community on a weekend," one woman said to another. "Oh, what beautiful wreaths!" She lifted the big one Rose had made of princess pine — a long, drapey green ground cover that made easy, beautiful wreaths. She gave the briefest glance at the price tag. "This will be perfect on my front door."

Another woman stepped forward. "What darling birdhouses! I have to have this one!"

"I'm giving Sallie a necklace for Christmas. This little box would be perfect to put it in."

Rose was kept busy taking money and giving change while Luke helped putting the purchases into cardboard boxes and plastic bags.

"I should have brought more cash with me today," one woman complained. "Maybe we can come back tomorrow."

"We won't be open. We'll be at church."

"Oh, that's right. It's Sunday tomorrow."

"I can take a check," Rose offered.

"Really? You don't know me."

"I trust you."

The woman drew her checkbook out. "I'll give you some ID."

"Not necessary."

"Such sweet people. No one trusts anyone anymore." The woman handed her the check and beamed at her. "Your little boy is darling."

"Thank you."

"Well, we'd better get going, get out of your way. I see you have more customers stopping."

Luke looked up. Two more cars were parking out in front of the house. "Looks like it's going to be a *gut* morning."

They sold out before 11:00 a.m. Luke walked to the road and took down the sign, then helped Rose carry the thermoses and a tired Daniel into the house.

"Looks like we'll have to make lots more for the next sale," he told her as she fixed them lunch.

"Oh, I nearly forgot!" she exclaimed when

173

she'd sat at the table. She dug into her apron and produced a stack of bills.

"What's this?"

"Your share for the birdhouses and trinket boxes."

He pushed the money back into her hands. "Absolutely not. I'm not taking it."

A pushing session ensued.

"I want to make this farm a success for you and Daniel," he said simply.

She stilled, and tears welled in her eyes. "*Danki,* Luke."

"Don't cry," he said, uncomfortable. "I can't stand it when a woman cries."

"*Mamm?*" Daniel's bottom lip quivered.

"Happy tears, Daniel. Happy tears."

Reassured, the boy dug into his sandwich.

Relieved that she'd blinked back the tears, Luke picked up his sandwich. Yes indeed, it had been a *gut* morning.

THIRTEEN

Lillian looked up in surprise when Rose and Daniel walked in the back door of her house that afternoon.

"How did the sale go?"

"We sold out before lunch."

"That's *wunderbaar.*" She rose. "I was just having a cup of peppermint tea. Want some? The water's still hot."

"*Ya,* please."

Daniel tugged at his *aenti*'s apron. "Where's John?"

"He should be getting up from his nap soon." Lillian smiled down at him. "If you give me a hug I might let you go wake him up."

He bounced on his toes. "Hug! Hug!"

Chuckling, she bent and let him wrap his arms around her neck. *"Danki, lieb.* Now go wake John. Just don't scare him to death, *allrecht?*" She poured a mug of hot water, set it before Rose, then took her seat.

They watched Daniel tiptoe up the stairs, heard steps overhead on the ceiling, then there came a shout and bedsprings bounced. Feet hit the floor and the boys scrambled down the stairs whooping.

"Well," Lillian said, taking the noise in stride. "I wonder how monkeys got into my kitchen."

The boys looked at each other and made monkey noises and crouched on the floor.

"Maybe they got out of the zoo?" Rose asked, playing along.

"I was thinking of making some hot chocolate for our boys. But I only see monkeys in my kitchen and monkeys can't have hot chocolate."

The boys stood and grinned. "Can we have some hot chocolate?" John asked her.

"May we?"

"May we?"

"*Schur*. Sit."

She fixed the hot chocolate, added extra-cold milk, then brought a bag of miniature marshmallows to the table. Both boys giggled as they added marshmallows until they toppled from the cup onto the table.

Rose dipped a teaspoon into Daniel's cup, tasted it, then nodded. "Now you can drink it."

"Have you thought about *schul*?" Lillian

asked Rose.

"*Schul?*"

"They start next fall." She paused. "I can see you hadn't thought of that."

Rose swallowed. "Not — not really. Not exactly." She let out a breath. "Time is going so quickly."

"And it just goes faster and faster. They'll be in *schul* before we know it." Lillian patted her hand. "When Annie started *schul*," she said as she sipped her tea, "it felt so strange. John kept me busy, of course. But I worried so about her. Would she like it? Would she miss me? I couldn't wait for her to get home."

"And did she miss you?" Rose asked quietly, glancing at Daniel.

Lillian laughed. "Not a bit from what she said. She never stopped talking when she got home. And there was not a word about missing her *mudder.*"

"How did you feel about that?"

"Glad. We're supposed to be teaching them how to leave the nest."

There was a blur of color at the window. A cardinal perched on the windowsill.

"Do you have a lot of cardinals in your yard this time of year?"

"No more than the other types of birds." Lillian glanced in the direction of the window. "Why?"

"We have one that's been hanging around the yard."

Daniel laughed. "Birds don't hang, *Mamm*. They fly."

She smiled at him. "So they do."

"I'd see cardinals whenever I thought about *Mamm* and *Daed* after they died," Lillian said thoughtfully.

"Can we —" John stopped. "*May* we go outside and play?"

Lillian plucked a paper napkin from the basket on the table and wiped at his marshmallow mustache. *"Schur."* She waited as Rose helped Daniel with his jacket and the boys had gone outside. "Luke said he might not have seen Daniel hanging from the window if a cardinal hadn't flown at him that day."

Rose stared in surprise. "Really? He didn't tell me that." Although, now that she remembered, he *had* started to tell her about a bird pestering him. He just hadn't finished the tale, obviously. Perhaps because he knew how affected she'd been by the whole window incident. "Interesting."

Lillian turned the flame on under the teakettle. "So maybe Sam is watching out for you and his *sohn*?"

"Or our parents."

"I think it's Sam."

It was a nice thought. But it made Rose miss him to think that. She sighed wistfully.

The teakettle whistled. Lillian got up, turned off the flame, and poured them both more hot water. Rose dunked her tea bag in her mug.

"I don't know —" she started.

The back door flew open. "*Mamm!* There's lots of acorns out here!"

She pressed a hand to her heart. "Daniel, don't scare your *mudder* like that."

"Sorry." He turned to Lillian. "Can I —" he stopped, started again. "May I take some home?"

"*Schur.* I'll get you a pail."

"John too."

"Of course." She reached into a cupboard, found two pails, and handed them to Daniel, who flew back out as quickly as he'd come.

"He made some simple ornaments with acorns, and people bought them, so he's excited," Rose said. She laughingly described her attempts to corral his exuberant crafting. "Still," she finished, "so much of what we made and sold were things anyone could make."

"You're not giving yourself enough credit. You always had a gift for making beautiful wreaths. Much better than mine."

"Why don't you make some for me to sell this week?"

"No time. But you're welcome to take whatever you can use from our backyard."

"That would be *wunderbaar.*"

"If you're finished with your tea, we can gather some things now."

Rose quickly gulped down the last drops and put her mug in the sink. "You'll never guess what Luke did." She turned to look at Lillian, surprised that she'd blurted out what she did. "He made some birdhouses and little wooden boxes that were sold and wouldn't take the money for them."

Lillian paused in shrugging on her jacket. "Really?"

She buttoned her own jacket. "He said he won't take a wage until after the harvest either."

"Interesting. But I'm not surprised. Luke's a generous man. Lovina's told me all he's done since he came here to help the family. I would never have suggested he help you with the farm if I hadn't gotten to know him, trust him."

She paused with her hand on the door-knob. "Rose? He bears another look."

"Another look?"

"As more than a helper. More than a friend."

They'd been *schweschders* too long for Rose to misread her. "I'm not ready for that. It hasn't been long enough."

"Maybe it's time to think about the future," Lillian said gently.

Rose lifted her chin and met her sister's gaze directly. "Like I said. It hasn't been long enough. *Kumm,* we need to see what the boys are up to."

Who knew if she'd ever trust her heart to love another man again? No one knew what pain she still felt over losing Sam.

No one but another widow.

Luke was waiting for Rose when she drove the buggy into the driveway. He had bad news for her.

He hated delivering bad news.

She climbed out of the buggy and looked at him apprehensively. "What's wrong?"

"The oak tree has to come down."

"The oak tree? Why?"

"It's dying. It wouldn't be safe to leave it standing. A limb could fall and hurt Daniel or one of his friends playing in the yard."

"Are you *schur* it can't be saved?" She walked over to it and he followed her.

"I had Abraham come over and look at it

181

while you were gone. He agreed with me." He frowned as he saw her lips tremble. "He'll come back and help me cut it down tomorrow. I wouldn't suggest it if it didn't need to be done, Rose. And I'd never do it without your permission. Where's Daniel?"

"He's staying to have supper at Lillian's."

Luke shifted uncomfortably as she began to cry. "I'll plant another for you."

"But it won't be the same one."

She ran her hand over the bark and looked up at the bare branches. "I played under this tree when I was a little girl. Helped my *mudder* set up tables in its shade to feed everyone helping harvest. Daniel loves the swing."

Luke fumbled out a bandanna and handed it to her. "Look, there are some acorns under it." He bent and gathered them up, held them out. "I'll plant them and it'll be like the *sohn* of this old man here. Remember the old saying: 'Mighty oaks from little acorns grow.'"

He stared when she put her arms around the trunk and hugged it.

"One of the reasons I wanted to come back here was because things didn't change here," she said quietly. "Young men didn't die before their time. They raised their *sohns* and lived long, happy lives." She sighed. "At least that's the way I remembered it, being younger."

Then, as if she'd said too much, she looked embarrassed and stepped back. "Sorry, I know I sound like I'm overreacting. Sometimes I don't think I'm handling change very well."

"I think you're doing very well."

She sniffed and gave him a watery smile. "When I was at Lillian's she talked about our *sohns* going off to *schul.* It seems like he was just born a few months ago and soon he'll be old enough to go to *schul* with the other *kinner.*"

"That's months in the future," he told her, hoping to reassure.

"I know. But time seems to go so fast." She glanced at the buggy. "I need to unhitch Daisy."

"I'll do it."

She walked with him. "Lillian and I gathered up some more greenery for wreaths. I'll get that out before you put the buggy up."

"There's too much for you to carry by yourself."

"Maybe we should put everything on the back porch and I'll get it when I'm ready to do the wreaths. Otherwise Daniel will get into it when he comes home."

183

"*Gut* idea." He stacked two cardboard boxes, hefted them, and started for the house. She grabbed another and trailed behind him to the porch, where they set everything down. Luke thought she looked a little lost. A little lonely.

He gave the sky a quick scan. "You know, we have enough daylight left to make a *gut* start on the tree. Abraham said he'd come back if I wanted him to."

"You *schur*?"

He nodded. "I'll go give him a call." He went to use the phone in the shanty. While the bishop had decreed cell phones acceptable here, it was something he didn't feel the need for like some did.

Abraham came right over and soon they were working together, one of them climbing a ladder to saw the tallest limbs, then working with the two-handled saw to cut the trunk.

"Some of this — the part that's not diseased — can be saved for firewood," Abraham told him.

"That might make Rose feel better."

"What?" Abraham swiped at the sweat on his forehead. The day was cold but the work was hard.

"She was sad about us having to cut it down."

"Women. I'll never understand them. It's just a tree."

Luke started to tell him what Rose had said but decided against it. If she wanted his cousin to know, she'd tell him.

"Anyway, I told her I'd plant some of its acorns so there'll be another in its place one day."

"It'll take a long time for it to grow to that size again."

"There's no hurry."

Abraham gazed up at the darkening sky. "True. But we need to be getting going. The *fraa* will be getting supper on the table."

"I'll just let Rose know I'm leaving."

"Allrecht."

Luke opened the back door and saw Rose sitting at the kitchen table with a cup of tea before her. Her shoulders were slumped and she looked lonelier than he thought he'd ever seen her. She glanced up and he watched her smile quickly — a smile that didn't quite reach her eyes.

"Done already?"

"*Ya,* with cutting it down. I'll be doing some splitting and yard cleanup tomorrow."

"I'll see you then."

He lingered, hating to see her sad. "When's Daniel due home?"

She glanced at the clock. "Soon. I've been

185

enjoying the quiet."

Luke doubted that, but what could he say? "Well, then, I'll be going. *Gut nacht.*"

"*Gut nacht.*"

He drew the door closed but heard her call out his name. "*Ya?*"

"*Danki* for the kind words earlier. For not making me feel silly for an old tree."

"You weren't being silly. You have your memories of the tree. But Rose, another will grow, and you'll make more under that one."

She smiled and this time her smile reached her eyes. "True. *Danki.*"

Luke felt better as he walked out to Abraham's buggy. He didn't often feel he had the right words with her but today he thought he might have.

"Everything *allrecht*?"

"*Ya.* Fine." He leaned back in his seat, aware of a mild ache from the exertion of climbing the tree and cutting it. But it was a *gut* ache. One that affirmed that he'd done a *gut* day's work. "My *mudder* wants me to come home for Christmas."

"You should," Abraham said. "You didn't go back last year."

He nodded. "But I don't feel right about leaving when Rose needs me."

"I'll stop by and help her while you're

186

gone. It's the least I can do."

"It's too much on top of your own chores."

"Not this time of year."

Luke lapsed into silence, idly watching the passing scenery.

"Well?"

"I'll think about it."

"Don't think too long. Who knows if it's hard to get a bus ticket this time of year?"

"True. *Allrecht.* I'll make my decision tomorrow."

They arrived home, unhitched the horse, and went inside the house. The kitchen was warm, filled with delicious aromas and all the noise and clamor of a boisterous family.

It might be *gut* indeed to go back and see his family, catch up on all that had happened in his absence. Enjoy a family Christmas.

He'd go buy that ticket tomorrow.

FOURTEEN

Rose told herself she'd never done anything so stupid.

Then she frowned. It was wrong to call herself stupid. That was saying God had created someone stupid, and He didn't do that.

But one morning just days later Abraham's buggy was rolling down her drive with Luke in it, and she was regretting telling him he should go visit his family.

She'd seen the hesitation in his eyes and been determined to send him on his way without regret. Why, she'd even packed him a lunch with all his favorite food and Daniel had been present to give him a hug and a colorful handmade card.

"I'll be back later to help with chores," Abraham had assured her.

She didn't care about the chores. She'd manage somehow. Things were slow during winter. And besides, she'd managed when Sam had been ill and there wasn't always help at their farm, hadn't she?

There was just this feeling, this sinking feeling, in the pit of her stomach that Luke wasn't coming back. Family was so important, so compelling. Luke would go back to Ohio and they'd persuade him to stay . . .

Pasting a smile on her face, she turned to Daniel and saw tears welling up in his big blue eyes.

"Daniel? *Kind,* what's the matter?"

"Don't want Luke to go," he blurted out through trembling lips.

She gathered him up in her arms and carried him into the house. "I know, I know. But Luke wants to go see his *eldres* for Christmas. We want him to be happy."

"I want Luke for Chris-mas."

"Me too. But he'll be back soon." She set him down in his chair. "How about I make us some hot chocolate?"

He stared at the table, took a deep, shuddering breath. "Luke."

She hadn't thought he'd miss him this much. He'd been so young when Sam died. But now he was almost five. She hadn't considered how much time Luke had spent with him, unlike Sam at the end when he'd been so ill, so exhausted.

"Hot chocolate with marshmallows."

He wiped his nose on his sleeve and thrust

out his bottom lip.

"Then we'll read a story. The seed story."

Daniel laid his head on the table. He was inconsolable.

She fixed his drink, cooled it with some milk, then set it before him with a little bowl of miniature marshmallows. He sniffed, eyed the marshmallows. And then began picking them up and dunking them into the cup. A couple of sips later, he looked a bit happier. By the time he drained the cup he had cheered up completely. He looked at her and grinned.

She smiled back and wiped his white marshmallow mustache off with a paper napkin, then let him choose two cookies and eat them so slowly she felt she sat there for hours. Finally he finished, and she cleaned him up. They headed upstairs for the story and his nap.

The sky had darkened, and rain began falling. After lunch they curled up on her bed with a quilt and his favorite story and she read it to him until he fell asleep. She listened to his slow, even breathing as she watched the rain slide down the glass. And felt like weeping.

What if Luke didn't come back? What if the pull of his home, his family, was too much and he stayed? For all she knew, there was a woman back there who cared for him. Who he cared for.

She shook her head and sighed. Well, it was done. Luke was on his way. If he came back he came back. There was nothing she could do now.

Tired, unbearably tired, she slept.

When Daniel stirred, she woke and found her arm had gone to sleep under his head. The room had darkened. Daniel turned his head to look up at her.

"*Mamm* took a nap!" Obviously finding it funny, he chortled.

"I did." Love stirred in her as she stroked his hair. He was such a happy, happy *kind.*

"I'm *hungerich!*"

She ticked his tummy. "You're always *hungerich!*"

He giggled. "Beanie weenies!"

"You're going to turn into a beanie weenie one day. I'm just going to have to eat you up, little piggy!" She pulled up his shirt, exposing his plump tummy, and blew on it, making him twist and giggle harder.

"Stop, *Mamm!*" he cried as tears ran down his cheeks. "I'm *hungerich!*" he repeated.

She glanced at the clock on her bedside table. It was time for supper. They'd slept for hours, probably because they were warm and snuggly under the quilt she'd drawn over them.

They went downstairs and she looked into the refrigerator and wondered what she'd fix. She'd been too distracted to think about it earlier. A brief check of the contents revealed a container of beef vegetable soup. She took it out and poured it into a pan to warm then got a skillet out. Soup and grilled cheese sandwiches would make a perfect supper on a cold night.

Daniel looked up from his coloring book. "Beanie wienies?" he asked hopefully.

"You are obsessed," she told him and ruffled his hair. Before his current obsession with beanie wienies, he'd eaten gallons of macaroni and cheese for months. She wondered what the next fixation might be. "*Nee,* we're having Three Bear Soup and grilled cheese sandwiches."

Once when he'd had a cold and been fretful, she'd persuaded him to eat the soup by calling it Three Bear Soup after the fairy tale and the name had stuck.

He nodded and went back to his coloring.

Rose turned the flame on under the iron skillet and dropped some butter into it. As she waited for it to melt, she glanced out the window and wondered where Luke was now. Had he eaten any of the sandwiches she'd packed for him? The cookies she knew were his favorites?

She shook her head, focused on placing the cheese sandwiches in the skillet, and watched them brown. When they were done she cut Daniel's into quarters to make it easier for him to pick up and sat down to eat the simple supper with him.

And tried not to think of how many times Luke had sat in the chair at the head of the table and shared a meal with them.

If he didn't come back she'd have to get used to it being just Daniel and her again. A wave of sadness fell over her at the thought. She tried to shrug it away. The two of them had had many meals as a family after Sam died. It didn't take a *mann* to make a family. It was nicer to share a life with one but until such time as God sent another along, the two of them would be just fine.

If God sent another man along. The Amish believed that God set aside a special someone for a person. But she couldn't help wondering if he had *only* one for each. She knew widows who'd married again so surely not.

And even if God didn't have someone in mind, the local bishop would be eager to play matchmaker — always subtly, of course. The one back in Ohio had urged

193

her to consider another man shortly before she'd moved and it probably wouldn't be long before the bishop here did so as well. Marriage was strongly encouraged.

"Mamm?"

"Hmm?"

"More soup?"

"Schur." She rose, ladled more soup into his bowl, and told him to blow on it so he wouldn't burn his tongue.

After supper they made a batch of peanut brittle. She let Daniel have a piece and packed away the rest for a gift for Christmas.

The evening stretched long before her after Daniel went to bed. The house was quiet. Too quiet. She worked on gifts as she sat before the fireplace in the living room, knitting a sweater of a soft blue for Lillian. Her *schweschder* was always so busy making clothes for her family that she didn't do enough for herself. Rose hoped she'd like the sweater. She'd tried it on before she added the sleeves. At least it was easy to know how it would look and fit on her since they looked so alike and were the same size.

She smiled as she remembered someone once asking her how she felt about being a twin. "I've only ever been a twin," she'd confessed. "So I wouldn't know."

How *wunderbaar* it would be to celebrate

Christmas with Lillian and her family this year. Her spirits, which had flagged a bit since Luke's departure, rose at that, and she found herself feeling more cheerful as she sat before the warm fire and worked on the sweater while the winter wind howled around the house.

As Luke rode the bus he found himself remembering how he felt when he left Rose's farm earlier.

He hadn't been able to look back as the buggy left Rose's drive three days before Christmas.

He didn't dare. If he did he was afraid he wouldn't be able to leave.

Abraham's horse had stopped at the road and waited for his signal to proceed once a car passed. Luke glanced out and saw a cardinal perched on the mailbox. It tilted its scarlet head and regarded him with its bright black eyes. Then it flew off.

"Traveling light," Abraham remarked, jerking his head at Luke's small suitcase.

"I'm coming back."

Abraham spared him a look. "Never doubted that."

"Besides, I still have some clothes in Ohio. I'll be bringing them with me when I come back."

"Gut."

"Guess I'm glad I mailed my presents a week ago or I'd be toting them along."

They shook hands at the bus station and he watched the buggy roll away. He didn't have long to wait for his bus. He handed his suitcase to the driver who loaded it into the baggage compartment, then climbed aboard and found a window seat. The bus filled quickly with people wearing happy expressions and carrying shopping bags. They were obviously going somewhere for the holidays and happier about it than he was.

"This seat taken?"

Luke jerked out of his daydreaming and stared up at an older *Englisch* woman. "No. Please, sit."

Luke wasn't *hungerich* yet but he couldn't resist taking a peek inside his lunch box. Sure enough, Rose had packed his favorite sandwiches and cookies and tucked in a thermos of coffee.

The driver closed the door and soon the bus was moving out of the station and onto the road.

"We're on our way!" the woman said cheerfully. "You going home for Christmas?"

Luke nodded.

"Me too," she beamed.

He wasn't the best at making conversation with strangers but he didn't need to worry. The woman introduced herself as Mae and chattered nonstop.

"I've always admired the Amish," she told him. "Peaceful, hardworking people. We need more like 'em in this country, we do. I like how family's important. Country went down the drain when we got television, it did. Why, my Henry, God rest his soul, all he did from the time he came home from work was watch the tube. Ate his dinners on a tray in front of it. Barely spoke to me and the girls. He retired and never left his recliner. Now he's gone and I don't turn that television on, not even to watch the soaps, I don't."

The Amish were talkers but Luke began to wonder if the woman was going to take a breath. It was going to be a long trip if she stayed aboard the whole way. Thankfully, she got off four hours later at her stop and no one filled her seat.

Luke turned his attention to the passing scenery. The relative silence gave him time to think. What the woman had said about family was true. Family *was* all-important. He'd been taught that from birth. But he'd come to think of Rose and Daniel as family. He hated the miles that were separating them, the distance during such a holy time of year. He'd given his word, though, and so he'd spend Christmas with his family and enjoy it. Who knew how long a time it might be before he returned since he intended to make his home in Lancaster County — hopefully with Rose and Daniel.

When Luke stepped off the bus tired, his muscles cramped, it was all worth it the minute he saw his *dat* waiting for him at the bus station. He wrapped Luke in a big hug and tossed his suitcase into the back seat. "Your *mudder*'s been cooking and baking ever since she heard you were coming. But it looks like Lovina has been taking *gut* care of you."

It wasn't the time to tell him that he ate a lot of meals at Rose's. And her home had become more than a place of work.

"Luke!" His *mudder* greeted him with a hug — and tears — as he came through the door to their house. He patted her back and gave his *dat* a helpless look. But his *dat* was no help. He just grinned and helped himself to a cup of coffee and sat at the kitchen table.

His *mudder* finally let go and wiped her tears with a tissue she pulled from her apron. She began unbuttoning his coat as if he were a *kind* again until he laughed and

198

shook off her hands. He hung his coat and hat on pegs by the back door, sat at the table, and let her flutter around her kitchen putting a meal before him.

Everything smelled wonderful. The sandwich and cookies Rose had packed had been eaten hours ago and he was starved.

"I made your favorites."

His *dat* just grunted. "Food's his favorite."

"Same could be said of you," she told her *mann* tartly as she set another loaded platter before their *sohn*. But there was a twinkle in her eyes.

Finally she sat. But she didn't move to fill her plate or lift her cup of coffee. She simply sat staring at him.

"Eat," he told her. "I'll bet you haven't touched a thing you've cooked today."

"It's just so *gut* to see you again," she told Luke. "Parents are supposed to let their *kinner* fly, test their wings. But it's so hard when they fly so far."

He grinned. "*Mamm,* I'm twenty-eight. And it's Pennsylvania not the end of the world."

"Kinner are always kinner."

"It's not so far, *Mamm,*" he assured her. "Not so far at all. And it won't be so long without a visit again, I promise."

Who knew . . . If things went the way he

hoped, maybe he'd be bringing Rose and Daniel here to meet his family.

He ate, enjoying the food and the comfort of a room he'd grown up in, and listened to his *mudder* chatter about all the family coming for Christmas Eve the next night.

"It's going to be a *wunderbaar* time with you here," she said and sighed. "So *wunderbaar*."

Luke nodded but his thoughts drifted back to Lancaster and one woman. A week seemed like forever.

FIFTEEN

Daniel camped out at the front window an hour before family was due to arrive. "Chrismas is here," he told her, his eyes alight with excitement.

Rose smiled as she put another log on the fire. "It is."

She gazed around the room. She'd spent hours *redding* it up, dusting and polishing furniture. She'd bought little votive candles at the dollar store and set them in little glasses among the evergreen boughs on the fireplace mantel and now they glowed and scented the room.

A big comfy armchair was positioned before the fire. She'd placed the family Bible on its cushion. Amos would sit there very soon and, with family gathered around in this old house for the first time in years, would read the story of one child whose birth had changed the world.

She couldn't help glancing over at Daniel,

201

the child who had changed hers, and thanking God for the precious gift of his life.

"When are they coming?" he asked, growing impatient.

"Soon."

A noise caught his attention outside. He bounced on the chair she'd let him pull over to the window and then his shoulders sagged and he sighed — a big, very childlike sigh. "Not them," he announced sadly.

"They'll be here soon."

She walked over to look out the window with him. Truth be told, she was feeling excited too. This was their first Christmas back in the home she'd grown up in and even the old house seemed to be waiting.

What was Luke doing right now? Were he and his family gathering round for the reading of the sacred story from the Bible? Was there a feast laid out to be consumed afterward? How would they like the gifts he'd made and shown her so proudly?

He'd wanted her and Daniel to open his gifts to them before he left but she wouldn't allow it. They would open them when he returned, she told him firmly.

She hoped he'd return . . . but she had no guarantee.

She told herself it was in God's hands.

"They're here!" Daniel shouted. He

jumped down from the chair and had the door open before she could stop him.

"*Kumm,* they're going around the back," she told him, closing the door.

He raced to the back door and threw it open. "John!"

"Daniel! I brung Chris-mas cookies!" He held out a plate with brightly decorated cookies. "We baked them today!"

"Brought," his *mudder* corrected. Her amused gaze met Rose's. "Say 'Merry Christmas,' John!"

"Merry Chris-mas, *Aenti* Rose! Merry Chris-mas, Daniel!" he chirped.

"Chris-mas cookies, *Mamm!*" Daniel exclaimed.

"Why don't you two go put them on the table," she told them with a chuckle. She looked at her *schweschder.* "Next to the other ones we baked today. Gee, I hope we have enough. Evidently they're the most important thing."

Lillian laughed. "Amos is bringing in the baked ham as soon as he unhitches the buggy. The *kinner* and I have lots of *gut* things to eat."

Annie trooped in carrying a dish she set on the table. There was a flurry of movement as jackets and hats and bonnets were shed and then the *kinner* scampered into

203

the living room.

Lillian set down her dish and shed her outerwear. She hugged Rose. "It feels so *gut* to have you home for Christmas. To celebrate here in the home we grew up in." She sighed and stood back. "It's the start of many, many happy Christmases here. I just know it."

Amos came in with a big roaster pan. "Merry Christmas, Rose." He turned to Lillian. "Where do you want this?"

She took it from him and set it on the stove while he brushed snow from the shoulders of his coat before he took it off and hung it on a peg.

"Coffee, Amos?"

He rubbed his hands together. "*Ya. Danki.* Cold night."

He took the mug from her and headed into the living room. They followed and settled into chairs. The *kinner* were already seated on cushions on the floor before the fireplace. Daniel looked up at her from his seat, his little face beaming. It did her heart *gut* to see how happy he was to be with his cousins on this holy night. He'd never celebrated one with his extended family.

Amos eased into the big armchair beside the fire, set his mug of coffee on a table, and opened the big leather-covered Bible.

"Now the birth of Jesus Christ . . ."

The *kinner* listened, rapt, as he read. Rose glanced over at Lillian and their gazes met. There were tears in Lillian's eyes. Rose reached over and took her *schweschder*'s hand and squeezed it. Lillian always rushed around like a busy little bee and seemed so practical, taking care of everything. But tonight her emotions were obviously on the surface.

Amos closed the Bible and gazed at the *kinner.* "And that's the story of Christ's birth we celebrate tonight."

Annie sighed. "I love that story."

"Me too," Daniel spoke up. "It's almos' as *gut* as the seed story."

"Seed story?" John asked him.

Daniel jumped up. "I'll show you."

"Later," Rose told him. "Now it's time for us to eat."

"Eat! Eat!" crowed Daniel.

"Chris-mas cookies!" John added.

"You'll eat something more than cookies," Lillian told him as they all headed for the kitchen.

Warmth and delicious aromas filled the kitchen. Amos carved the ham and they all piled their plates high with slices and baked sweet potatoes and corn pudding and Lillian's yeast rolls. The *kinner* chattered so

205

much Rose wondered how they managed to clear their plates. Then it was time for the special fruitcake baked from her *mudder*'s recipe. And of course lots and lots of Christmas cookies.

"Another slice of cake?" Rose asked Amos.

"*Nee, danki.* I'm stuffed." He grinned. "Looks like even our *kinner* have finally gotten enough to eat."

Schur enough, they sat back in their chairs, replete and looking sleepy.

"Let's help *Aenti* Rose clean up and then we'll head home," he told them.

Rose had glanced out the window and seen the snow was coming down harder. "Best you get on the road. I can clean up."

"But —"

"*Nee.* Get everyone home and in bed. We'll see you tomorrow."

"Bright and early."

Daniel pouted. "Don't go."

"They'll be back tomorrow."

"With presents," Lillian promised.

A flurry of movement arose as coats and hats and bonnets were donned and hugs given, and then they were gone. Daniel went upstairs to brush his teeth and don his pajamas. Rose put away leftovers and put the dishes in the sink to soak while she tucked him in. When she went to his room she found him stretched across his bed, his pajamas pulled on but not buttoned.

He was sound asleep.

Smiling, she buttoned his pajama top and pulled his quilt up over him and tucked it in. He stirred and opened his eyes. "Merry Chris-mas, *Mamm.*"

She kissed his forehead. "Merry Christmas, *lieb.*"

"Not tired." But he couldn't hold back a yawn.

"Bed."

He giggled. "Story."

"One."

He fell asleep on the second page of his favorite bedtime tale.

"*Nee*, not tired at all," she murmured, leaning down to kiss his forehead. She yawned. "I'm tired and not afraid to admit it."

She walked to her room, changed into a nightgown, and climbed into bed. It had been a *wunderbaar* evening but an emotional one.

Nothing had changed.

Luke sat and listened to his *dat* reading the story of the birth of Christ and let his gaze sweep around the room. Oh, everyone looked a little older, and his *bruders'* and *schweschders' kinner* had grown like weeds in the time he'd been gone. But the scene in the living room — the evergreen-bedecked mantel, the big pots of poinsettias, the presents stacked on the table that the *kinner* eyed and were told wouldn't be opened until tomorrow — everything was so much like it had been before he'd left to help Abraham.

The old farmhouse hadn't changed and wasn't likely to until a younger generation took it over and added on if they needed to.

After the tradition of reading the story was over, the family eagerly descended on the big kitchen table laden with a large baked ham, vegetable dishes, pies, and so many different Christmas cookies. It was a *wunderbaar* visit, he reminded himself as they all dug in and enjoyed the good food and even better company. But he found himself homesick for a place that wasn't even his home.

Later that evening, he looked up at a knock on his bedroom door.

"You're packing?"

Luke turned at the sound of his *mudder*'s voice. "*Nee.* Just sorting through some things, taking a few shirts back with me. But I do need to get back soon. Abraham took over my chores so I could come and he has his own farm to take care of."

She sat on his bed and watched him pack. "Tell me about her. This woman you work for."

"She's a widow. Has a four-year-old *sohn.*" He folded the new Sunday shirt she'd sewn for him and placed it in his suitcase.

"I know that much. You wrote me that in one of your letters."

Luke looked up and studied her face. He saw her curiosity but more, the gentle patience and understanding. "I went to work for her and fell in love with her."

"And have you told her?"

He shook his head. "It's too soon. She's still grieving."

"How long has it been?"

"About a year and a half."

"Love doesn't count the years."

"Nee." He sat on the bed beside her. "She tries to hide it from everyone."

"It might take a long time for her to want to get married again," his *mudder* said softly. "Have you thought about that?"

He nodded. "I'll wait. I'll wait as long as it takes."

"Luke? Are you coming?" his *dat* hollered up the stairs.

"I'll be right there."

He tucked the remaining shirts in the suitcase sitting on a chair at the end of his bed.

She hugged him. "I love you. Think about what I said."

"I will. And *Mamm*? I'm hoping I can bring them to visit next year."

She smiled and there were tears in her eyes. "Me too."

Sixteen

Friends and family began arriving early the next morning.

Daniel couldn't have been happier. Once again he took up his post at the front door. When their visitors walked in with presents instead of food as they had the night before, he was beside himself.

"John! Annie! We got presents for you!" he cried and ran to the tree to retrieve them. "And *Aenti* Lillian! A big one for you! And *Onkel* Amos! It's not so big as *Aenti* Lillian's but it's really nice. It's a —"

"Daniel, don't tell him what it is!" Rose rushed to say. "Let him open it!" She chuckled. Her *sohn* could *not* keep a secret.

He danced on his toes, too excited to sit.

John tore the brown wrapping paper from his present and found two wooden puzzles. He immediately began working on one of them. Daniel joined him, finding it more fun than waiting for Annie and his *aenti* and his *onkel* to open theirs.

The two boys worked on the puzzles while Lillian opened her gift. "Oh, Rose, how lovely!" She pulled it on immediately. "Amos, look!"

"Very pretty," he said with a smile. "It matches your eyes."

Daniel looked up from the puzzles. "*Onkel* Amos, open your present!"

He obliged by pulling at the string that bound his gift. Daniel ran over and stood at his side, watching with wide eyes as Amos unwrapped the paper. "I helped make it!" he told his *onkel,* his eyes shining. "*Mamm* said it's your favorite."

"Peanut brittle has been my favorite since I was a little boy like you," Amos said as he picked up a piece and gave it to Daniel.

"I like it too!" He turned to John. "Here, Annie, you have some too! *Aenti* Lillian?"

"*Nee, danki,* I'll have some later," Lillian told him.

Rose frowned. Lillian looked pale. "Are you feeling *allrecht*?"

"*Ya.*"

But a few minutes later she rose quickly and rushed to the bathroom. Rose followed and knocked on the door. "Lillian?"

The door opened. "Don't fuss. Mornings are just a little rough."

"I have some ginger ale in the refrigerator for you."

Lillian gave her a shaky smile. "You remembered."

Rose looped her arm in her s*chweschder*'s. "Go sit in the living room and I'll get it for you."

Once she got Lillian settled in a chair by the fire, Rose went into the kitchen and poured a glass of ginger ale for her *schweschder.* She felt a moment of envy for Lillian. She herself had never experienced morning sickness or the miracle of birth.

Stop it, she told herself. You have Daniel and that is more than you ever might have had.

A burst of laughter came from the living room, intruding on her thoughts. Her very self-pitying thoughts.

"*Aenti* Rose, we're waiting for you!" Amos called.

Smiling, she poured him a cup of coffee and took it and the ginger ale into the living room.

"*Mamm*, open your present!" Daniel insisted, holding out the package.

She sat and patted her lap. "Here, you help me."

He climbed up into her lap and helped her open it. Then he stared at the envelopes with drawings of vegetables and fruits inside.

"They're seeds I gathered from *Mamm*'s kitchen garden the last year she was alive," Lillian explained. "I saved them hoping you'd come back and plant them one day."

Tears rushed to her eyes. She blinked at them, tried to say something, but she was overcome by emotion.

"*Mamm?*" Daniel patted her cheeks. "Don't cry."

"Happy tears," she whispered. "Happy tears. *Aenti* Lillian gave us seeds to plant in the garden when it gets warm. See, green beans and squash and lettuce and strawberries."

"And punkins?"

"And punkins."

John held out another package. "We got you gardening gloves too."

"He doesn't keep a secret any better than Daniel," his *mudder* said with a sigh.

Rose laughed, her heart lighter. "*Danki,* all of you. Well, who wants hot chocolate?"

"Me!" the *kinner* chorused.

She fixed the hot chocolate and they had no sooner finished it than the next round of visitors arrived, bringing in a drift of cold air and snow and arms full of presents.

Hours later, after the last visitor had left,

the last present had been unwrapped, and there were only crumbs on the platter that had held cookies and candy, Daniel wandered over to the front window.

"Luke?"

Rose shook her head. "Luke's with his family, remember?"

"I want him to come home."

She started to explain that he *was* home but Daniel was rubbing his tummy and looking fretful.

"He'll be back soon," she reassured him, hoping not just for him that it was true.

"When?"

She took his hand and led him over to the calendar that hung on the kitchen wall. "This day," she said, pointing to the thirtieth.

Daniel counted the days. "Five days?"

"Five days."

He stuck out his lower lip. "That's a long time."

"Not so many. They'll go by fast. You have new books to read and new games to play with. We can read one of those new books tonight when you go to bed."

She moved to the refrigerator and took out some plastic containers of leftovers from the night before. As she made sandwiches from the ham Lillian had brought she thought about the day. It had been her first Christmas back in her old home, one she'd never thought she'd experience when she married Sam.

She cut a sandwich in half, placed one half on a plate, and set it before Daniel. The other half went on a plate for herself, and then she served them both some soup she had warmed.

Daniel's head nodded over his plate before he'd finished. Company had worn him out. She scooped him up in her arms and carried him upstairs. Her little boy, always a bundle of energy, snuggled against her with a contented sigh.

"Nice Chris-mas," he murmured.

"Very nice," she agreed.

"Again tomorrow?"

Rose laughed and kissed his downy head. "*Nee,* two days was enough." She set him on the bed and tugged off his shoes and socks. "Pajamas, then brush your teeth."

When he sat there unmoving she helped him, then led him into the bathroom down the hall to brush his teeth.

"Story," he said, climbing into bed.

She took the three new books from the bedside table. He'd carried them up earlier like the precious treasures they were for him. He chose one and patted the space next to him on the bed. So she settled beside him and opened the book and read to him as the wind blew snow against the window and the old house settled in for the night. He was asleep before she turned the third page.

"Merry Christmas, Daniel," she whispered as she leaned down to kiss his cheek. She lifted her gaze. "And Merry Christmas, Sam."

Two days later, Luke gathered his courage. "I thought I might head back today," he told his *dat* as he helped him in the barn.

His *dat* nodded as he brushed the coat of his favorite horse. "Not surprised. You're already on the road."

"What?"

His *dat* looked at him. "Your *mudder* used to say that to me when I was going on a trip to a horse auction or a hunting trip. She'd say that I was already gone, I was already on the road, that I hadn't been paying attention for hours."

"Sorry." He hesitated. "You think she'll mind me leaving before I had planned to?"

"Nee."

"It's been *gut* to be back but I have a lot to do back home." Then he winced. "I mean, this is home but that's become what

217

I think of as home now."

"But the farm there isn't yours. You just work there. Wouldn't do for you to think of it as yours. That Rose could remarry, you know."

He nearly dropped the bucket of water he'd been carrying. "I know." It was his worst nightmare. "Anyway, would you mind giving me a lift to the bus station?"

"I think I could squeeze it into my busy schedule." His *dat*'s tone was sardonic.

"I'll go on in and finish packing up my stuff, then. Unless you need me to do something else."

"Nee."

Luke started out of the barn.

"Sohn?"

He turned. *"Ya?"*

"Breakfast first."

"Oh, yeah. Right."

"Already on the road," he heard his *dat* say as he opened the barn door.

His *mudder* was in the kitchen putting breakfast on the table. Luke shrugged out of his jacket and hung it and his hat on a peg by the door.

"I made pancakes," she told him with a smile.

His favorite. Guilt swamped him. He walked over to the sink and washed his hands. "I'm going to head back today."

She paused as she lifted a pancake with a spatula and then she set it down on a plate. "Today?"

"Ya." He walked over to hug her. "I had a *wunderbaar* time but I need to get back." He poured coffee into three mugs and set them on the table. "Abraham is helping Rose with my chores while I'm gone."

"Well, we've enjoyed having you here." She set the plate of pancakes down on the table, then sat to sip her coffee. "So, have you packed already?"

He nodded. "Mostly."

"I'll make you a lunch to take on the bus."

"Danki."

"You even talk like a Lancaster," she teased but her eyes were sad. *"Danki* instead of *denki."*

His *dat* came in then and after discarding his outerwear and washing his hands he joined them at the table.

"So, you left me one pancake," he grumbled as he looked at Luke.

His *mudder* rose and went to the oven. "You know I always keep yours warm in the oven until you come in." She transferred a stack of them onto a plate and set it before him. "Luke tells me he's leaving today."

"You were the one who told me you

thought he'd leave early," his *dat* reminded her as he poured syrup over his pancakes.

Luke looked up in surprise. "You did?" He remembered what his *dat* had said about already being on the road. His *mudder* knew her men.

Sighing, she pulled his lunch box from a cupboard and put it on the kitchen counter. "I did." She poured the last of the coffee into their mugs, started another pot on the stove, then went to the refrigerator and pulled out sandwich makings.

Finished with his breakfast, he set his plate and mug in the sink. "I'll go up and get my suitcase."

He went upstairs, gathered his things, and found himself gazing around the room. It was the room he'd slept in from the time he'd been a *kind*.

"Did you check your closet to make sure you didn't forget anything?"

He turned. "I will, *Mamm*." But he had taken everything he wanted. "Why didn't *Daed* turn this into a sewing room?"

She smiled. "It's yours until you don't want it anymore."

"I want to stay there. I want to marry Rose."

"I see. She's special, this Rose?"

"Very special."

A flutter of red caught his eye. A cardinal perched on the windowsill and peered in at them.

"Maybe you'll bring her to meet us soon."

Luke dragged his attention away from the bird and looked at her. "Or you could persuade *Daed* to bring you to visit."

"He doesn't like to travel. But I'll do my best." She held out her arms, and he went into them. "Be well. Be happy."

"I will." He hugged her hard and then grabbed his suitcase and left the room. He couldn't leave if he saw his *mudder*'s tears. And he knew she'd feel worse if she saw his.

He found his *dat* drinking coffee when he went downstairs and set his suitcase by the back door.

"Sit down and have another cup."

"Nee, danki."

"You *schur* are in a big hurry to get back to Lancaster County."

"Don't want to miss the bus."

His *dat* gave him a sardonic look.

"Always *gut* to get there early. Never know what you'll run into with traffic and weather this time of year," Luke said.

He got a grunt from his *dat* at that. "So maybe you'll invite us down to meet this woman you work for."

221

"When's the last time you wanted to get on a bus and travel?"

"Might if you invited us." His *dat* got up and put on his jacket and hat. "Have you forgotten we went there to visit family when you were fifteen?"

"Hardly. I wouldn't have gotten to know my cousin Abraham better or realized how much I liked the area if we hadn't."

"Still say they should have stayed in Ohio."

Luke grinned. "Never give up on that, do you?"

"Land prices are better here."

"No argument there. But Lancaster County is where I want to be."

On the road he found his thoughts wandering. Rose was still grieving for her *mann*, but one day he hoped she'd really see him, see how much he cared for her, and wanted to marry her. He wanted to help her raise her *sohn* and take care of the farm. Have more *kinner* with her.

His savings could go toward making some improvements to the farm or be set aside for a rainy day.

He felt a nudge in his side. "What?"

"Haven't even climbed on the bus and you're already gone."

"Sorry. Just thinking of what I need to do when I get back."

"You always were one to be thinking and planning." His *dat* pulled over to the side of the road and allowed a car to pass, then pulled back out. "Still some months before spring planting. Unless spring's coming earlier to Pennsylvania than it used to."

Luke chuckled. "*Nee.* I'm spending my free time building furniture to earn some extra money, and sticking it in the bank. I've had to do a lot of repairs too. Farm sat empty for years after Rose's parents died. Her *schweschder*'s *mann* did what he could, but no one can take care of two farms." He didn't tell his *dat* that he'd refused to take any wages from Rose until the crops came in. That was his business.

He fell silent and watched the familiar scenery pass by. "It's been *gut* for Rose to be back. She and her *schweschder* are *zwillingbopplin* and very close."

"It's *gut* she went back home then. Family's best when you're grieving." He pulled into the bus station parking lot and turned to stare at Luke. "Sounds like you care a lot for this widow you work for. You hoping she'll look in your direction?"

"*Ya.*"

"Sometimes it's hard to measure up to a dead man."

Luke huffed out a breath. "Well, that's blunt."

"No point dancing around the truth, is there?"

"Nee." He glanced over at the bus station. "Well, I guess I'd better be going."

"Glad you came. Meant a lot to your *mudder.*"

Luke hugged his *dat* and was surprised to see him blinking hard when he backed away.

"Love you, *Daed.*"

"Love you, *sohn.* We'll see you soon."

He nodded and picked up his suitcase. "Do."

SEVENTEEN

Rose woke early the day before Luke was expected back. Never one to lie abed when there was work to be done, she got up and dressed. She peeked into Daniel's room and saw he was still asleep, his quilt made of his *dat*'s shirts tucked up under his chin.

Tiptoeing down the stairs — avoiding the creaky step — she went to the kitchen. She loved her *sohn* and he was a *gut* one, but how she cherished that first cup of coffee and a quiet half hour to herself. It was as golden a time as the shorter and shorter period in the afternoon when he napped.

She filled the percolator and set it on the stove. A pan of water went on another burner for oatmeal. Soon the kitchen was filled with the burble of water and the scent of coffee. She poured oatmeal into the pan and stirred it before she turned down the flame and set the timer. The moment the coffee stopped perking she poured a cup and sat down with it.

Dawn light filtered through the kitchen window. She wondered when Luke would board the bus to return to Lancaster County. Then, once again, she wondered *if* he would return. Family was so important. Who knew better than her? As much as she had come to depend on him, as much as she needed him to help with the farm, she couldn't blame him if he stayed. She wouldn't blame him.

She'd just never forgive herself for telling him he should go. She put her head in her hands and called herself a fool for the hundredth time.

Something made her look up. A cardinal sat in the window and peered at her. She wondered if it was looking for breakfast. She and Daniel had filled the feeders yesterday. Thinking of him, she glanced at the clock. He was usually up by now. She rose, stirred the oatmeal, and turned off the timer before it could buzz.

And glanced out the window. The bird had flown away. Funny, she didn't remember seeing one hang around the yard so much when she was growing up.

She had time for a second cup of coffee before Daniel came downstairs rubbing his eyes, his hair standing up in spikes.

"Hungerich, Mamm," he told her as he climbed into her lap.

All God's creatures were *hungerich* this morning, she thought as she remembered the bird. "I made oatmeal for you."

"Mmm."

She kissed the top of his head. "I can get it for you if you get into your chair."

He gave her a hug, then slid down and went to his chair. She fixed him a bowl the way he liked it: with a spoonful of brown sugar and raisins and milk. Her own bowl got a spoonful of brown sugar and milk.

And so they started another day with a simple breakfast, just the two of them. It was another ordinary day, a slower-paced one now that winter had them in its thrall.

An hour later she was cleaning up the kitchen and Daniel sat coloring at the kitchen table when there was a knock on the back door.

"Guder mariye," said Luke as he walked into the room.

Speechless, Rose stood there as Daniel launched himself at him and Luke swung him up and around and around.

"Well, someone's happy to see me," Luke said when Rose continued to stare at him, silent. He set Daniel down, picked up the dish towel Rose had dropped, and handed

227

it to her. "I came home a day early."

"*Ya,* I see."

He grinned. "Surprised you, huh?"

"You could say that." She set the cloth aside to wash.

"Coffee smells *gut.*"

"I'll pour you some."

"Luke!" Daniel gazed up at him adoringly as he clung to his leg.

"*Ya,* it's Luke," she said, smiling. "Daniel, let Luke sit down and have some coffee."

"I colored a picture for you," Daniel told Luke as he settled back at the table. "See?"

Luke bent down to admire it as Rose poured the coffee and set it on the table far away from Daniel and his coloring book.

Luke shook his head. "Rose, he looks like he grew while I was gone."

"*Nee.* Only in shoe size. I have to go buy him some new shoes soon."

She poured herself another cup of coffee and sat, watching as Luke and her *sohn* talked. Snow dusted Luke's hat and the shoulders of his coat. He glanced up at her and caught her looking at him.

"Daniel, let Luke take off his hat and coat."

Luke chuckled as he shed the coat and hat and hung them up. "Mighty cold out there." He sat and wrapped his big hands around the mug then took a sip. "Mmm, it's *gut*. My *mudder* packed a thermos of coffee for me for the trip but I ran out many miles before Pennsylvania."

"Did you have a nice Christmas with your family?"

"Chris-mas?" Daniel paused in his coloring and his blue eyes went wide as saucers. "*Mamm!* Presents!" He proceeded to rattle off everything he'd gotten. "You got present for me?"

"Daniel, it's not nice to ask for presents —" she began. But Daniel was already down from his chair and running for the living room. He returned full of smiles and bearing the gift they'd wrapped for Luke.

"Merry Chris-mas!" he cried and thrust it into Luke's hands.

Rose grabbed Luke's mug before it got knocked over. Then she saw the expression on Luke's face — a mixture of surprise and . . . was that awe?

"Open it!" Daniel cried, dancing on his toes. "Open it, Luke!"

He unwrapped the paper and found an insulated coffee mug filled with a cellophane bag of peanut brittle.

"Me and *Mamm* made the brittle!" Daniel told him proudly. He was so happy she didn't have the heart to correct his grammar.

"I figured the mug would help keep your coffee warm when you worked out in the barn when it's cold."

"I love it," he said. "I really love it. The candy and the mug."

Daniel just beamed.

"Now would you like your presents?"

"You didn't have to get us anything."

He just gave her a look. "*Kumm,* you'll need your coats." He looked at Rose. "Aren't you coming?"

"*Schur.*" Curious, she bundled Daniel up and donned her coat and bonnet. What on earth was Luke up to?

Luke watched Daniel race toward the barn.

He'd missed that *kind* so much. His *mudder* too. And this place.

"Door, Luke!" Daniel cried as he tugged at it.

Luke opened the door to the barn and Daniel walked inside. "I don't see anything."

"Why, I left it in here before I went to Ohio." He winked at Rose and walked over to Daisy. "Have you seen Daniel's Christmas present?"

Daniel stared up at him. "Horses don't talk!"

"What's that, Daisy?" Luke leaned closer to her and pretended to listen to her. "Uh huh, that's right. I forgot where I put it. Thanks for watching out for it for me." He walked over to an empty stall and Daniel let out a shriek when he saw what was inside.

"A box! A big box!"

Luke laughed. "There's something inside it," he told Daniel and lifted the box away.

"*Mamm!* A whee-barrow!" Daniel ran to grasp the handles of a child-sized wheelbarrow and pushed it out of the stall. "I got a whee-barrow!" Before she knew it he was out of the barn and racing it around the yard.

"He loves it," she told Luke as they hurried to follow him. "I think he likes it better than the sled I gave him." She watched him and wondered if she'd ever seen him so happy. Then she remembered manners. "Daniel, did you forget something?"

Daniel stopped. "*Danki,* Luke!" He ran over with his arms out. Rose watched as Luke bent down and accepted his hug.

"Well, that was more of a success than I expected."

"He's always been happy with everything," she said, then stopped, appalled at what she'd said. "I didn't mean —"

"I know what you mean," he told her. "He

was pretty happy with the cardboard box."

"I came home one day and found Sam reading a seed catalog to him," she said, watching as Daniel began to put handfuls of snow into the wheelbarrow. "Now it's one of Daniel's favorite books. Imagine. A seed catalog."

She looked at him. "Lillian gave me seeds from our *mudder*'s kitchen garden for Christmas. I can't wait until Daniel and I can plant them."

"That reminds me." He went back into the barn and returned with a package wrapped in brown paper and string. "This is for you."

Daniel came running over to see. "Present?"

"For your *mudder.*"

"Open it, *Mamm*!" Daniel cried, jumping up and down. "Open it!"

Rose pulled off the wrapping to find an oval wooden sign that said *Rose's Handmade Gifts.*

"*Mamm*'s name," Daniel said. "R-O-S-E. Rose."

"I made it from the wood from the tree I cut down," Luke told her. "You can put it up on the front door on the days when you want customers, take it down on the days you don't."

She traced the lettering with her fingertips. "It's lovely. I hadn't thought this far yet . . ."

"You can put it up whenever you're ready. The things you made were beautiful. Remember how people liked them."

"*Danki.* I love it." She glanced down and saw that Daniel's cheeks had turned bright pink from the cold.

"Looks like it's time to go in," Luke murmured.

Rose nodded. "Daniel, time to put the wheelbarrow up."

"I wanna stay outside," he whined.

"We can play with it again tomorrow."

"Mamm!" He thrust out his bottom lip and looked mutinous. It was a look she seldom saw.

"Hot chocolate and gingerbread."

"I *schur* would like some hot chocolate," Luke said. "And you made gingerbread?"

"*Ya.* And I bought mini marshmallows."

With a big sigh Daniel began pushing the wheelbarrow toward the barn. Luke helped him remove the snow before they stored it. They emerged with Daniel chattering a mile a minute about Christmas.

Inside, Rose cut big wedges of gingerbread while the milk heated on the stove. She set a slice before Luke. "I can't wait to hear about your trip. When Daniel runs down."

"I'm enjoying hearing about his Christmas."

"He was more excited this year than he's ever been," she told him. "I think it was because he was around his cousins."

And maybe, she thought guiltily, because she'd made more of an effort to make things different. Maybe she was coming out of the fog that had seemed to cling to her after Sam died.

She watched as Daniel stuffed an enormous bite of gingerbread into his mouth. And then realized Luke was staring at her.

"How was your trip? Was your family happy to see you?" she asked quickly. Then blushed. "Silly question. Of course they were. How was everyone?"

He told her about the visit, describing the bus ride, how the family farmhouse had looked. How all his *bruders* and *schweschders* had converged on it for supper when they heard he was back.

"I always thought a big family would be fun."

"You can't imagine the noise. And the nosiness."

She smiled. "Lillian can be pretty nosy. And she always seems to know what I'm thinking."

"That twin thing, huh?"

"*Ya.*"

"Anyway, it was a nice visit. I'm glad I went."

"Were they sorry when you left?" she asked quietly.

He shrugged. "You know how *mudders* are. I think mine was half hoping I might come back for *gut* but she understood. I invited them to come visit."

"That would be *wunderbaar.* I'd love to meet them."

"We'll see if they take me up on it. *Daed* doesn't like to travel."

"*Mamm?* More marshmellies?"

"A few more." She got up to get them and when she poured them from the package pretended to spill a few more of them. Daniel giggled as the marshmallows bounced on the table. He snatched them up and dropped them into his cup.

"Love marshmellies," he told Luke.

Luke chuckled as he took a paper napkin from a basket on the table and wiped at the white mustache over Daniel's lip. "I noticed."

Such a funny kid. His *bruders* and *schweschders* had *kinner* he'd enjoyed visiting while in Ohio but none charmed him as much as this *kind.*

"You like marshmellies?" Daniel asked him.

"Schur."

Daniel grabbed the bag before she realized what Rose was doing and tried to pour some into Luke's cup. A few plopped into the mug, but more fell helter-skelter all over the table and bounced along its surface. Luke was the first to react and grabbed the bag. "Whoa, there. I think that might be enough, *danki.*"

Daniel's eyes welled with tears. "Sorry, *Mamm.* I'm sorry!"

She took the bag from Luke and put it to the side. "It's *allrecht.* But let me do that next time."

Then she looked at him as she obviously remembered she'd made a joke of letting a few of the marshmallows fall when she poured them for Daniel earlier.

A knock on the back door made them look up.

Sarah poked her head in. *"Guder mariye!"* She glanced over. "Luke, I didn't think you were due back for another couple days."

"I wasn't. Came back early."

"Naiman, look who's here!" she exclaimed and turned to let him enter.

"I see," Naiman said as he wiped his feet on the mat. His gaze met Luke's. Luke

236

didn't see the same welcome in the man's eyes that he saw in Sarah's.

Maybe he'd come back just in time.

EIGHTEEN

Rose smiled as Isaac, Sarah's *sohn,* shed his
jacket and hat and scrambled up into a chair
next to Daniel. "Isaac? Would you like some
hot chocolate?"

"*Ya!*" he cried.

"Isaac?" his *mudder* said quietly.

"Please." He grinned up at Rose. "And
danki."

Rose ruffled his hair. "You're *wilkumm.* No
one can get enough hot chocolate in the
winter." She poured him a mug and added
some milk to cool it down so he could safely
drink it.

"We have marshmellies!" Daniel told him.
"How many you want?"

Luke made a grab for the bag before Daniel could pick it up. He poured enough to
coat the surface of the drink and chuckled
when Isaac giggled. Rose watched his ease
with the *kind* and sat again at the table.

And was surprised when she happened to

glance at Naiman and saw him glaring at Luke. Puzzled, she frowned.

"So, tell us about your trip," Sarah invited, smiling at Luke. "How was your family?"

"Growing," he told her as he chose a cookie and offered the plate to Isaac. "The family's gotten bigger. My *bruders* and *schweschders* had more *kinner.*"

"You don't miss home?" Naiman asked.

"This is home now," Luke said simply.

"Paradise?"

There it was again, thought Rose. *A strange . . . tension between the two men.*

"Of course."

"So you intend to stay?" Naiman pressed him. "You won't be taking over the family farm?"

"One of my *bruders* will do that."

"Well, I'm glad you'll be staying here in our community," Sarah told him, smiling at him.

Rose intercepted Daniel's reach for a fourth cookie and his protesting squawk so she didn't get to hear Luke's response. "That's enough cookies. Now, you and Isaac go play with your new puzzles in the living room."

The boys scampered off leaving the adults to talk. When she realized that Sarah was engaged in a conversation with Luke she

239

turned to Naiman with a smile and asked him about the Christmas holiday with his family.

And all the while she listened to him, she was ashamed to admit that her attention kept straying to another man . . .

If he noticed, Naiman didn't show it. He talked easily about his parents and the visits with his *bruders* and *schweschders*. Still, after a moment she realized with some embarrassment that he'd stopped and was staring at her.

"I'm sorry, what did you say?"

He sighed and his eyes were sad. "Nothing important."

Rose glanced at Luke and caught him looking at her. Her gaze slid to Sarah, and she saw disappointment in the other woman's eyes.

"Sarah, it's time we were going," Naiman said.

"Isaac isn't going to be happy," she murmured. "He's been begging to come over."

"I'll tell him we want you to visit this week," Rose promised. She walked with Sarah into the living room, where the boys huddled over one of the puzzles.

"Isaac, *kumm,* time to go!"

Isaac looked up at her, his lower lip thrust out. "*Mamm,* I want to play with Daniel."

"Five more minutes," Sarah said after a moment. "Then we must go." She turned to Rose. "He only has eyes for you, you know."

"What?"

"Luke. It's so obvious. He only has eyes for you."

"I — *nee*."

"It's true." Sarah managed a smile. "You're just not ready to see it. I wasn't."

"I —" Rose didn't know how to respond.

"I'm sorry Naiman isn't being friendlier to Luke," Sarah said. She glanced over her shoulder, hesitated, then turned back to Rose. "He told me he's worried that Luke is interested in you because of the farm." She bit her lip. "Maybe I shouldn't have told you that."

"Nee, it's *allrecht*. Naiman doesn't need to worry. Luke is a *gut* man. He came here to help Abraham after he was hurt, remember? And he's helping me and won't take any pay until the crops come in." She made a face. "Maybe I shouldn't have told you that."

"We'll keep this conversation a secret," Sarah said and they laughed. "Let me help you clean up in the kitchen."

They made quick work of the dishes while Luke and Naiman somewhat indifferently discussed farm equipment. That done, they walked back into the living room to collect Isaac. Sarah told her *sohn* they'd return in a few days and bring one of the toys he'd received for Christmas and was able to get him to put on his coat and hat to leave.

"*Danki* for stopping by," Rose said as Naiman donned his outerwear. Guilt made her blush as he nodded and shepherded Sarah and Isaac out to his buggy.

She closed the door and turned to find Luke studying her. "What?"

"That was uncomfortable." He paused, studied his hands. "Naiman doesn't like me much."

"I'm *schur* you're wrong." She picked up a colander and turned to investigate the contents of the refrigerator. Gathering up vegetables, she moved to the table to begin peeling and chopping.

"He seems very . . . protective of you."

"I've known Naiman all my life," she said, picking up a knife to peel carrots and potatoes. "We grew up together. He's just a friend."

Silence fell between them. Rose peeled a potato and watched the brown skin fall in a spiral toward the table.

"We did date a few times," she admitted. "Before Sam visited. After he arrived . . . ."

She trailed off. "I didn't see anyone else. Sam always said it took just one look for him. It didn't take much more for me." She blushed. "Sarah wrote me that Naiman dated someone else for a time. I thought when I moved back I'd find he'd married, but I guess he hasn't yet found the woman he wants for his *fraa*."

"I see."

She continued to chop vegetables. "I'm making pot roast for supper this evening. Are you staying?"

"Are you inviting me?"

"What a question. Of course. But if Abraham and Lovina were expecting you since it's your first night home . . ." She left the question open. There suddenly seemed to be a strange distance between them.

"They're not expecting me for supper. I told them I'd be taking over my chores here again. Speaking of which, I should be getting out to the barn and taking care of them."

"*Allrecht*. Why don't you take some coffee with you? In your new mug."

"*Gut* idea." He took it to the sink, washed it, then filled it with coffee. "See you later." He plucked up an apple from a bowl on the counter and tucked it into his coat pocket.

She looked at him and smiled. "I'm glad

243

you're back, Luke."

He nodded, his gaze intense. "Me too."

Rose stopped working and sat back in her chair. The only sound in the room was the ticking of the kitchen clock. She should have trusted that Luke would return instead of worrying that he'd stay with his family. Why had she worried so? Wasn't that arrogant of her to think God didn't know what He was doing? He wouldn't have led her back here only to wonder how she would manage the farm.

She shook her head and got back to work on the vegetables until the kitchen door opened and Lillian sailed in on a gust of cold air.

"So Luke is back." She wore a big, self-satisfied grin.

"The Amish grapevine is fast as usual."

"I didn't need it," Lillian said as she pulled off her bonnet and coat and hung them up. "I felt your emotions this morning."

The twin bond had always been so strong. Rose should have known she'd come over immediately.

"You're not going to say I told you so, are you?"

Lillian lifted her chin, pretended to consider it. "*Nee.* I don't have to, do I? Maybe you'll listen to me next time."

Rose tried not to smile. "Maybe."

Laughing, Lillian leaned down and hugged her.

"Your cheek is cold. Sit, I'll make you some tea."

Daniel ran into the room. "Where's John?"

"I didn't bring him."

His lower lip thrust out. "Oh." He turned and rushed back out.

"Well," said Lillian.

"I'm sorry," Rose began but Lillian just waved her hand and laughed. "I bet John would behave the same way if you showed up at my house without Daniel."

Lillian started to sit then saw the sign Luke had made for Rose lying on the nearby kitchen counter. She picked it up and studied it. "Where did this come from?" Her eyes danced with merriment.

Rose set a cup of tea on the table. "I'm sure you can guess."

"Tell me everything," Lillian demanded, settling into a chair. "Everything."

Luke walked to the barn thinking about Rose saying that she'd stopped dating Naiman after meeting Sam. That it had taken Sam just one look. She'd blushed when she said that.

He'd wanted to say that one look was all it had taken him too. One look. But he didn't dare.

Daisy and Star stuck their heads over their stalls and greeted him with neighs. "*Ya,* it's me," he said, rubbing their noses affectionately. "Missed you."

Star nudged him with her nose. Her nostrils flared as she pushed at his jacket.

"Did you miss me or the apples I bring you?"

Star snorted.

"Rude question," he agreed. Drawing out the apple, he cut it into pieces and fed them to the horses. "She said she was glad I was back. Daniel was too. I missed them so much. I'm not leaving them again." He frowned. "She says that Naiman is a friend but I can tell he wants to be more. Just like he can tell I want to be more than the man who works for her."

Star pushed at his empty hand. "All gone. And it's time to get to work." He opened the stall door and led Star into an empty stall, then set to work shoveling out the dirty straw and throwing it into a wheelbarrow. Soon the exertion had him shedding his jacket and rolling up his sleeves. Not the most pleasant work, but necessary. He scattered fresh straw, topped off the hay racks, filled the food and water buckets, and moved on to Daisy's stall.

Once he was done with the cleanup and feeding he turned to a new furniture project — a chest of drawers. Furniture making was satisfying, paid well, and was a logical way for Amish men to make some money during the long winters. After all, they didn't go to the mall and buy furniture for their homes — they made it, just as the women sewed most of the family's clothing and quilts for their beds.

The barn door slid open and Rose walked in. Luke's spirits lifted — and then he squinted against the light that streamed around her from the open barn door until she shut it. This woman didn't have the same slender grace that Rose had. She appeared a little heavier than Rose and held one hand protectively over her stomach.

It was Lillian, he realized. Some might have trouble knowing which was which, but after the first time he'd met the two of them, he'd quickly spotted the differences between them. It wasn't just that Rose was slimmer and more fragile in appearance. There was a certain way she smiled, the way she tilted her head. A certain way of moving.

In the week he'd been away it seemed that Lillian had gained weight. Her stomach was rounder beneath her apron. Embarrassed, realizing he shouldn't have noticed, he focused on her face. It wasn't done for an Amish man to discuss a woman's pregnancy unless it was with his own *fraa*. "Lillian."

"I'm glad you're back."

"I wouldn't have left but Rose insisted," he found himself saying.

Lillian smiled. "Rose has called me bossy but she *schur* knows how to get her way when she wants. I'm glad she talked you into going home to be with your family. It's so important. Family, I mean. Did you enjoy your visit?"

He nodded and gave her the same update he had Rose as he sanded the chest of drawers. Lillian had talked to him a lot about his family when he first came to help Abraham. She'd asked him so many questions about why he wanted to stay here when they were in Ohio. When she'd learned he was looking for a farm she'd talked to him again and mentioned her *schweschder* might need someone to help her when she moved here.

And his life had suddenly changed.

"Well, I'm glad you're back." She paused, became pensive. "Sometimes I wish that things could have been easier for Rose, that Sam could have lived. But in calling him home, God brought my *schweschder* home.

And you, Luke. This is your home now, *ya?*"

And then she was giving him a gentle smile and walking out of the barn. The door slid shut. He stood there for a long moment staring after her, wondering what that was all about. Then, shrugging, he went back to work on the chest of drawers.

The hours flew by. He put a coat of stain on the piece and took a break for lunch, then gave it another coat when he returned. Then he looked at the order for another commission and began cutting out the wood for it while the stain dried. The custom cradle was easy and one he didn't often get requests for. Perhaps people thought it was too old-fashioned these days or an item they didn't find as useful. He remembered watching his *mudder* tuck younger *bruders* and *schweschders* into one and keep it rocking with a nudge of her foot as she quilted or mended clothing.

As he worked his thoughts circled back to Lillian and how he'd noticed her growing pregnancy. She had such a contented air about her. What, he wondered, had Rose looked like when she'd been expecting Daniel? She always seemed so serene and happy when her *kind* was in the same room and knew so well how to handle his moods and behavior. Did she ever think about getting remarried and having other *kinner*?

The barn door slid open again, and this time when a woman walked in he could tell immediately it was Rose. Well, it was easy since Daniel bounded in beside her.

"Daniel and I are walking over to Lavinia's house to check on her," she said. "She's been laid up with a sprained ankle. We'll be back in about an hour."

Her gaze fell on the wood in his hands and she stiffened. He looked down, then up at her.

"I got a commission for it," he told her. "I've only made a few of them. People just don't seem to ask for them these days."

"Nee," she said slowly.

"Boppli," Daniel cried.

"Ya, it's for a *boppli,"* Luke agreed. "Did you have one for Daniel?"

She nodded. "Sam made it. I put it up in the attic. Well, we're off," she said abruptly. "We'll be back soon." Grasping Daniel by the hand, she hurried out.

Was it his imagination that she'd looked uncomfortable when she'd seen that he was making a cradle?

With a shrug he went back to work. Time passed quickly and before he knew it he heard the dinner bell ringing on the back porch. He pulled on his jacket and hat and left the barn. Rose stood on the back porch holding Daniel who was madly clanging the dinner bell. When he saw Luke he giggled.

"Luke! Supper!"

Rose set him down and he scrambled inside. "He wouldn't stop begging until I let him do it."

"Funny kid." He held the back door open and followed her inside. "How was Lavinia?"

"Doing better. She was happy to have the food Daniel and I brought to her. We didn't stay long, though. He had a little trouble sitting still and she's elderly."

"You should have left him with me."

"To play with your saws and hammers while you work on furniture?" she asked with a smile as she shed her coat and bonnet.

"Don't forget the awl." He caught Daniel by his jacket collar as he tried to race into the other room. Daniel giggled and turned his attempt to help him out of his jacket into a wrestling match. Luke ended up with the jacket but Daniel shrieked with laughter as he escaped with his hat.

Rose smiled at them as she washed her hands. "Daniel, give Luke your hat to hang up, and go wash your hands."

Daniel pulled off his hat to reveal hair

standing up in tufts, making him look like a rumpled little chicken. He handed the hat to Luke and ran out of the room as Luke hung it on a peg and turned to watch Rose pull out a roasting pan and set it on the stove. He hadn't thought he was all that hungry, but as the scent of the pot roast drifted toward him he realized he was ravenous. No one made a pot roast better than Rose.

Not that he'd dare ever tell his *mudder* that.

Rose put the roast, potatoes, and carrots on a platter and set it on the table, then frowned. "Something wrong?" she asked him.

"*Nee.* That smells *wunderbaar.* How can I help?"

She gave him a surprised look. "You don't need to do anything."

He just stared at her.

"Sorry, I'm not used to having help. Sam avoided the kitchen unless it was time to eat."

So her *mann* hadn't been perfect. Too often Luke had found widows often remembered them as much better than they'd been.

"You could slice some bread," she said.

"Let me go get my saw."

"Very funny." She got a knife from a drawer and handed it to him.

He sliced the bread, she set the table, and Daniel returned to swipe a slice of bread from the basket before Luke could stop him. As Luke settled in his seat at the table he closed his eyes and sent up a prayer of thanks. He was home, truly home. As Lillian had said, God had sent him where he belonged.

The wind tossed a flurry of snow against the kitchen window. Rose shivered. "It seems like it's been winter forever and it's only the end of December."

"It'll be spring soon," he promised.

Her mouth quirked into a smile. "You were here last spring. You know it's over in the blink of an eye."

"That reminds me," he said as she handed him the platter of pot roast. "I had a lot of time to think on the bus. Maybe tomorrow we should look over the plan for spring planting again. I have an idea."

"*Schur.*" She fixed Daniel's plate and set it before him. "It's *gut* to have a well-thought-out plan."

He took a bite of pot roast and chewed it thoroughly. Seemed to him that it was time to make a plan to win her heart.

NINETEEN

"I saw my first robin today!" Rose told Lillian. "That means spring's coming soon, right?"

"Schur," Lillian agreed placidly. She rubbed the mound of her abdomen. "Whatever you say."

Rose tossed a spool of thread at her. "It *was* a robin. Really!"

"It's going to be some time before we see a robin," Lillian told her.

Snow splattered the window as if a giant hand had tossed it. It was cozy here by the fire. The boys played with toys in a corner of the living room while Annie read quietly on the sofa.

"If you *do* see a robin, you might knit the poor thing a sweater."

Rose giggled at the thought. "I'm just feeling a little restless. Luke and I have so many plans for spring. Planting, I mean." She felt heat rush into her cheeks and glanced down at her quilt.

"I noticed Luke drove you and Daniel to church again."

"It makes sense like he said. He's already here for morning chores so he said we should go together. Daniel and him and me, I mean."

"Daniel *schur* loves him."

"He's so *gut* with Daniel."

Lillian knotted her thread, clipped it, then threaded her needle again. "Sam would want you to marry again, give Daniel a *dat.*"

"It's too soon. You and I have talked about this."

"Sam's been gone coming up on *two* years," Lillian reminded her quietly.

"*Ya.* Too soon." She stood. "I'm going to get us some tea."

Going into the kitchen, she filled the teakettle, set it on the stove, and turned up the gas flame. She wasn't ready to tell anyone — even her *schweschder* — that she had feelings for Luke. They felt like the first stirrings of seeds in earth, pushing their way up to the surface and basking in the warmth of his regard.

She wasn't naïve. She could tell that he cared for her. It showed in all the little ways he made *schur* they were comfortable and safe. There was a stack of wood on the back

255

porch that was more than they needed for the rest of winter. He checked the windows and doors where wind and wet could come in and took such *gut* care of the animals.

And sometimes she caught him watching her with that special look a man had when he'd found a woman pleasing. She hadn't forgotten what that was or how it made a woman feel. She'd felt frozen as the earth outside this cold winter but inside she was beginning to sense her heart thawing.

The kettle screeched, and she turned the flame off, poured mugs of boiling water, and dropped tea bags in two and packets of hot chocolate in the others for the *kinner.* A plate of cookies went on the tray.

When she walked into the room, she found Lillian sound asleep. John looked up and started to speak. She shook her head and shushed him. "Your *mudder* is taking a nap."

"Then we don't have to?" he asked with a mischievous grin.

"Naps are *gut* for everyone," she said and put their hot chocolate on the floor beside them. "Careful, don't drink it yet because it's hot. And don't spill."

She sat and sipped her tea and once again thought about how tired Lillian was. She decided that when Amos came to pick them up, she would try to pull him aside and ask him if she seemed more tired than she had in previous pregnancies. Lillian had always been healthy but it seemed this pregnancy was more wearing on her than others had been.

Then again, she hadn't been here the last time Lillian had been expecting. Lillian and her *mann* had unexpectedly shown up in Ohio for a visit and Lillian had looked exhausted. Just a few days later she'd gone into premature labor and the twins came early, the midwife who'd come at their call had told them.

She shouldn't have been traveling at that stage in her pregnancy, the midwife had admonished. But she'd done it for Rose — and for Sam.

Rose frowned as she remembered how she'd broken down on the phone talking to Lillian. Sam's chemo was wearing him out and Rose was still trying to care for him and the farm as well. She hadn't even had to call Lillian — she'd gone out to the phone shanty to call the doctor's office with a question and found a message from Lillian on her answering machine. Lillian had sensed her distress and urged her to call right back. And as much as Rose tried not to, she'd broken down and confessed her fear that Sam wasn't getting better. The chemo was taking such a toll on him that she was scared to death that Sam was giving up.

Lillian and Amos had shown up several days later. Their visit had been a gift of support and more.

Rose looked over at the boys and marveled at them. The way they seemed to have a language of their own as they talked and played, a similarity in gestures and expressions.

All of it reminded her of herself and her *schweschder*.

Lillian woke with a start and smiled sheepishly as she straightened in her chair. "Sorry. I guess I fell asleep." She reached for the teacup Rose had set on the table beside her.

"Let me get you a fresh cup. That's probably cold."

"That's *allrecht*. When you're a *mudder* you eat cold food and drink cold drinks." She sipped as she turned her head to watch the boys sprawled out on the rug near the fire. "It's *gut* they're together. They enjoy each other so much."

"I was just remembering when you came to Ohio. It gave Sam a reason to keep fighting."

Lillian nodded. "I'm glad. Amos and I have never regretted it."

"You seem so tired lately. What does the doctor say?"

"That I'm doing well. That every pregnancy is different."

"You'd tell me if something was wrong?"

"Of course." She finished her tea, picked up her quilt, and began to sew again. "I know you're restless for spring but I'm enjoying this slower time. Things will be busy soon enough when planting season comes."

"I know."

Amos came to pick them up, and Rose found herself agreeing to let Daniel have a sleepover at John's house. And just like that the house became quiet — so quiet she didn't know what to do with herself. She picked up the cups and took them to the kitchen to wash, then glanced at the clock. This was the time when she usually started supper. She had no enthusiasm for fixing anything, though. Perhaps there were leftovers she could scrape together.

She had her head in the refrigerator when she heard the kitchen door open and jumped back in surprise.

Luke frowned as he stepped inside and saw

Rose press a hand to her throat. "Sorry! I didn't mean to startle you!"

"It was just so quiet. I thought everyone had gone."

"I never leave without letting you know."

Rose nodded. "My thoughts were just a million miles away. I'm not used to Daniel being gone."

"I saw him leave with your *schweschder.*"

She closed the refrigerator door. "It's his first sleepover. He's never been away from home before."

"I guess you wouldn't want to hear how happy he looked as he climbed into the buggy."

"*Nee*, I know. He ran out of the house."

She sat at the table looking a little sad and lonely. "I decided not to watch him leave. I know we have to let go sometime. But I didn't think it would start this early." She sighed. "I believe I told you Lillian reminded me he and John would be starting *schul* in the fall."

"They're the same age, *ya*?"

"*Ya*. Near." She stood. "Would you like some coffee? I haven't started supper yet."

"Why don't we go out? You're always cooking for me."

"I don't mind. It's the least I can do when you work so hard."

"Daniel's having fun tonight. Why shouldn't you? We could go to that Italian place that just opened up. Everyone's been talking about it. I heard it's *gut* and the prices are reasonable." He patted his pocket. "Got paid today by the furniture store and Lester gave me three more orders. We can call it a celebration."

She glanced down at her dress. "I'm not dressed to go out."

"You look fine to me but I have to go home and change, so there's time to put on something else if you want. I'll be back for you in half an hour. If you don't mind my taking your buggy."

"Of course not."

Luke watched her hesitate and found himself holding his breath. He'd tried so hard to be casual but he felt anything but.

"I guess we could."

"*Wunderbaar.* I'll be back in half an hour." He left before she could change her mind, hitching the buggy up quickly and urging Daisy to go a little faster than was probably safe on roads that still had some snow on them.

When he got to Abraham's he dashed inside, found Lovina in the kitchen preparing supper, and told her he was going out again. He took the stairs two at a time to rush into his room and put on his Sunday best.

She gave him a knowing smile when he clattered down the stairs. "Hot date?" she teased.

He flushed. "Just supper with Rose. Daniel's on a sleepover and I thought she'd like to get out."

"Where are you going?"

"That new Italian place in town."

"Heard the lasagna is *gut.*"

"Can't be better than yours," he said loyally as he edged toward the door.

"I'm *schur* it is. I heard the owner's from Italy. Have fun."

Luke found his heart racing as he urged Daisy back home. This was the first step on his plan to win Rose's heart. Now if he managed to keep from looking overeager and remembered his table manners . . . . He hadn't been out on a date in a long time and never one so important.

When he pulled back into the drive, Rose came out wearing her coat and bonnet. She climbed into the buggy and smiled at him. "That was fast."

"I'm *hungerich,*" he said then wished he could call back his words. He sounded dumb.

"Me too."

"Lovina said she heard the lasagna is *gut.*"

"I'd like to try it. Daniel has me make spaghetti and meatballs so often, I don't think I'll order that."

"Or beanie weenies."

She laughed. "I doubt that'll be on the menu."

"Nee."

"I've never had tiramisu. Fannie Mae said she had it there and it was the best dessert she'd ever had. And you know she's famous for her chocolate cream pie."

"Then you should have lasagna and tiramisu."

"And I'll have to roll home." She grinned as she gazed out at the passing scenery. "Snow's let up. I was telling Lillian I can't wait for spring. It's been a long winter."

"It's always a long winter here, isn't it?"

She nodded. "And spring is so short if you blink you miss it. Then summer's a long season."

"It's much the same back where I come from. But I like it here better." Because here was where she was. But he didn't dare tell her that.

Rose shivered when a gust of wind buffeted the buggy. He reached into the back for the blanket and gave it to her. She spread it over her lap.

"You're not cold?"

He shook his head. "I'm fine."

The parking lot of the restaurant was nearly filled with a combination of *Englisch* cars and Amish buggies but he found a place to park. Inside it was warm and cozy with checkered cloths on the tables and candles stuck in Chianti bottles casting a soft glow. The scents were spicy and delicious. It didn't take long for them to be seated at a table and there was a basket of crunchy breadsticks to munch on while they waited for their food.

They'd shared many meals together in her Amish farmhouse kitchen but no matter how she treated him like a friend, it was still her home and he was working for her. But here they were equals. And a couple like so many of those sitting at tables around them.

Some of those other couples were obviously more romantic than others. He saw some holding hands as they sipped a drink or ate their supper.

He couldn't help hoping Rose noticed . . .

She glanced around and then shook her head and laughed ruefully.

"What?"

"I keep expecting Daniel to pop up at my elbow," she told him as she picked up her napkin and placed it on her lap. "I can't remember ever having a meal without him. If I try to cut up your food or move your glass away from your elbow, just tell me to stop."

He grinned. "I will. And I promise I won't talk with my mouth full."

"Lillian was telling me we *mudders* so often eat cold food because we're tending to our *kinner* at a meal. Not that we mind," she added quickly. "It's just a fact of life."

"Well, tonight you get to eat a hot meal you didn't cook and your supper companion won't keep you jumping," he promised.

She studied her menu and he studied her over the top of his. The candlelight cast a soft glow over her rose petal skin and soft pink lips. When she gazed up at him and caught him staring, her eyes looked bluer than they ever had. "What looks *gut*?"

"Everything," she confessed. "But the prices —"

"Don't worry about it. We're celebrating. And it's my way of paying you back for so many delicious meals in your home."

"You work so hard. It's the least I can do. And I'm *schur* the food here is better than my cooking."

"Don't say that. You're a *wunderbaar* cook."

Luke decided it was safer to order the

lasagna than risk eating spaghetti and dropping it in his lap. They talked easily as they ate. He'd been afraid conversation might be stilted because it was a date and then realized maybe Rose didn't think of it that way.

Well, that was *allrecht.* Whatever it took to ease his way into her life was just fine with him.

"How's the lasagna?"

"Delicious. Yours?"

"The same." He grinned. "Probably came from the same pan, *ya*?"

She laughed. "*Ya.* Next time I'd like to try the chicken parmigiana. It sounded delicious."

Next time. He hoped there'd be a next time. "We'll try it."

"Save room for dessert," their server stopped at their table to say. "You must try our tiramisu and our zabaglione."

So of course they had to try them. Rose ordered the tiramisu and Luke the zabaglione and they sampled a little of each other's.

He took the long way back, and she didn't object. The moon was big and full and bright, the woods deep and mysterious along the country road leading home. Everything was fine until they approached

Abraham and Lovina's farm on the way home.

"Why don't I drop you off here?" Rose asked him.

Luke shook his head. "Then you'd have to unhitch the buggy."

"I know how to do it," she said with a grin.

"It wouldn't be gentlemanly."

"But you shouldn't have to walk home."

"I don't mind. It's not far. And remember I ate my food and then finished yours. I need the walk." He kept the buggy rolling along, refusing to argue with her about it, and delivered her to her front door.

"*Danki* for supper," she said, smiling in that quiet way of hers before she got out of the buggy. "I had such a nice time."

"Me too. We have to do it again sometime."

Luke waited until she was safely inside before he unhitched the buggy, put Daisy in her stall, and gave Star a final pat for the night on his way out of the barn.

He walked home feeling more content than he could ever remember being.

TWENTY

She couldn't settle.

Rose found herself roaming the house, looking into Daniel's room even though she knew he was at Lillian's, aimlessly wandering around feeling restless. Finally, she changed into her nightgown and tucked herself into bed. She tried reading for a little while and found herself listening for . . . she didn't know what. There were only the usual noises of an old house settling, the wind soughing against the window.

She hadn't expected to feel so totally alone without Daniel there. While it wasn't anything like the first terrible night she'd spent without Sam, it was a little wrenching to know she didn't even have a little person in the house. Restless, she got up, slipped on her robe, and went downstairs to fix a cup of chamomile tea.

As she sat with the tea at the kitchen table, her thoughts circled back to her evening with Luke. It was the first time she'd gone out with a man since Sam. Oh, it hadn't been a date, but still, it was time spent with a man other than her late *mann* and she couldn't help feeling a bit unsettled. Had it been her imagination that he hadn't looked at her as a friend did as they enjoyed their meal? She wondered if it had just been that so many of the couples around them had seemed to be there on dates, sharing a romantic evening.

She couldn't even think about having a date with a man. It felt too soon. Felt too strange. She had a *sohn* to raise. A farm to get going again. There were so many reasons why she couldn't ever see herself dating, let alone married again. *Ya,* she was attracted to Luke but . . .

How could she tell a man what she'd told no one but her *schweschder*? Deep inside herself she had buried any dreams of marrying again, having another *kind.*

With a sigh she got up, poured the cold tea in the sink, and went back upstairs. She slipped into bed, turned off the bedside battery-operated lamp, and pulled her quilt up high over her shoulders. When sleep finally came it was filled with dreams that made her toss and turn. When she woke, she couldn't remember them but felt vaguely uneasy and restless. Conflicted. Being out with Luke had made her think about him in a different way. But that didn't mean she wanted to think about dating . . . marriage.

She dressed and found herself automatically going to Daniel's room to wake him for breakfast. It took a moment to remember that he'd had a sleepover.

Luke came in for coffee while she was eating breakfast.

"Have you eaten?"

He nodded. "So, when's Daniel due home?"

"I'm picking him up in a little while."

"I'll hitch up the buggy when you're ready." He sipped his coffee. "So how was it last night without him? You said it was his first sleepover."

"Quiet." She smiled. "And when I got up this morning I forgot he wasn't here and went to his room to wake him." She sighed. "I'll admit there are times that I long for some peace and quiet but last night it was too quiet."

She rose and put her breakfast dishes in the sink. "I guess I'll go get him now. It was nice of Lillian to have him over when she has a big family and she's so tired lately."

"And you miss him."

"*Ya,* of course I miss him."

"Rose?"

"Hmm?" She squirted dish liquid into the sink and turned on the tap to fill the sink with water.

"I had a *gut* time last night."

"Me too."

"I'd like to do it again."

She turned and met his gaze, saw the interest she'd seen and questioned the night before. "I don't think I'm ready to date yet, Luke. And I don't know when I will be."

"*Allrecht,*" he said slowly. "Then are you ready to be friends? Because I enjoy your company."

Rose didn't know what to say. "I — *danki.* I just think that if you're looking for a *fraa* you shouldn't look in my direction." She stared down at the mug in her hands and used the sponge to rub at it so she didn't have to look at him. "Maybe you should think about someone else. Sarah —"

"*Nee,*" he said quietly but firmly. He put his mug in the sink. "I'll go hitch up the buggy. I'm missing Daniel too."

She didn't look up until she heard the door open and then shut. Only then did she realize that she'd been holding her breath. She let it out and watched him walk to the barn. He was a handsome man. And such a hard worker. He could have any *maedel* he wanted. She'd seen them looking his way at church, at singings and work frolics.

She sighed. Why couldn't things have been easier? She knew Sam would want her to be happy. He'd insisted on talking one day about the future when his test results had come back and they hadn't been *gut.*

"I want you to get married again if I die," he'd said and she'd burst into tears and refused to talk to him about it. He'd insisted she listen to him and so she'd sat and done so. She was a *gut fraa,* he told her, and a *gut mudder.* He wanted her and Daniel to be happy.

She'd been so grateful the doctor had walked into the hospital room and interrupted their conversation. And as the chemo failed and he grew weaker, it was easier to avoid another such discussion.

She sighed again. She'd been lucky that she had Daniel after Sam was gone. She'd have had no place else to give all the love she'd felt for her *mann.* Her family lived in another state. And besides, it was a different kind of love she was missing now — the love you felt for your partner, your life companion.

Another man would want more *kinner.* And —

The door opened, interrupting her thoughts. "Buggy's ready."

She dried her hands and pulled on her coat and bonnet. *"Danki."*

When she walked into Lillian's kitchen she was glad she hadn't listened to Lillian's offer that Daniel could stay as long as he wanted. Lillian sat at the kitchen table overseeing the *kinner* eating breakfast and looked so pale and tired.

"Hi, *Mamm*!" Daniel cried when he saw her.

"Hi, *lieb.*"

She bent to kiss the top of his head then sat beside Lillian and touched her hand. "What's wrong? And don't tell me nothing."

"I just had a bad night," Lillian confessed quietly. "I can't talk about it right now."

"Allrecht. Why don't you go rest and I'll see to the *kinner?*"

When her *schweschder* nodded and did as she suggested without protest Rose was even more concerned. Lillian was the rock in the family, always looking after everyone else and almost vibrating with energy. She *never* took a rest.

Amos came in a few minutes later after doing chores. "Where's Lillian?"

"Lying down. If you'll watch the *kinner* I want to talk to her."

"*Schur.*"

Rose found Lillian lying on the bed. "Tell me what's wrong."

Lillian's eyes were filled with fear. "I'm spotting."

"Did you call the midwife?"

"*Nee.* She's not in until 9:00 a.m."

"I'll go call her."

"Her number's in the book by the phone."

"You rest and try not to worry."

Rose rushed downstairs and pulled Amos aside to tell him she was calling the midwife. It was only when she got outside to the phone shanty that she realized she'd been so worried she'd forgotten her coat. She shivered as she waited for the office to answer.

"It's not uncommon in pregnancies," the midwife reassured her when she came to the phone.

"You don't think we should bring her into the office?"

"No. Have her rest, stay off her feet, and give us a call if the bleeding gets worse."

Rose thanked her and hung up but she didn't feel reassured. But she summoned a smile as she walked back into the kitchen. The *kinner* had finished breakfast and scattered to other rooms in the house.

"The midwife says make Lillian rest and call if the spotting gets worse."

Amos nodded and looked relieved.

"Listen, why don't I take the *kinner* back to my house so Lillian can have some peace and quiet? You make *schur* she doesn't get up and do anything, *allrecht*?"

"I will."

"I'll bring them back after supper. And I'll bring supper back for you and Lillian."

They rounded everyone up, got them into jackets and hats, and she watched them clamber into the buggy. She smiled and waved at Amos and wondered if she'd survive an afternoon with all the *kinner*.

Luke was in the barn making a dining-room table when he heard a buggy coming in the driveway. He walked outside and watched Daniel and then Lillian's *kinner* tumble out and race, laughing and yelling, toward the house.

"Brought home some extras, did you?"

She didn't smile. "Lillian's not feeling well. I said I'd have the *kinner* over so she can get some rest."

"Sounds like you won't," he joked as he heard a high-pitched scream. "Get any rest, I mean."

"Lillian was so exhausted I felt I needed to give her time to rest. It's the least I can do."

"Go on in before one of them gets into mischief," he told her as they heard a wail.

Luke unhitched Daisy and led her into the barn. Best to avoid the house for a few hours. He went back to work and if he wondered occasionally how Rose was faring, he was man enough to push the thought away and focus on the wood.

The need to warm up and have a cup of coffee finally drove him inside. He opened the kitchen door cautiously and found it a hive of activity. The *kinner* crowded around the kitchen table stirring big pottery bowls filled with batter. Rose was bending down to take a pan of cookies from the oven.

She glanced up at him with a smile. "Good timing. The first cookies are done."

"I came in for hot coffee," he told her a little defensively.

"Oh, then you don't want a cookie?"

"I do!" Daniel cried. "I'll eat Luke's cookie if he doesn't want it." He gave Luke a big grin.

"That's so nice of you," Luke told him, chuckling.

Rose used a spatula to transfer cookies to a plate. "I'm *schur* Luke wants one, Daniel.

He loves cookies just as much as you."

Luke reached for a cookie she'd just placed on the plate. "They're not cool enough to eat!" Rose warned him.

He tossed it from one hand to another. "Ouch! That's hot!"

"You're supposed to be setting a *gut* example," she admonished.

"Mmm, it's *gut*."

"Sit and I'll pour you a cup of coffee."

Luke did as she told him, sitting next to Annie who was stirring batter in a big bowl. She opened a bag of chocolate chips and poured. "Oops," he said, bumping her elbow so she spilled some of the chips onto the table. He grabbed them up and popped them into his mouth. "Delicious."

"*Aenti* Rose! Luke's stealing the chocolate chips!" Annie protested and giggled.

Rose put her hands on her hips and stared at him. "Do I have another *kind*, Luke?"

Shoving a few of them in his mouth, he grinned at Annie. "They're so *gut* I can't wait for them to go into cookies."

"I want some!" John said.

So of course everyone wanted some. Rose reached into a cupboard and found another package. She portioned out chips into outstretched hands and gave Luke a stern look when he held out one of his big hands.

"You're the one that started this. I don't think you should have any."

"You're right," he told her and tried to look penitent. But he had trouble biting back a grin.

She set the plate of cooled cookies in the center of the table and went to the refrigerator to get a gallon of milk. The kitchen got quiet as everyone filled their mouths with the treats. Luke kept an eye on the *kinner* as Rose pulled finished cookies from the oven and set another tray in to bake. But although he kept an eagle eye out for John bedeviling his *schweschder* and made certain no one ate raw cookie dough — gee, he'd eaten lots of the stuff when he was a *kind* but now *mudders* were saying it wasn't safe — a cup of milk got knocked over and it and the ensuing tears had to be mopped up.

"That's it for the cookie baking," Rose announced as she set the last tray on top of the stove and turned off the oven. "Now what shall we do?"

"Build a snowman!" Daniel announced.

"Not today," his *mudder* told him. "The sun's melted the snow to slush. Another time."

She shot Luke a look that said she hoped there'd be no more snow.

"Can we read stories?" Annie piped up.

"I got a *gut* story!" Daniel told her. "I'll get it. Luke will read it to us, won't you, Luke?"

He blinked at the suggestion. And then, as he saw the adoration in the *kind*'s eyes, found himself agreeing.

"I'll get it!" Daniel scrambled down from his chair and raced up the stairs to his bedroom.

"Walk!" Rose called after him and then shook his head. "That *kind* hasn't walked since he learned how. Everything's been a race ever since."

Daniel was back downstairs in no time clutching his favorite story. He thrust it into Luke's hands.

"A seed catalog?" Luke asked, gazing up at Rose.

"Remember I told you I came home one day and Sam was reading it to him," she told him. "He'd been looking at it, and when Daniel woke from his nap he wanted his *dat* to read it to him."

Luke felt something stir in his chest at her quiet words. He looked down at the dog-eared catalog. It had obviously been well loved.

"Looks like a *wunderbaar* story," Luke said. "Why don't we go in the other room by the fire and read it?"

Rose gave him a smile that warmed his heart.

So Luke settled into the big chair by the fire with Daniel standing at his side and his cousins sprawled on the rug around him and read them the seed catalog story. Well, it was no story, of course, just descriptions of a variety of seeds.

"Corn!" Daniel pronounced as he pointed to a photo of a plump ear of corn.

"*Ya*, corn," Luke said, nodding. "And this particular seed is resistant to disease and produces a high yield." He read on, waiting for the *kinner* to get bored with the descriptions of best planting times and pricing details but they listened dutifully. There were seeds for wheat and barley and oats and soybeans and potatoes. As he turned the pages and read Daniel pointed out each crop and had some of the words memorized.

Luke caught a glimpse of Rose as she peeked into the room to see how they were doing. Her gaze softened as she watched them from the doorway. Annie stood and wandered over to her to ask a question and the two of them disappeared into the kitchen.

"I didn't know *kinner* could find a seed catalog so interesting," he said ruefully when Rose came out of the kitchen a while later.

"They just love being read to." She smiled at the *kinner*. "I made hot chocolate," she announced. "Anybody wants some they should join me in the kitchen."

Luke sat there for a long moment studying the catalog in his hands. Funny what *kinner* got attached to. He'd wondered how much Daniel remembered of his *dat*. Somewhere deep inside was the memory of Sam's voice making a simple sales catalog interesting to a toddler.

He found himself wondering what it would be like to be a *dat*. He'd grown to love this sweet, funny little *sohn* of Rose's in the short time he'd been here. Like the rest of his friends and family he believed *kinner* were a gift from God, one to be cherished. A man was truly blessed if he had a *fraa* and *kinner* to care for and guide in faith and love.

Normally he thought himself a patient man but he wished God's timing and his own were the same. He wanted Rose to turn to him, to see he was the man God had set aside for her, and marry him. Daniel would be a *sohn* to him, the first of many *kinner* he hoped he and Rose would be blessed with.

"Luke!"

Startled from his thoughts, he looked up.

"*Mamm* made hot chocolate!" Daniel grasped his hand and tugged on it. "*Kumm!* We have marshmellies!"

Grinning, Luke allowed himself to be drawn into the kitchen, noisy with Lillian's brood, and sat at the table to enjoy the warmth of the drink and the kitchen. It was a *gut* day for *schur*.

TWENTY-ONE

Spring had sprung.

Rose knelt in the dirt in her kitchen garden and took a deep breath. *Schur,* it was a breath of air that held the not-so-pleasant aroma of manure from the nearby fields. But it was so *wunderbaar* to finally be outside planting the seeds Lillian had given her. And planting seeds from her own garden in Ohio.

She wasn't the only one working in the kitchen garden. Daniel was happily planting the seeds she'd given him in his own corner of the garden.

Her *sohn* was a born farmer. Every so often he'd look over at her and laugh and laugh.

Luke worked in the fields with his cousin Abraham and a couple of other men. Once they finished the spring planting here, they'd move on to their farms and Luke would help them.

A flurry of movement caught her eye. She smiled. A robin, *schur* sign of spring. Lillian had teased her when she said she saw one a week ago and jokingly asked her if she was going to knit it a sweater. Well, no one could deny this bird watching her from the nearby fence post was definitely a robin. And the day was warm enough it didn't need a sweater.

And neither did they. Daniel had insisted on shedding his once he saw the men were in their shirtsleeves. Rose had shed hers after the effort of planting warmed her.

A buggy rolled up the drive. Rose finished covering the seeds she'd planted and watched Lillian get out of the buggy. She was moving slower these days. A sonogram had revealed that she was carrying *zwilling-bopplin* . . . again.

"Daniel, *Aenti* Lillian is here!"

He merely grunted, too absorbed in dropping a seed into the hole he'd dug.

"John's here."

He looked up then and waved him over.

She stood, brushing the dirt from her hands, and hurried to take the picnic basket Lillian carried. "I told you that you didn't need to bring anything."

"I wanted to. And I'm doing fine. I told you the doctor says we're all doing well."

"You need to be careful not to overdo."

"I'm not."

"Daniel, John, *kumm,* we're going to fix lunch," Rose called, and they followed them into the house without protest. That told Rose Daniel was *hungerich.*

"How does it feel to be carrying *zwilling-bopplin* again?" she asked as she helped Lillian take off her sweater once they were inside the house.

"Zwilling . . ." Daniel began and then frowned. "Bop-bop."

Lillian laughed and bent to kiss the top of his head. *"Zwillingbopplin,"* she said slowly and carefully. "Two *boppli."*

"Two?" he asked, gazing at her stomach with wide eyes.

"Two," John told him, nodding.

"Go wash your hands," Rose told him and watched as they ran off. She turned back to her *schweschder.* "Sit."

Lillian did as she told her and began unpacking the basket. "I made two chicken pot pies and an apple *schnitz* pie."

"That's a lot. *Danki."*

Her *schweschder* shrugged. "It was easy to sit and make piecrust and roll it out. It'll be nice to make some pies with rhubarb and strawberries soon."

Rose turned on the oven to heat the pot

pies and filled the teakettle with water. "I'll make us some tea." She busied herself getting out mugs while the water heated.

"I'm so glad it's getting warmer again."

Rose poured boiling water into the mugs and carried them to the table. "I love spring." She sighed as she gazed out the window. "The light's different. The air. It's all about new beginnings. I planted most of the seeds you gave me for Christmas. Some of the ones I brought from my kitchen garden in Ohio too."

Daniel walked back into the kitchen waving his hands. After inspecting the job he'd done washing them, Rose handed him a dish towel. He never seemed to remember to dry his hands on the towels in the bathroom. Or if he did it was when he hadn't done the best job on washing them and the towels ended up with dirty handprints on them.

Her *sohn* climbed into his chair and grinned when she handed him a carrot stick to munch on. John walked in a few minutes later and, after Lillian inspected his hands, joined Daniel at the table. He took the carrot Daniel offered and finished it. Rose opened a drawer and got out coloring books and crayons she kept in the kitchen, and the boys began coloring.

"So, the planting is going well?" Lillian asked her as she sipped her tea.

"Luke thinks they'll be done this afternoon." Rose glanced out the window and saw the men were still working. She'd give it a few more minutes and then call them in.

"Luke planted *lots* of seeds," Daniel informed Lillian. "I did too."

"I planted green beans," John said. "They're my favorite."

"Mine too," Daniel told him.

"And peas." John slung a companionable arm around his cousin.

"I like them too."

"Two peas in a pod," Lillian murmured with a smile.

The back door opened. Rose looked up as a man stepped inside — tall, wide shouldered, with an easy grace in his movements. With the sun forming a nimbus behind his head it was hard to see his features at first. And then she saw it was Luke standing there. "Ready to feed us lunch?"

"Schur."

She watched as his gaze slid to the two boys sitting with their heads close together at the table, absorbed in their own conversation as they colored.

"Hi, Luke," Lillian said.

He looked at her. "Hi, Lillian. *Allrecht,* Rose, we'll be along in a few minutes." He closed the door behind him.

She sat there, not moving.

"Rose?"

"Ya?"

"Rose?"

She turned, frowning. "What?"

Lillian just smiled. "Nothing."

"Wipe that smug smile off your face," she admonished. "I know what you're thinking." She got up and opened the cabinet for plates.

"You do, do you?"

She got out plates and began setting the table. "I might have been a little slow but I figured out you did some matchmaking," she said quietly so the boys wouldn't hear her.

"Me?" Lillian looked at her with an innocent expression. Then she ruined it by laughing. "Well, you have to admit it worked out well."

"We've gone out a few times. That doesn't mean —" She stopped. Daniel had glanced up from his coloring and was looking interested in the conversation. "Little pitchers," she told Lillian, inclining her head.

"Pitchers?" Daniel frowned in consternation.

"Time to put the coloring books away," she told him. "We're about to eat." She chose knives and forks and set them beside each plate. "There, we're all set."

"I believe you are," Lillian said giving her a level look. "I believe you are."

Rose glanced out the window. "They'll be coming in now." She picked up a knife and cut the apple *schnitz* pie into portions. "Hope there's a piece left to send home to Amos. It's his favorite."

"I made two. It's as easy most times to make two as one."

Rose walked over, gently patted Lillian's baby bump, and smiled. "Is it?"

Lillian laughed. *"Ya,"* she said and she gazed fondly at John and Daniel.

"Something wrong?"

"Hmm?" Luke looked over at Abraham. "Oh, *nee,* just thinking."

"Guess that explains the strange expression. You don't do it much."

Luke elbowed him. "Very funny. Cousins *schur* knew how to tease. "Let's head in for lunch." As they walked, calling the others, he found himself thinking about another set of cousins sitting in the kitchen with their twin *mudders.*

"Tomorrow we can start at the next farm,"

Abraham said as they met up with several of the men.

"That will be *gut*," Abraham said. "Supposed to rain later this week."

Luke stood looking at the fields. This was what he had longed for all those long months of winter — being out here, his hands in the soil, planting seeds, working the land. He'd always loved to farm and even though the land he stood on didn't belong to him, it was his to tend and help prosper.

"Let's go in to lunch," Abraham said.

He nodded and walked with everyone else to the house. The men all washed their hands before they went in. When they went inside, Luke saw two pies with golden brown crusts set in the center of the table. Pie for lunch? Then he caught the rich scent of chicken and gravy. Ah, Lillian's specialty — chicken pot pie.

Bright-red juice oozing from some cuts in the top crust of a third pastry told him there was a fruit pie for dessert. Pie and pie. Could life be better?

"Cherry," Lillian said when she saw the direction of his gaze.

"Sounds *gut*. Anything you and Rose make is *gut*."

She chuckled. "Hungry men will eat just

about anything."

"Not true," he told her firmly. Yet she wasn't far off the mark.

They gathered around the table, gave thanks for the meal, and then there was little conversation as men who'd worked hard satisfied their hunger and the *kinner* — always *hungerich* — did the same.

Luke ate two generous servings of the pot pie and still had room for the *schnitz* pie. There was no lingering over a second cup of coffee, though. The men were eager to finish the planting and get home to their afternoon and evening chores.

So, with thanks to Rose and Lillian they were out the door and back to work.

Hours later the men left the fields and Luke led the horses back to the barn and unhitched them. It felt *gut* to be done with the planting. It was just the start of a lot of work to come, of course, but nothing could begin until seeds were planted, prayed over, and left to sprout.

With the horses fed and watered, Luke shut the barn door and stood looking at the fields, then at the farmhouse where Rose would be cooking supper.

But neither belonged to him. Not the way he wanted.

The sky was turning gray, matching his

mood. No rain was forecast for today but the air was still a bit chilly for spring and dark would come soon. He found his steps slower than usual as he walked toward the farmhouse. Light shone brightly from the kitchen window.

A flash of red caught his eye. He spotted a nest of cardinals in a bush as he walked. A lone male perched on the porch railing and seemed to be watching him. Where was his mate, he wondered. He'd often seen the lone male here on the farm, but now that it was spring and birds and animals were building nests, mating for the season, he didn't see the mate to this one anywhere in sight. Perhaps she was off scouting for a location for their nest where they'd raise their hatchlings.

Did cardinals mate for life? He couldn't remember. Some birds and animals did. Many of his Amish friends loved bird watching, but it hadn't really been an interest of his. Instead he'd focused on the land.

He paused and looked again at the fields. This land was rich, and crops grew well. If God granted it, there would be a *gut* harvest, one that would put the farm back to its original prosperity. Lillian had told him that while it was small, it had always provided for her family as she and Rose grew up.

He sighed with satisfaction. Planning what they'd plant, working together, had been everything he'd hoped for. And a glimpse of what they could have together . . .

Turning, he passed the kitchen garden that Rose and Daniel had spent much of the day planting. There would be fruits and vegetables from seeds Lillian had saved and some from Rose's Ohio garden growing in the rich soil.

Looking up, he saw the light beaming out of the kitchen window and watched as Rose appeared in it, looking out. He didn't know if she saw him, but it didn't matter. His heart lightened as he caught the glimpse of her as she stood at the sink.

The long winter of waiting for her to see him, really see him, had finally happened. He'd eased her into going out for buggy rides, for meals. They'd even gone for an outing with Daniel to a pizza parlor. He felt like his plan to win her was finally happening.

Spring always felt like the true beginning of the year to him. Not January. It was the time when the earth woke up and he got to do his most favored thing: plant seeds that would come to life.

He was moving more quickly toward the house, opening the door to the brightness and the smile lighting Rose's face, hearing Daniel look up from his coloring book and cry, "Luke!"

And he told himself it might be a long time until fall harvest when he could marry her and be a *mann* and a *dat* if God willed. But for now, he had those he held dear in his heart close. And he felt he was in theirs.

"So, the planting is done," he said as he washed his hands at the sink. "We start at Matthew's farm next week."

Rose handed him a clean dish towel to dry his hands. "It feels *gut* to know that the farm will be back in use again. I know my *mudder* and *dat* would be happy to see it." She turned as the oven timer dinged. "Sit, supper is ready."

He didn't need to ask what it was. The scent told him. *Allrecht,* when he'd come inside for a cold drink a little while back he'd peeked in the oven.

"I colored this for you, Luke!"

He looked at the page and wasn't surprised to see that Daniel had colored a picture of a farmer holding an armful of corn as he stood in a field.

"Daniel went out this morning expecting to see if any of the seeds he planted yesterday sprouted already," Rose told him as she set a platter with a golden roast chicken on the table.

"It takes time for *gut* things to happen," he told the boy and ruffled his hair. "For them to sprout and bloom and grow." His gaze met Rose's. "Once you were just a hope and a dream and then you were a *boppli* and you grew and grew —"

"And now I'm a big boy!" Daniel exclaimed. "John and me go to *schul* soon."

"That's right." They were so close in age, he thought, and remembered how the two of them had sat with their heads together that afternoon. Something niggled at the back of his mind, but then Rose was sitting down and looking at him expectantly. He wasn't the head of this family — yet — but she looked to him for the blessing of the meal.

Soon Daniel was chattering and Luke was carving the chicken, done to a golden turn, and placing slices of the meat on plates . . . and the thought just slipped away.

He turned down a second helping of pie. "I'm going to head on home unless there's something you need me to do."

"*Nee,* you did so much the last few days," she told him. "*Danki* for helping bring the farm back to life."

"I'm happy to do it," he said and meant it. Rose rewarded him with a big smile.

He was more tired than usual walking home afterward but that wasn't surprising. Planting took a lot of hard labor and even though winter was spent in making furniture and repairing tack and things that couldn't be seen to in harvest time, he was bone-weary.

A buggy pulled up beside him. The bishop leaned out the window. "Out walking late. Want a ride home?"

"I'd love one, *danki,*" he said and climbed inside. He knew what was coming and it didn't take long for the questions to start.

"So, I hear you finished planting at Rose's today."

"Ya." The Amish grapevine was faster than . . . Well, it was fast.

"How are things coming along?"

"As you say, we finished planting today," he said, knowing that wasn't what was being asked but biting the inside of his cheek to keep from grinning. Two could play this game.

"You know what I'm asking."

He turned and gave the man a direct look. "They are coming along very well."

"That's *gut* to hear," Vernon said, nodding as he looked ahead at the road. "I hope that you'll be one of the first couples I'll marry after the harvest."

"That's my hope as well."

"When a woman has a *kind* a man takes him on as well."

"There's nothing I'd love more."

"Gut, gut." He pulled into the driveway of Abraham's house. "Until you're married you'll continue to be circumspect. *Ya?"*

"I will." Luke knew what the man meant, and he had no desire to have anyone think he wasn't careful of Rose's — and his — reputation.

"Well, see you in church on Sunday."

"See you. And *danki* for the ride." It had been short and the conversation brief but they'd come a long way in many regards, Luke thought as he got out of the buggy and walked up to the farmhouse.

Abraham and Lovina were sitting at the kitchen table having a last cup of coffee for the evening and some quiet time together. He said *gut nacht* to them and hurried upstairs, unwilling to intrude even though they never let him feel he was doing so. He showered and pulled on pajamas and then sat on his narrow bed and pulled out his journal. In it he wrote the details of the planting and then turned to the back page where he kept an accounting of his funds.

The furniture making had plumped his bank account. It would have been plumper if he'd accepted a wage from Rose but he wasn't willing to do that until the harvest came in. And he wouldn't then if it wasn't what he hoped it would be.

He closed the book, tucked it under his pillow, and slipped under the quilt.

All was going according to his plan. Well, to His plan, really. On that thought he closed his eyes, said his usual prayer of thanks, and let sleep take him.

TWENTY-TWO

Rose didn't need a calendar to know it was spring. The planting was done and now she was seeing evidence of the too-often brief season that announced rebirth.

She walked out on her porch and smiled as she watched daffodils bob their sunny yellow heads in the mild spring breeze. She spotted a nest tucked under an eave of the porch and watched a *mudder* robin flitting in and out of it. Squirrels raced after each other in the boughs of a nearby maple tree that bore new leaves.

And Luke had brought her a clutch of wild crocus he'd found in the field one day. A line from a poem in a slim volume of poetry Sam had given her when they were dating popped unbidden in her mind as she remembered that day. *"In the spring a young man's fancy lightly turns to love."* She smiled at the memory of how she'd felt when Luke handed the flowers to her — like a *maedel* getting her first flowers from a young man.

But she wasn't young, and she'd loved and lost just a few years into her marriage. She'd almost immediately felt fearful at how her heart had leaped so quickly. It was becoming more obvious to her Luke had developed strong feelings for her.

"*Mamm,* I'm not sleepy."

She turned. Daniel stood there rubbing his eyes, obviously tired but not willing to admit it. "Lie down with a book until I come get you. You don't have to sleep. Just rest."

He gave her an aggrieved expression and walked back into the house, his shoulders slumped as if being punished. She wouldn't be able to convince him he needed to nap much longer. He always told her he was a big boy and didn't need a nap even when she knew he — even she — needed one after a long morning working in the kitchen garden and doing chores.

She sat in a rocking chair and drew in a deep breath then shook her head ruefully when she caught a whiff of manure from the fields mixed with the heady scent of the purple hyacinths in a pot nearby on the porch. It was warm enough that she needed just a thin sweater today.

A heavy winter coat wasn't the only thing

she'd shed with the warmer weather. She felt lighter these days and realized she'd finally begun to shed the burden of grief she'd carried. Grief had become a comfortable, familiar weight she'd become accustomed to, so much that it was a friend and part of her.

Sam hadn't been her only loss but she couldn't share her unspoken grief with anyone but Lillian.

A buggy rolled up. Sarah climbed out and waved to her before she reached inside and took out a basket. She smiled as she climbed the steps to the porch. Really smiled.

Rose wondered if Sarah too was feeling a lifting of the invisible veil of grief she'd been wearing as a widow. She'd lost her *mann* close to three years ago. There was no timetable to grief, Rose had learned by attending a grief support group back in Ohio. It had no predictable steps or stages like the stairs Sarah climbed to the porch. Its only predictability was its unpredictability.

"I brought Isaac over to play with Daniel like we agreed," she told Rose as she settled into a rocking chair.

Rose looked past her. "Where is he?"

Sarah laughed. "Asleep in the back seat. He nodded off on the way over here. But of course he didn't need a nap."

"*Nee,* of course they don't need naps," Rose agreed.

"Where is Daniel?"

"In his room resting. Because he doesn't need a nap either. He's a big boy, he says."

"Well, we'll have a few minutes of peace and quiet then." She reached into her basket and pulled out some balls of yarn and a pair of knitting needles. "I'm making some baby caps for the mud sale being held at the fire department. I thought if I did them in pastels people might still be interested in buying them even though the weather is getting warmer."

"I think you're right. Daniel wore a cap well into summer because he got a lot of ear infections when he was a *boppli.*" She stood. "I'll get my quilt, and we can work out here if you're comfortable," she said. "It's finally warming up."

"That'd be nice."

She slipped inside for the tote bag with the lap quilt she was making for the sale and returned to the porch. As she neared the door, she heard voices. Sarah and Luke. She had her hand on the screen door but found herself pausing.

The two were talking about spring planting — nothing very interesting — but she watched Sarah, watched the way she looked at Luke and the way he looked at her. The last time Sarah had visited with her *bruder,* she had very definitely been flirting with Luke. But Luke hadn't displayed any interest in her and she'd stopped.

Now, though Rose looked for it, she didn't see any flirting on Sarah's part. And staring hard at Luke, she saw he was talking to her in a friendly manner but showed no interest in her as a woman.

She pushed open the door and walked out onto the porch. Luke looked up and she saw the warmth in his eyes.

For her.

"I came in for something to drink," Luke told her.

"I'll get you some iced tea."

He held up a hand. "I can get it." He went inside.

"Allrecht." Rose turned to Sarah. "Can I get you anything?"

She shook her head. "*Nee.* Sit."

Rose sat down and picked up her quilting. "So."

She looked up. "So?"

Sarah glanced over her shoulder at the door. "You and Luke," she said in a lowered voice.

"Me and Luke what?"

"You know."

303

"*Nee,* I don't." But she knew what Sarah was getting at.

"*Allrecht,* I'm being nosy." Sarah smiled. "I guess I want to see another widow find happiness."

Rose looked at her then. Looked hard. There was something different about Sarah. She didn't have that haunted look in her eyes. Instead there was a quiet glow about her.

Sarah smiled. "Eli and I have been seeing each other. I didn't think I could ever be interested in another man after my *mann* died. I was wrong." She blushed.

"I'm so happy for you." Rose reached over and touched Sarah's hand.

"Do you think God has more than one man set aside for us?"

Now it was Rose's turn to glance at the door. "I don't know."

"I don't know if anything will come of it." Sarah focused her attention on her knitting. "But I don't want to live alone the rest of my life. I liked being married, having a partner. And I want more *kinner.*" She looked up. "Don't you?"

Rose felt a pang in her heart. "*Ya,*" she admitted.

It wouldn't ever happen. But it wasn't something she could tell Sarah. There were some things in your heart you couldn't share with another — even a dear friend.

"Oh, look who's awake," Sarah said, her voice light and filled with laughter as she gazed out at the buggy where her *sohn* peered at them from the window. "Well, we had a few minutes of peace and quiet. *Kumm,* Isaac!" she called to him, sounding indulgent.

The screen door squeaked open. "*Mamm,* I had my nap!" Daniel announced.

Rose set down her quilting and held out her arms to Daniel. He climbed up into her lap and she hugged him tight. Then he saw Isaac coming up the walk and immediately squirmed to get down. She let him go and sighed. *Ya,* she wanted more *kinner,* but . . .

Luke couldn't imagine a nicer day.

Well, if it was a few degrees warmer, it would have been nicer. But he had the day off — well, the afternoon, now that church was over — and a beautiful woman he loved sitting beside him in the buggy.

And she'd packed a basket of food so they could have a picnic outdoors. The chilly outdoors. When he saw her shiver he wondered if it was such a *gut* idea after all.

"*Schur* you want to do this?"

"It'll be fine once we get out in the sun.

Spring is a short season here. Best to enjoy it before we get a long, hot summer."

So they took the long way to a park she'd mentioned and had the place to themselves.

"I brought chili and corn bread and hot chocolate to warm us up," she told him as she unpacked insulated containers from the wicker basket. "When we come back in the summer I'll bring fried chicken and potato salad. Summer food."

Luke liked that — her talking about them coming back in the summer. It meant she thought of them together then. Maybe it was time to talk about it.

He thought about what to say as he spooned up the chili and found it warm and just a little spicy. "We'll come back in the summer?" was the best he could come up with.

Rose blushed again. "If you want."

"I want." He set down his spoon. "Rose, I want us to be together — forever. I want us to get married after the harvest."

The way she stared at him, her spoon suspended halfway to her mouth, told him she hadn't been expecting him to say that.

"We haven't known each other that long," she finally managed to stammer.

"From what you said it's been longer than you knew Sam."

306

"That's true. I hadn't thought of it that way." Now she put down her own spoon and gazed off at the pond. "I guess you think about such things more when you get older, when you've lost someone. It becomes harder to trust your feelings, I guess."

"Look at me, Rose. Tell me what you see."

She met his gaze and finally nodded. "I know you care about me."

"*Nee,* Rose, I more than care about you. I love you, Rose. You and Daniel. I want you to marry me. I want to raise Daniel with you."

He watched her bite her bottom lip, a nervous habit of hers. "I don't know what to say."

"Say yes."

She closed her eyes, opened them again, and he saw the sheen of tears. "I need to think about it, Luke."

"*Allrecht,*" he said, although he didn't feel that way. It hurt that she didn't immediately say yes. "We have time."

Looking relieved, she nodded. "Fall is a long way away."

"Don't make me wait that long for you to say yes."

"I won't."

Luke picked up his spoon and began eating again although his appetite had fled.

After a moment, Rose picked up her own spoon and ate. But he noticed that when he looked away for a moment as another buggy approached the park, she put her bowl into the basket and he didn't think she'd finished her chili.

He scraped his bowl clean and forced bites of cornbread past the lump in his throat. When she offered cookies for dessert he took one and dropped pieces of it when she wasn't looking.

"I'm sorry I've upset you." She rubbed at her temple as if it hurt.

"I'm fine. If you need time I understand." He put as much sincerity in his voice as he could and he must have convinced her because her frown cleared and her hand fell to her lap.

A couple of ducks waddled over from the pond and busied themselves under the table. Rose leaned down and watched them. "They must have found something from people before us," she told him.

He hoped she didn't see the pieces of chocolate chip cookie he'd dropped. Then, stricken with guilt, he hoped chocolate didn't make ducks sick. Surely there weren't enough chocolate chips in one cookie?

They talked idly about the church service that day, the news about the different members. But he knew he'd ruined the mood. He gazed at the sky hoping he could use it as an excuse. "Looks like we'll get some rain this evening."

She didn't even glance up at the sky but packed up his bowl and spoon. When the ducks came out from under the table and quacked and looked at her, she took the piece of cornbread she hadn't eaten and tossed chunks of it to them.

They got back into the buggy and on the long way home traveled through a covered bridge. Pain stabbed him in the chest again as he remembered the local custom Amish couples followed there — as they traveled through the structure, out of sight of prying eyes, couples dared to kiss.

But not them. Their buggy rolled through and the boards rattled and when they emerged on the other side into the sunlight, he saw that Rose's head was bent. Her bonnet hid her expression but he figured it wasn't any happier than his.

They stopped for Daniel at Lillian's house and for once Luke saw him dragging his heels as he walked back to the buggy with his *mudder.* She put him into the back seat and when Luke looked over his shoulder, Daniel had his arms folded across his chest and his lower lip stuck out in a pout.

"I wanna stay and play," he muttered tear-fully.

What a day. No one was happy.

When they got home Luke unhitched Daisy from the buggy and Rose told Daniel to go inside while she retrieved her basket and purse. As she turned she saw a dark sedan pull up in front of the house.

"I wonder who that is," Rose said.

Luke glanced down the driveway. "Probably a lost tourist. I'll go see."

A woman dressed in a business suit got out and looked in their direction. Luke recognized her and froze. "Rose, see to Daniel," he told her quickly. "I'll help the lady."

Rose nodded and headed toward the house. Luke hurried down the driveway.

"Hello!" the woman called. As he got closer he saw her brows draw together in a frown, and then her expression cleared. "Mr. Miller?"

His steps slowed. *"Ya?"*

"I thought I recognized you. I was just driving around the area." She tapped her forehead with one finger. "God gave me this great memory for faces. I'm Mimi Forstein. Forstein Realty."

She glanced at the farmhouse and then at him. "So, you bought the farm?"

310

Back when he'd first arrived in Lancaster County to help Abraham, Luke had visited her office looking around for property. There hadn't been any in the Amish community available and so he'd wandered into her office to ask what might be up for sale nearby. The realtor had mentioned she'd talked to Lillian about listing her parents' property for an *Englisch* buyer, but that Lillian had declined and so it wasn't for sale. She'd then offered to show him two other farms that bordered the Amish community, but they'd been too expensive for him. He'd immediately gone back to Abraham, however, and asked about the vacant farm. Abraham had told him to talk to Lillian and given him her address. And that's how he'd come to be working for Rose.

"No," he told the realtor. "I work for the woman who owns it. She returned to the area and she's living here now."

"Well then," she said, her smile still in place. "Whenever you're ready to buy a place of your own, if you don't find anything in the Amish community, let me know. I'll do my best to help you." She produced a business card and handed it to him.

Luke took it from her and watched her climb back into her car. Then he turned and walked to the back door. Rose stood at the stove stirring something in a pot that smelled incredible.

"Who was that out front?"

He hesitated. "Someone asking for directions. I'm heading on home. I'll see you tomorrow."

"You're not staying for supper?"

"*Nee, danki.* I think I'll eat with the family tonight. I haven't seen much of them lately."

If she was disappointed — if she felt anything — she didn't show it. "*Allrecht.* Have a *gut* night."

He nodded and tried not to look at the three place settings on the table as he passed it. There was just no way that he wanted to eat another meal and be as uncomfortable as he'd been at the picnic.

Twenty-Three

Rose did her best to stick with her routine the next morning. After all, doing that had gotten her through all she'd endured since Sam had gotten sick. She'd gotten up at her usual time, dressed, made breakfast, and fed Daniel. Then they'd gone out and worked in the kitchen garden — something both of them loved.

And then she made the mistake of looking up and seeing Luke working in the fields and the whole uncomfortable conversation they'd had at the picnic had reared its ugly head.

What was she going to do?

She sat back on her heels and thought about it. She suddenly knew she needed to talk to Lillian. And it wasn't just because her twin was her first and best friend in the world as well as being her *schweschder*. It was because she needed advice that only Lillian would understand . . . what she said

313

and did would affect Lillian. She couldn't tell Luke why she couldn't marry him without asking Lillian if she had her permission.

"Daniel?"

He looked up at her and gave her a sunny smile . . . and watered his shoes with his watering can.

"Look out, *sohn*! You don't need to water your shoe."

He glanced down and giggled. His bad mood hadn't lasted for more than a few minutes after they'd gotten home yesterday. So she wasn't at all surprised that he was in his usual sunny humor today.

"Let's go visit *Aenti* Lillian."

"*Ya!*" he shouted and dropped the watering can. The water inside splashed both sneakers.

"We should take her a treat," Rose told him, getting up and dusting off her hands. "What shall we take her?"

"Ice cream!"

"*Gut* idea. And maybe some of our daffodils? Let's go clean up."

They went inside, and Rose washed their hands and helped him change into clean clothes and dry sneakers. Then she went into her room and quickly changed her dress; she knew from experience that given enough time Daniel could find some way to get messy again.

They went out in the front yard and Rose clipped some daffodils and piled them in a basket Daniel carried for her. Back inside, she grabbed the ice cream, tucked it into a cooler, put a package of cones in a tote, and they were ready.

Luke walked over from the fields when he saw them going toward the barn with the baskets.

"We're gonna go see *Aenti* Lillian and John!" Daniel told him.

"I'll hitch up the buggy for you."

Rose hated the way he avoided looking at her. "We can do it. No need for you to stop work."

"I don't mind." He disappeared into the barn.

Daniel bounced. "Me and John are gonna play."

"John and I," she corrected automatically.

"John and I."

A few minutes later they were on their way. Crops sprouted in the fields they passed. Men worked in their shirtsleeves and occasionally looked up and waved. Daniel waved back and couldn't sit still.

"I love it here, *Mamm.*"

"I know you do, sweet boy."

"I don't wanna go back to Ohio."

She reached over to stroke his hair. "We're not going to do that. We're here to stay."

"Gut."

They pulled into the driveway of Lillian's house and Rose had to snatch at Daniel's collar as she stopped the buggy. "You know you're to sit still until I say you can get out," she said sternly.

"I'm sorry." He waited a beat. "Now?'

She waited another beat then nodded. "Now."

He climbed out and bolted for the back door of the farmhouse. When she went inside Lillian grinned at her as she looked around the kitchen. "He's already upstairs."

They gazed upward at the sound of pounding feet. "So much energy," Rose said with a sigh. She studied her *schweschder*'s face. Lillian looked better but Rose was still concerned she was overdoing. "Sit. I'll make the *kinner* cones."

First she took the daffodils and put them in a vase, filled it with water, and set it on the table. "Daniel and I picked these for you."

Lillian smiled. *"Danki."*

Next, Rose unpacked the contents of her basket and pried the top off the gallon of ice cream. "Should I put a pickle in yours?"

Lillian sat heavily. "Never craved them when I was pregnant." She rubbed a hand over her baby bump and smiled. "But I *do* crave ice cream. Can't get enough."

Rose got out a bowl and scooped up the chocolate chip ice cream — Lillian's favorite — and set it before her with a spoon.

"You gave me too much!"

"You're eating for three."

"And already waddling," Lillian said with a sigh as she dug in.

Rose fixed a small bowl for herself and put the gallon container in the refrigerator freezer. "I'll call the *kinner* down in a few minutes. I have something I want to talk about with you."

She took a seat at the table but left her ice cream untouched. "I want you to promise not to say anything until I finish."

"That sounds serious." Lillian set her spoon down. "*Allrecht,* I promise I'll keep quiet until you finish."

"Luke asked me to marry him."

As she'd predicted, Lillian's face lit up. Her mouth opened and then shut.

"I know what you're thinking." Rose got up to pace the kitchen. "I'm *schur* from the moment you met Luke you thought he was the solution for everything for me — someone to help run the farm, someone who

317

might be my *mann* and a *dat* for Daniel. But Lillian, there's just one small problem."

She sat and gazed for a long moment at Lillian's baby bump and felt despair. "A man — especially an Amish man — wants something I can't give him. He wants *kinner*, Lillian. I can tell him I can't have *kinner*. But how do I explain Daniel? No one was ever supposed to know our secret. It could get out to the bishop, to other people who wouldn't approve —"

She rose and paced again. "Coming to Paradise was a risk. Daniel and John look enough alike, are close enough in age that there may be questions — especially once they start *schul*."

"Rose, come, sit. Stop wearing yourself out."

She took another turn of the room, then another. Then, catching her *schweschder*'s eye, she sank at Lillian's feet and put her head in her lap. "It's too much to think about. It's why I almost didn't come home." She sighed as she felt Lillian stroke her shoulders. Lillian, always a *mudder*.

"You never needed my permission to tell Luke. I trust him to keep it to himself. And Rose, I don't think you're giving him credit. I believe the man loves you and wants you whether or not you can have *kinner*. It's obvious how much he loves you and Daniel. I've watched him when he didn't know I was doing so."

Rose lifted her head. "You think so?"

"I do. Amos does too. We've talked about it."

"Amos would be *allrecht* if I told Luke about Daniel? About how the two of you gave him to Sam and me?"

"He is. You can ask him yourself, if you want."

"*Nee*, I trust you." She sighed. "I pray Luke understands and keeps our secret."

Lillian reached across and grasped her hand. "He's a good man, this Luke. I see how much he loves you and Daniel every time I'm in the room with you. His asking you to marry him was such a surprise?"

"*Ya.*" She used her spoon to make little designs in her ice cream. "I guess I was in such a fog for a long time after I moved back. Still grieving Sam. Trying to get settled here and get the farm going again. I came to depend on Luke to help me and I didn't really see him for himself until recently. And to think someone could care for me as much as Sam did . . . Well, I just thought of him as a friend."

"Do you still?"

"I'm not sure. All I know is I hurt him

319

and I'm sorry for that. But I need more time."

"You've got it." Lillian smiled. "No one can marry until after harvest." She glanced up at the ceiling. "Speaking of time. It's been too long and it's too quiet up there."

Rose got up and went to the stairs. "I guess no one wants ice cream," she called up.

There was an immediate stampede of feet as *kinner* clattered down the stairs. "We want ice cream!"

"I thought so," she said with a smile. "Everyone sit at the table."

Luke worked hard in the fields all afternoon but kept glancing over at the road hoping to see Rose and Daniel coming home.

He knew she was close to her *schweschder,* Lillian, but recently she'd spent more time over at her house. Men weren't supposed to notice when the women in the community were expecting a *boppli,* but he knew Rose was concerned about Lillian because several times she'd brought her *kinner* back to babysit them. But was that the reason she was visiting Lillian today?

Maybe it was her way of avoiding him . . .

She'd avoided looking at him when she came out carrying a basket and headed toward the barn to hitch up the buggy. He didn't think he was imagining her discomfort since he'd proposed. How he wished he'd waited a while longer to ask her. He'd just been so certain his proposal would be met with acceptance.

Luke rubbed at his chest. It hurt his heart — physically hurt his heart — to remember the shocked look on her face and how she'd turned him down. He was a man who'd always worked hard for what he wanted, who just kept going until he got it. But this — this was taking some real doing to get over.

Hope surged as a buggy approached from the opposite direction. When it rolled past and didn't turn into the driveway, his spirits plummeted.

Another hour passed, and still Rose and Daniel didn't come home. He took a break and went inside for something cold to drink and found it depressing to see the room empty. This time of day, Rose was always busy preparing supper. So often she looked up with a smile and asked him if he wanted to stay for supper with her and Daniel.

Maybe she wouldn't even come home for supper. She and Daniel might stay and eat at Lillian's. Well, if they did, he'd just do his evening chores and eat at his cousin's house. He was always welcome there.

But he didn't want to be there.

So he finished his cold drink, set the glass in the sink, and went back out to work in the fields. And to watch the road for Rose.

At least the seeds he'd planted were bearing fruit — corn and wheat and the other seeds were sending green sprouts and leaves and tendrils skyward. Rain was predicted later in the week and his fellow farmers expected a *gut* growing season. Rose's kitchen garden was doing well too. Daniel was quite the little farmer with the patch he carefully tended each day when he and his *mudder* weeded and watered it.

Time, he thought. It took time and a lot of patience to tend the land. A crop didn't spring up instantly. Everything didn't always thrive. Sometimes it rained too much or too little, or there was some blight and adjustments had to be made. Sometimes even with all the hard work you put in, things just happened. Crops didn't pay what they should.

Rose had said she needed more time.

He touched the bright-green leaf of a young corn plant. Could he take a deep breath and put his trust, his faith, in God's timing? Not his own?

He grimaced at the thought. He'd always

considered himself a patient man. Apparently he needed to be even more patient.

With a heavy sigh he headed to the barn to do the evening chores. Although he lingered over them as long as he could, he could no longer ignore the obvious.

Rose wasn't coming home for supper.

So he bid goodbye to Star and began the walk to Abraham and Lovina's house. Something bright red hovered to his right. He glanced up and saw the male cardinal flying along beside him in the gathering dusk. It wasn't the first time he'd had the bird as a companion and wondered why a bird would do such a thing.

The walk felt longer than it ever had — even those times he'd had to walk home after very long planting days. When he turned into the drive of what had been his home for the past months, he decided to check the barn first to see if Abraham was there and needed his help.

Abraham glanced up when Luke slid open the barn door. "Home early tonight?"

"*Ya*. Need some help?"

"*Nee. Danki.* Just finished." Abraham wiped his hands on a bandanna and began walking toward the open door. "Will you be eating supper with us tonight?"

"*Ya.*"

Abraham stopped. "You don't sound happy about that."

Luke bent his head and felt guilt swamp him. "Sorry. I just thought I'd be eating with Rose and Daniel tonight."

"Problem?"

He glanced up and saw sincere interest on his cousin's face. Dating was a private matter in the community but Abraham was not only a cousin — he was a *gut* friend. And Luke had never felt like he needed one more.

"I've grown to love Rose and Daniel," he began. "I asked her to marry me."

Abraham's face lit up. Then he took a good look at Luke, and it dimmed. "She said *nee*?"

"She might as well have."

His cousin waved a hand at a nearby bale. "Sit." He took a seat on another bale. " 'Might as well have' doesn't sound like *nee*."

Luke sighed heavily. "She said she needed more time."

"That's not *nee*."

"You're right, I guess."

Abraham gave him a sympathetic look. "Expected her to say *ya* immediately, did you?"

Luke reddened. "I guess."

324

"She's a widow, been through a lot. And she just moved back here, hasn't known you all that long," Abraham pointed out. "She didn't say *nee*. She said she needed more time. You have it. After all, there'll be no marriages until after harvest."

"I know."

Abraham leaned over and clapped him on the shoulder. "Give her some time. Neither of you are going anywhere."

He was right.

"So, *kumm*, let's go in to supper. The family will be glad to see you. And you know Lovina always cooks more than enough. I think she made chicken and noodles tonight."

Luke got up and followed him out of the barn. "No one makes chicken and noodles better."

"She made a strawberry rhubarb pie too. I saw it earlier when I went in for a cold drink."

It wasn't supper with Rose and Daniel but when he walked into the kitchen Lovina looked up and gave him a big smile.

"Luke! Are you joining us for supper?"

"If you'll have me."

"Of course, you're always *wilkumm*!"

He washed up and took his seat and when the youngest *kind* leaned over to grasp his sleeve with sticky fingers, he decided he was a lucky man to have this family.

Twenty-Four

It was nearly dark when Rose pulled the buggy into her drive.

When Luke didn't come out of the barn she had the feeling he'd gone for the day. She turned to Daniel who was watching her.

"Now?" he asked.

"Now."

He jumped out as she climbed out the other side. "Here, take the basket and go into the house."

Always a dutiful *sohn*, he did as she told him and raced toward the house. She shook her head and smiled as she unhitched Daisy from the buggy. That *kind* had so much energy even after running around with his cousins at her *schweschder*'s house for hours.

She was surprised that Luke had gone. He usually lingered after supper and evening chores. Perhaps he'd decided she wasn't coming home for supper and had gone home to eat with Abraham and Lovina and the family. It was just that he'd made such a fuss earlier about helping hitch the buggy she seriously thought he'd be here to help unhitch it.

Well, no matter. Every Amish *maedel* learned how to do for herself from a young age. During the time Sam had been ill she'd learned how to do even more. She'd grown up on a farm and been Sam's partner wherever needed. Amish *fraas* worked in the field not just the home. She'd cared for their livestock, and only when he became so sick that he needed her care around the clock had she asked for and received the help of others with the farm.

Luke had left food and water for Daisy in her stall, so the mare went to it immediately. Rose gave her a rub and spoke to her quietly before she left the barn and closed the door. She went into the house, climbed the stairs, and started a bath for Daniel. It wouldn't be long before their nighttime routine of bath, reading a story, then bed would be over and she'd face another night alone.

Tonight the thought of being alone bothered her much more than usual for some reason. She should have been used to it. After all, she'd soon have been a widow for two years.

She sighed. "Daniel! Bath!"

He came running. Bath time and story time were favorites of his even when he resisted actually going to bed.

She poured in some bubble bath while he shed his clothes and climbed in. Every bath toy had to be added to the tub of course. While he splashed and told her about playing with his cousins she sat on a stool beside the tub and listened. He wasn't old enough to trust leaving him alone yet or to wash himself. She wasn't *schur* how she'd feel about the time he'd need her less.

After she washed, rinsed, and dried him off she sent him to put on the pajamas she'd laid out on his bed. She cleaned up the bathroom and when she went to Daniel's room found him studying something she hadn't seen before.

"What's that?" she asked as she sat beside him.

"Luke gave it to me." He held out a seed catalog. "Read it to me?"

Her fingers shook a little as she took the catalog. She hadn't known Luke had done this. That day when she'd babysat Lillian's *kinner* . . . She remembered how he'd read them Daniel's seed catalog when her *sohn* brought it to him. He'd obviously remembered how Daniel loved that catalog, probably noticed how it was well loved. Shabby, actually, from all the handling.

Rose settled back against the headboard, read the cover to him, and then turned to the first page. As she continued, Daniel occasionally stopped her to pronounce a word that a photo pictured — "Corn!" or "Wheat!" — and some of the words written underneath. She smiled. It was so *gut* to see his enthusiasm about books and to know it wouldn't be much longer before he'd be reading them himself. She loved being a *mudder* but knew letting him do things for himself was the best thing she could do for him.

Daniel nodded off midcatalog so she set the book on his nightstand and slipped from the bed. She bent to kiss his cheek and pull his quilt up to his shoulders. Tiptoeing from the room she went downstairs to brew a cup of tea and take it to her favorite chair in the living room. She sipped at the tea — a calming chamomile — and picked up the quilt she'd begun for Lillian's *zwillingbopplin.*

Then she let it fall into her lap. She stared down at her flat stomach. *Nee,* she would not think about how she needed to talk to Luke and share with him that she couldn't have *kinner.* He was a *gut* man who deserved to turn to another woman he could marry and have a family with.

Lillian had said she could share that Daniel was not her child — that he was Lillian and Amos's. She'd said she didn't think the news would make any difference to him. Rose wasn't so *schur* about that. It was obvious Luke loved Daniel. But how would he feel about him not being her birth child? How would he feel about them not being able to have their own *kinner*?

She sighed. So much to think about. She cared so much about Luke. But trusting him with her heart, with her *sohn* . . . Life was so different from what she'd thought it would be. Decisions were so much harder.

Well, she'd told Luke she needed more time, and he hadn't been happy. And maybe he wouldn't be happy with what she had to tell him. But Lillian was right — she needed to tell Luke about Daniel. And even if he was *allrecht* with that, she still felt she needed more time to make a decision about getting married again. She couldn't let herself be pressured about something so important.

Encouraged by her decision, she picked up the quilt and began sewing again. The task soothed her and made her smile to think about how it would cover Lillian's *kinner*.

When she climbed the stairs to her solitary bed she felt calmer than she had since Luke had asked her to marry him. She didn't want to be a widow forever but she wanted to make the right decision. And when she climbed into bed she prayed that God would help her make it.

Both horses were in the barn when Luke got to Rose's house the next morning. Luke hadn't really expected otherwise. Well, to be honest, he'd worried about her and Daniel coming home late by themselves, or having trouble unhitching the buggy by herself. But he'd have heard if anything had gone wrong. The Amish grapevine was as fast as the *Englischer* Internet. And Rose was a smart woman. She knew how to unhitch the buggy.

He just so wanted to take care of them both.

With a sigh, he started on the morning chores. At least Daisy and Star were happy to see him and rewarded him with neighs and a rub of their noses as he fed and watered them and led them outside so he could clean out their stalls.

When he finished he went into the house for coffee and found Rose and Daniel in the kitchen. She looked up from the table where she sat watching Daniel frost a big cinnamon roll.

"Guder mariye," they said at the same time and Luke was relieved to see she didn't quickly glance away. He poured himself a cup of coffee.

"There's a plate of eggs and sausage warming in the oven," she told him. "And cinnamon rolls." She gestured at the plate of them in the center of the table.

Daniel looked up with a grin. "We made them!"

Luke used a pot holder to get the plate from the oven and take it to the table. He grinned at the smear of icing on Daniel's nose. "I see. They look delicious."

"Mamm, can I eat this one?" He pointed.

She smiled at him. "*Schur.* But then that's it. Two is plenty for one small boy."

He frowned. "I'm a big boy!"

Luke watched her bite back a smile. "You're right. And since Luke is even bigger I guess he should have three, *ya*?"

"Ya!" Daniel bit enthusiastically into the roll and got even more icing on his face. When his *mudder* went to wipe at it with a paper napkin, he giggled.

This, thought Luke. This was why he needed to stop feeling hurt and disappointed that Rose hadn't immediately accepted his proposal. He loved this woman and her funny little *sohn* and didn't want to lose them.

So he ate the breakfast she'd cooked him and listened to Daniel chatter as he kept forgetting his *mudder*'s telling him not to talk with his mouth full. It wasn't that the boy didn't listen to Rose, he mused. It was just that he was so full of energy, so full of life.

When Daniel finally took a breath, Luke looked at Rose. "I hope Lillian is well?"

"*Ya,* but I decided to stay and cook supper so she'd rest. Did you have supper with Abraham and Lovina?"

He nodded. "It was nice but I missed you both." He watched her blush and avert her gaze.

"Well, you're *wilkumm* to stay for supper tonight. I plan on making chicken and dumplings."

"I love those."

"I know."

When she saw Daniel licking the plastic knife he'd been using to frost the cinnamon rolls, she took it from him. "Finish your milk," she told him and watched as he did as she told him. "Go upstairs and get dressed. I put your clothes on your bed for you. Then we'll go out and work in our garden."

Daniel slid from his chair and raced up the stairs.

"He never walks when he can run," she said with a sigh.

"He'll slow down one day."

"When?"

"I was about fourteen," he admitted. "Then my *mudder* claimed I turned into a slug and didn't want to move more than I had to."

"I find that hard to believe. You still have a lot of energy."

Luke finished his breakfast and wiped his mouth on a napkin. "Well, I got over my slug period."

She laughed and it did his heart *gut* to hear the sound.

"You only ate two cinnamon rolls," she said as she got up to clear the table.

"I'll have another later if I may."

"You may." She turned from the sink. "Daniel showed me the catalog you gave him. We read it last night before he went to sleep."

"He's really a born farmer. I guess he got that from his *dat.*"

Did he imagine a shadow fell over her face at his words?

"*Ya* — and his *mamm,*" she said after a

335

long moment. "Luke —" She broke off at the clatter of feet on the stairs.

Then there came a crash, and Daniel was tumbling down the stairs. He grabbed at a banister as she raced to the stairs to try to stop him. The banister broke off and he landed at the bottom of the stairs. Blood spurted from his arm as he lay there, still.

"*Mein Gott,* Luke, he's bleeding!" she cried as she knelt and pressed her hands to Daniel's arm.

He knelt beside her, took the dish towel he'd grabbed, and held it down hard on the wound. "Rose, go call 911."

She raised her eyes to him and he saw horror in them.

"Rose. You have to keep calm to help him. Go call 911, tell them what happened, that we need an ambulance. I'll keep the pressure on this but he needs to get to the hospital quickly."

She nodded, got to her feet, and raced out the door to the phone shanty.

Luke prayed as he held the dish towel down hard and watched as it grew dark with blood. He'd seen the big sliver of wood before he pressed down on the wound but something told him not to try to remove it. The thing had obviously pierced an artery but removing it could well make the wound bleed worse.

Rose rushed back into the room and knelt beside Daniel again. "They're on their way. The dispatcher said to keep the pressure on, to tie a tourniquet above the wound if we could."

"Hold this and I'll get another towel to do that." He waited until she leaned over and put her hands over his before gently easing his out from under them. Her face was white as a sheet and her hands shook but she did what he said with a fierce, determined expression.

He grabbed another clean towel, tied it above the wound, and it seemed that he saw the blood flow less freely.

"Daniel, wake up," she begged.

"Maybe it's best he's out," Luke said, although he wasn't so *schur.* "He might be frightened if he saw all the blood. Listen, Rose, maybe you should go out to the drive and wave down the ambulance."

"I'm afraid to leave him," she whispered and looked at him with such wide, frightened eyes.

"I can keep more pressure on this."

"You're right." She pushed herself to her feet and raced out the door.

After what felt like an eternity but was no more than minutes later he heard the wail of sirens approach the house, and Rose came running back followed by paramedics. It was hard to let go of Daniel, but he stepped back so the man and woman could do their work.

"Good job on the tourniquet," the man told them as he checked out the tightness and then took a quick, careful look at the wound.

"There's a big splinter —" Luke began.

"They'll take that out at the hospital. Best not to disturb it and make the bleeding worse. It's arterial," the woman said tersely.

Luke sent up a silent prayer of thanks that he'd felt he shouldn't touch the splinter.

"Has he regained consciousness since he fell?"

"No," Rose said, faintly at first, then stronger when the man glanced up at her. "Is that bad?"

"They'll do a CAT scan at the hospital. I wouldn't worry until the doctor says to."

Two more paramedics came in with a gurney and carefully they lifted Daniel onto it while guarding his arm. They rolled the gurney out of the house as Rose and Luke followed them. He watched while the gurney was loaded into the ambulance. A paramedic turned to them. "We can take one of you."

Luke helped Rose climb inside and then stood as the doors closed. He watched as the vehicle sped out of the driveway, turned onto the road toward the hospital, and the siren blared. Soon it was out of sight.

He turned and saw a cardinal sitting on the porch rail watching him. Strange how the bird always seemed to be around. Shrugging, he went into the phone shanty to call for a ride. He might not be Rose's *mann* or Daniel's *dat* yet but there was no way he'd let Rose go through this by herself.

His ride arrived twenty minutes later. Luke got in, and as the vehicle backed down the drive he saw the cardinal leave its perch on the porch and follow. Strange, he thought, then forgot about it as he worried about how Daniel was faring.

TWENTY-FIVE

Rose began shaking minutes after she hurried into the hospital after the gurney.

The emergency room staff was waiting for them since the paramedics had called ahead and given them Daniel's information. She was gently urged into a chair outside the exam room and watched as the nurses and paramedics transferred Daniel to another gurney and began unwrapping the wound.

A woman came to sit beside her. She had a clipboard in her hands and told Rose she needed information and permission to treat Daniel. When she noticed Rose shaking she stopped and frowned. "Are you cold?"

She was chilled to the bone but knew it wasn't because of the temperature of the hospital. *Schur,* it was kept cold, but the real problem was being in a hospital, smelling the antiseptic and the fear that reminded her of those months when Sam had been so ill. It didn't seem to help to remind herself this wasn't the hospital where Sam had endured long hours of chemotherapy. It was a hospital, period. And a hospital had been the place that hadn't saved Sam.

"I can get you a warm blanket," the woman offered.

"No, I'm fine, thanks." Rose bit her lip. "When can I go in and see my *sohn*?"

"They'll let us know. Right now they need room to assess him." The woman was kind but brisk. "Your son's name?"

Rose answered all the woman's questions, just wanting to be with her *sohn*. She described Daniel's accident and what she and Luke had done to stop the bleeding.

"We don't have health insurance but —"

The woman raised a hand. "We've treated many members of your community here, Mrs. Troyer. We've never had any trouble being paid for our services."

Rose nodded. The community always rallied around to care for each other and share the financial burden of medical treatment.

The woman with the clipboard left her. A few minutes later a nurse hurried up to her.

"We've got the bleeding stopped but your son's lost a lot of blood," the nurse told her. "The doctor feels he needs a transfusion but he has a rare blood type and we're a little low on it right now. The blood bank has been contacted —"

"Daniel has a twin," Rose interrupted her. "Could he give the blood?"

The nurse pursed her lips. "I doubt he'd be allowed to do so. Children are too little to donate. We should be hearing back any moment from the blood bank. In the meantime, we're taking your son up to surgery."

"Surgery?"

"He nicked an artery so it's more than the doctor wants to repair here in the emergency room. We'll take him for a quick CAT scan on the way."

"Can I see him?"

"Sure. Give us a few minutes." She went back into the exam room.

Rose felt someone sit in the plastic chair beside her. She turned and saw that it was Luke.

"Daniel has a twin?"

Stunned, she stared at him.

"John?"

She nodded slowly. Before she could say anything, she heard her name called. "I have to go." She hurried over to the nurse beckoning her and walked beside the gurney. Daniel looked so small and pale on the big rolling bed. She felt her shaking increase.

They went into an elevator and the doors closed. The walls seemed to shrink and it was hard to breathe. Calm down, she told herself. You need to stay calm for Daniel.

Daniel had been a gift from Lillian and Amos. But more, from God. *Oh, please, God, don't take my* sohn. *I can't lose him too.*

"You okay, Mom?" the nurse asked.

Rose blinked. "Yes, I'm fine."

"Try to relax. You did a good job stopping the bleeding and the paramedics got Daniel here quickly. He's in good hands now."

"I know." She took a deep breath. "It's just . . . I'm so scared."

"It's hard. I have children of my own and even though I'm a nurse there are times I feel helpless too. But the doctor who's going to do the surgery is one of the best in the state."

"If Daniel would just wake up."

"Sometimes it's a blessing that the patient is unconscious — especially if it's a child. They get frightened. The doctor will know more after the CAT scan. Try not to worry. We're going to do everything we can for him."

Rose clung to the woman's words and her confident air.

When the doors opened, they went down the corridor to a room where a technician came forward with a smile. "You stand right there in the hall and we'll be done in no time."

So she stood there and waited, and when they emerged with Daniel, she followed them into another elevator. When they reached the operating room the nurse gave her a moment to kiss Daniel and tell him she'd be waiting for him when he came out of surgery.

One of the nurses showed her into another waiting room. A few minutes later she returned with a warm blanket and wrapped it around Rose's shoulders. Rose nearly wept at the gesture of comfort and thanked her with tears in her eyes.

"It's my pleasure. I saw a man sitting next to you in the emergency waiting room. Is he a relative? I can tell him he can come up here to be with you."

He wasn't a relative and yet he was the closest to being one — he wanted to be one, didn't he? And he'd helped save Daniel. She'd have tried to stop the bleeding if she'd been by herself but there would have been no way she could have gone out to the phone shanty to call 911.

"Thank you."

The nurse nodded and left her. Rose wondered if she'd done the right thing. Would Luke demand an explanation about

Daniel and John? She'd wanted to tell him but right now her nerves were stretched thin.

Minutes later Luke appeared and rushed into the room. "How is he?"

She swallowed hard. "They took him into surgery, said stitching up the artery wasn't something they do in the emergency room. I haven't heard if they got the blood they need for a transfusion yet."

He sat beside her and took her hand. "Let's pray. God will provide."

Grateful, she clung to his hand and closed her eyes. She'd expected questions, maybe even recriminations. Distance. Instead he offered comfort and a reminder that praying, turning to God, was the answer.

Peace settled over her.

Luke sat with Rose and they waited. The room was so quiet they could hear the ticking of the wall clock.

"I'll get us some coffee," he said after a time. He didn't like how she was shivering even though she had the blanket wrapped around her shoulders. "I passed a machine on the way here."

"Danki."

"Any news?" he asked when he returned with two cups.

"Nee." She accepted the cup from him and wrapped her hands around it. "I know you have questions —"

"Now's not the time. Let's just concentrate on Daniel." He drank his coffee and wondered how anyone could call the stuff that. "Did you want me to call Lillian?"

She bit her lip. "I'm afraid to." She sighed. "I think I should wait until I know more. I wouldn't want her to feel she needs to come here to be with me. Not in her condition."

"I agree. I called Abraham when I was downstairs and asked him to go by and feed and water the horses. I had to tell him we were here but to please not tell anyone, that it was up to you to do that."

"Danki."

He took another sip of his coffee and grimaced. "Listen, I can go get you some tea or a soft drink or something. This stuff is really nasty."

That coaxed a smile out of her. "It's not bad. It's warming me up." She used one hand to pull the blanket more securely around her shoulders. "It's hospitals. I hate hospitals since Sam got sick and we had to go to one in Ohio for chemo so often."

"I'm sorry," he said quietly. "Let's hope Daniel doesn't have to stay long and we can take him home soon."

346

The doctor came in. He was a tall, lanky man with tired eyes. "Your son came through surgery just fine. He does have a mild concussion but kids tend to bounce back from these things better than adults."

"But he didn't wake up."

"He was coming around just as he was wheeled into the operating room," he assured her. "He'll have to stay tonight, maybe another day or two but I expect him to have a full recovery."

"The transfusion?" Luke asked. "They said they were having to call the blood bank?"

"All done. They had what we needed."

Rose sagged and Luke grasped her around the waist.

"When can I see him?"

"He's in recovery. The nurse will come for you."

"Thank you, Doctor."

He nodded and left the room. Rose sank into her chair and wept with relief.

Luke reached for the box of tissues on a nearby table and handed it to her. Tears unnerved him. "You heard the doctor. Daniel's going to be *allrecht*. There's no need to cry now. Rose, don't cry. You'll make yourself sick."

She wiped her eyes and blew her nose.

"You all say the same thing."

Baffled, he stared at her. "Who?"

"Men. Sam said the same thing when the doctor told us he had leukemia."

He watched her walk over to the wastepaper basket and toss away the used tissue. She sniffled and sat again.

"Well, this was *gut* news."

Rose sighed. "I know. It's just relief." She pulled several more tissues from the box and set it aside. "Now if I can just see him."

An hour passed before the nurse came for Rose. She was allowed just ten minutes in recovery with him then she was walking back into the waiting room.

"He's going to be put in a room soon," she told Luke. "They're letting me stay with him. You should go home."

"I don't want to leave you."

"I'll be *allrecht.* They won't let both of us stay."

Resigned, he nodded. "I'll be back in the morning, after chores. Maybe they'll let Daniel go home then."

"I hope so."

"Do you want me to call Lillian?"

Rose bit her lip. "I don't want to worry her. But I have to. I wouldn't want her to hear about it from someone else." She used the phone that sat on a nearby table and left a brief message on the answering machine. Lillian would find it when she checked for messages in her phone shanty the next morning.

"Well, I'd rather have told her in person but that's better than nothing, I suppose," she told Luke when she hung up the phone.

"I'll stop by her house in the morning."

"That would be *gut*." She sighed. "*Danki* for your help. If you hadn't been there I don't know what I would have done. I couldn't have left Daniel to call 911."

"God watched over him."

She nodded. "Well, we'll see you in the morning."

Luke watched her leave the room and it was even harder than when she'd said she needed more time after he asked her to marry him. He wanted to stay with her, look after her. But he didn't have the right.

He took the elevator downstairs and stopped at the information desk in the lobby. While the *Englischer* who had driven him to the hospital had told him to call him when he needed a ride home, he didn't want to bother him at this hour. He approached the desk and waited until the receptionist hung up the phone. "Do you have the number of a taxi company?"

The receptionist smiled. "Sure. Would you

like me to call them for you or do you have a cell phone?"

"Please call them for me. Thank you."

He went outside and sat on a bench to wait. The air was warm with spring and smelled so much better than it did inside. He hadn't had the experiences Rose had with hospitals but the hours he'd spent here today had been more than enough. He drew in the spring air and then sighed heavily. He didn't want to leave, but when the taxi pulled up a few minutes later he got inside.

The driver asked for his address and started the meter. "Hope everything's okay," he said, jerking his head toward the hospital.

"Yes, thank you." What else could he say?

The drive was short. He was grateful for that since he had just enough money to cover the fare and a tip. He trudged inside and found Lovina sipping a cup of tea.

"How's Daniel?"

"He's going to be *allrecht.* They're keeping him at least overnight, maybe another day. Rose got to stay with him." He checked the percolator and found there was coffee in it.

"I can make you fresh," she began.

"*Nee,* this is fine. Anything's better than the stuff at the hospital."

"Have you eaten?"

He shook his head as he sat at the table. "Wasn't *hungerich* while I was there."

"Let me fix you a sandwich."

"I can do it."

"Don't be silly. You've had a hard day."

Abraham walked in as she was putting a sandwich together.

"*Danki* for taking care of my chores at Rose's."

"Happy to. Tell me about the boy."

So he told them what had happened. He found his hands shaking a little on the mug of coffee in his hands as he detailed how he'd felt seeing Daniel fall, about how the boy had bled so badly, and how the surgeon had said that he'd stitched him up. "Rose called and left a message on Lillian's answering machine, and I'll go by first thing in the morning to make *schur* she knows. I'm hoping we can bring Daniel home tomorrow."

"We'll pray for that," Lovina told him as she placed the sandwich before him.

He eyed it. "I feel guilty. I didn't think to get Rose something to eat before I left. So she's had nothing since lunch."

"I stayed with one of the *kinner* in the pediatric unit last year," Lovina said as she sat at the table again. "The nurses were very kind to me and brought me something to

351

eat and drink as I sat up with my *kind.*"

Somewhat relieved, Luke bit into the sandwich and found he was hungry after all.

When he climbed up the stairs and got ready for bed he wondered if he'd be able to sleep. But the stress of the day had been exhausting. His head touched the pillow and he was sound asleep.

TWENTY-SIX

Her little boy was cranky.

He didn't want to stay in bed. He fussed about the bandage on his arm. And he couldn't be coaxed to eat.

It had been a very long day. Two very long days.

"Someone's doing very well indeed," Patty, one of the pediatric nurses, told Rose as she tried to persuade Daniel to eat some macaroni and cheese.

She rolled her eyes. "I hope you're right. He's never been this cranky."

"The doctor's making his rounds now." Patty set aside the dish and pushed a bowl of Jell-O closer. "I have a good feeling he'll be . . ." She hesitated. "Discharged."

Daniel poked his spoon at the Jell-O and watched it jiggle. He put a spoonful in his mouth and looked thoughtful as he squished it around, and then he swallowed and grinned. Soon the dish was empty.

"Don't worry, he'll eat what he should soon enough." The nurse glanced at the tray sitting on a table before Rose. "Now, when are *you* going to eat? You need to keep up your energy. This little one is going to be running you ragged sooner than you think." *Home* she mouthed and grinned. "I'll go check on that doctor for you. When I come back I want to see some clean plates."

Rose picked up her fork and forced down a few bites. When she glanced up from her plate, she saw that Daniel was eating his macaroni and cheese. Relief swamped her. Now if only the doctor decided they could go home.

"Luke!"

Surprised, she turned and saw him standing in the doorway with a gift bag in his hands.

"Daniel!" He walked over and hugged him. "How are you doing?"

"I wanna go home, Luke."

"I know. I brought you something."

Daniel took the bag and pulled out a book. "Look, *Mamm*! A new book! I don't have this one!"

"I'll read it to you in a minute," Luke promised him. "Just let me talk to your *mudder* for a minute, *allrecht*?"

Daniel nodded and began turning the pages.

Luke turned to Rose. "I didn't bring anything for you because you said you didn't need anything."

Rose smoothed her dress over her knees. "I was grateful you went by Lillian's yesterday. She brought me clean clothes and visited with us." She sighed. "It wasn't easy to tell her what had happened but she took it well. She said accidents are going to happen with *kinner.*"

"What does the doctor say?"

"He hasn't been in yet today. The nurse says he's doing rounds. She went to see when he's coming in to look at Daniel."

"Well, let's hope he has *gut* news. Daniel's *schur* looking *gut* today. I didn't expect him to be bouncing back so quickly."

"I know. He's been cranky, and the nurse says that means he's getting better."

"Daniel's never cranky."

She smiled. "I know."

He sat in the chair beside her and she saw his gaze go to her tray. "I felt bad when I got home the other night and realized I hadn't gotten you anything to eat before I left. Lovina told me when she and one of her *kinner* were here last year that the nurses took *gut* care of the parents too. I'm glad to see she was right."

"Well, I didn't get any Jell-O like Daniel but the pie looks *gut.*"

"I'm *schur* it isn't as *gut* as the ones you bake."

"You flatter me." She glanced over at Daniel. He'd fallen asleep clutching his new book. "He's done that all day. Awake for a time and then he falls asleep. I was told not to worry, that it's not necessary to keep him awake every minute because he's got a mild concussion. I guess that's a *gut* thing because when he's awake he's been a bit cranky. Sam was like that. He hated lying in bed not being able to do much."

She got up and paced the room. Actually, she was much like her *sohn* and Sam. She didn't like being idle either. "I wish the doctor would come in." She walked to the open doorway and peeked out. He wasn't in the hallway.

"*Kumm,* sit," Luke said. "You look tired."

"Just what a woman wants to hear," she told him ruefully. But she sat. "Eat the pie for me, will you? The nurse who brought the tray for me wanted me to eat."

"So, then, you should listen to her."

"I'm not *hungerich.* And I ate the macaroni and cheese and the vegetables."

He took the plate from her — just as the

nurse walked in and gave him a reproachful look. "She told me to," he told her.

"Uh huh." She walked over to study Daniel. "Another nap?"

"He's been asleep for a few minutes."

"The doctor should be in shortly," she assured Rose. "He's seeing his last patient before Daniel."

"Thank you."

"You're welcome. I have a feeling we'll be saying goodbye to you and your son soon."

"I hope so," Rose said fervently. "I'm sorry, I didn't mean it that way."

But the nurse just laughed. "I know that. No one wants to be in the hospital." She left the room.

"I just want to go home," Rose told Luke. "I want to take my *sohn* home."

"I know. I fixed the banister. And cleaned up."

Rose closed her eyes, remembering the blood. "Daniel has *got* to learn to walk, not run. Especially down the stairs."

"He's a boy. I'm not *schur* how long that will take."

"The day he nearly fell out of his bedroom window I thought Lillian would be upset with me. A *mudder*'s supposed to protect her *kinner*. But like Lillian said, accidents are going to happen to *kinner*."

Rose looked at him. "I was going to tell you about Daniel. Before the accident. We'll talk about it. But not here. Not now."

"*Nee.* Not now."

The doctor walked in. "So, I hear you want to leave our fine establishment," he said with a grin. He walked over to Daniel and gently shook his shoulder. "Daniel, wake up for me, please?"

Daniel opened his eyes and rubbed at them. He immediately looked over at Rose. "*Mamm?*"

"Right here. Dr. Landon wants to talk to you."

"Don't wanna talk," he responded with a pout. "Wanna go home. Luke, go home?"

"Ask the doctor," Luke told him. "He decides."

Daniel gave the doctor a hopeful look. "I wanna go home."

"I see. What's your name, young man?"

"Daniel."

"And how old are you?"

"Five."

"If I let you go home today do you promise you'll do what your mother tells you to do? You'll rest and let her take care of you there? You won't ask to go outside and play until she says it's okay?"

"*Ya!*" he cried enthusiastically.

The doctor turned and winked at Rose. "Well, since Daniel promises . . . I guess I can discharge him. Make an appointment to see his pediatrician in a few days. We'll give you some instructions before you go on how to care for Daniel, what to watch out for, and so on. He needs to be very careful of that arm. And try not to be the active little boy I'm sure he is for at least a week or so because of the head injury."

"Thank you, Doctor. I'll be sure to follow your instructions."

"Remember to take care of yourself too. Sometimes I think it's harder for the parents to go through what you have than your child. They bounce back pretty fast."

Rose remembered the nurse saying something similar.

She was so relieved that Daniel was being discharged that she didn't even mind the long wait for the nurse to come in with instructions. Luke went to get the buggy from the parking lot and pull it around to the front entrance. He was waiting for them when they finally got downstairs.

"So, where are we going now?" he asked Daniel.

"Home," said Daniel, his eyes shining. "Right, *Mamm*?"

"*Ya*," she said. "Home."

■ ■ ■

Luke said a silent prayer of gratitude when they pulled into the driveway.

Home. They were home.

He knew that Rose and Daniel had been well taken care of at the hospital and he knew God was in charge. But still, he'd worried that they weren't coming home . . . that some problem would come up with Daniel. Bad things happened in a hospital sometimes that the best doctors and their fancy *Englisch* skills and machines couldn't cure.

God didn't promise you what you wanted. Rose had found that out once. Luke had feared it could happen again and this time to the little boy Luke had grown to love as much as he loved Rose. He'd kept reminding himself of something one of the women in their church was fond of saying — that it was arrogant to worry because God knew what He was doing.

It hadn't helped.

So he lifted Daniel from the buggy and carried him inside and all the way upstairs to his room. He helped Rose change him into pajamas, careful of the bandage on his arm, and then told Daniel he'd read him his new book.

"Make yourself a cup of tea and sit down for a few minutes and relax," he told Rose.

"But —"

"Go," he said gently. "Let me help now that you're home."

She nodded and left them.

He sat on Daniel's bed and they opened the book. It wasn't a seed catalog but Daniel seemed to like the bright pictures and the story about a llama and his mama.

"A llama?" he said, frowning. "We don't have llamas here."

"*Nee,* we don't. But it's a pretty neat animal, *ya*? I got to see one at a petting zoo once, when I was a boy."

They only got through half of the story before Daniel was dozing off again the way Rose had said he did at the hospital. Luke could have left him for a few minutes and gone downstairs to talk to her, but he lingered, enjoying the way the boy's head rested in the crook of his arm. He yawned. The stress of the past couple of days was catching up on him. He'd had trouble sleeping and had spent his waking hours finding things to occupy himself so that he didn't think about the two he loved being out of sight at the hospital.

He'd just rest his eyes for a moment . . .

He woke when Daniel stirred. "Where's *Mamm*? I'm *hungerich*."

"I'll go find her. What would you like to eat?"

"Beanie weenies."

Luke chuckled. "Your favorite. You stay right here and I'll go ask her to make them. Then I'll come back and we'll finish the book, *allrecht*?"

"Allrecht." He picked it up and began looking at the pictures again.

Luke found Rose asleep in the kitchen. Her cheek was pillowed on her arms folded on the table. A cup of tea sat untouched nearby.

He studied her for a long moment, torn about waking her when she was obviously exhausted. Her cheeks were pale and there were lavender shadows beneath her closed eyelids. But he couldn't leave Daniel alone upstairs for long. The boy was too restless to be trusted to stay there without someone with him.

"Rose?"

She sat up, blinking and looking disoriented.

"You're home," he said quietly.

"Daniel?"

"He promised to stay in bed with his book while I came down and told you he is *hun-*

gerich and wants beanie weenies."

She chuckled. "What else is new? But I'm so glad he's *allrecht* I'd gladly make them daily. He'd eat them every night for supper if he could." She got up and went to the refrigerator. "I think I have what it takes to make him some."

"*Gut.* I'll go back up and stay with him while you cook."

"I'll fix us something different."

"No need. It's fine with me. I don't want you to go to any trouble. You're tired."

"I'll get some rest now that we're home. The recliner at the hospital and all the noise there kept me up."

"That and worrying over Daniel."

She tried to smile. "That too. I guess that won't go away until he's bouncing around like usual."

"True." He turned to go back upstairs.

"Luke?"

He turned to face her. *"Ya?"*

"We'll talk after he goes to sleep later."

"No rush," he told her.

Daniel had kept his promise and was lying in his bed reading his book when Luke returned.

"Your *mudder* is making you supper."

"Beanie weenies?"

"Of course."

363

He sat on the side of the bed again and continued reading where they'd left off when Daniel had fallen asleep. They'd finished that book and begun another Daniel requested when Rose came in with a tray. After a prayer Daniel fell on the meal, eating with a gusto that Luke saw pleased Rose.

"He wouldn't eat much at the hospital," she told him.

"I suspect he'll be making up for it here."

"I hope so. Well, this isn't the most nutritious meal but keeping him quiet and happy and eating is most important, right?"

"Right."

Daniel put his fork down and picked up the plastic bowl of fruit and spooned that up. When he drank his cup of milk without complaint Rose felt herself relax at last. He looked at her and grinned. "Cookie?"

"You'll burst."

He giggled. "Silly *Mamm*."

"Rose?"

She looked at Luke, saw the unspoken question and nodded.

"I'll get you a cookie," he told Daniel. "Biggest one in the cookie jar. Want more milk?"

Daniel nodded.

"Please?" Rose reminded him.

"Please, Luke."

364

He took the tray with him. When he returned he carried a plate with two cookies and a plastic cup filled with milk.

"Two?" She gave Luke a stern look.

"They were small so I brought two."

Daniel made quick work of them, scattering crumbs Rose ignored. He drank the milk and didn't complain when she used a napkin to wipe his milk mustache away. His eyelids were drooping by the time she finished.

"I'll sit with him while you go down and eat," Luke told her.

She opened her mouth to argue and then nodded. A few minutes later he joined her downstairs. "He's asleep."

"*Gut.* Supper will be ready in about ten minutes. It's not beanie weenies."

He grinned. "I'm disappointed."

Rose smiled. "Lillian must have been here. I found a chicken and noodle casserole in the refrigerator. I just made coffee. Want some?"

"*Ya.*"

She poured them both a cup and they sat at the table.

"I've never told anyone about Daniel," she began after a moment. "Only Lillian and Amos know."

"I wouldn't betray your confidence, Rose."

"I know." She traced a finger on the wood tabletop and avoided looking at him. "We'd been married for two years and we were beginning to get worried when we didn't have *kinner*. And then Sam found out he had leukemia. We were devastated. Chemo wasn't working, and one day I broke down on the phone to Lillian. A week later she and Amos came to visit. She was eight months pregnant with *zwillingbopplin* and had no business traveling to see us."

"She's your *schweschder*. Family does such things for each other."

She looked up at him. "True. But then she and Amos sat down and told us that they'd talked about it and they wanted to give us one of their *boppli*. We barely had time to take in such an offer before she was going into labor. And suddenly we had a *sohn*. We had Daniel."

He saw tears in her eyes and felt unmanned. "What an incredible gift."

"It was more than a gift." Her lips trembled. "Maybe it made Sam fight harder. He finally went into remission. It didn't last but we had another two years before he got sick again. So I feel Lillian and Amos gave us two gifts."

God had, he thought, but he stayed silent.

"After Sam died Lillian convinced me that

I should move back here." She took a deep breath. "Lillian was right. I'd never really liked it in Ohio. One of Sam's *bruders* bought the farm from me. I'm glad we moved back. I'm close to Lillian again. And Daniel loves being near his cousins. Especially John. It's like somehow they have a connection. As if they've never been separated."

"I'm glad you told me. I wondered that day when you watched the *kinner* for Lillian. The two boys played together and there was something about the two of them sitting so close together. Something niggled at my brain . . ."

"So, this is the reason I haven't been able to say yes, why I stalled and asked for more time."

"Because you wanted to tell me."

"*Ya.* I wanted to tell you about Daniel. And why I can't marry you."

"I want to help you raise your *sohn,* Rose. The fact that you didn't bear him doesn't matter to me."

"But don't you understand?" she cried. "I can't have *kinner.* I never got pregnant when I was married to Sam. That's why Lillian and Amos gave us Daniel."

"That doesn't matter to me."

She got to her feet and paced the room.

"You're so good with *kinner.* You deserve to have your own."

"I want you and Daniel."

Frustrated, she stared at him and shook her head. "You say that now. But how will you feel in years to come?"

"Rose. Sit. Please."

She sank into her chair.

"I want you to marry me. To let me help you raise your *sohn* and bring this farm back to what it was when you grew up here. Please, Rose. Be my *fraa.*"

"You're relentless."

"*Ya.* Marry me, Rose."

She laughed and shook her head and said the words he felt he'd been waiting for forever. "*Ya.* I'll marry you, Luke."

TWENTY-SEVEN

Rose woke feeling stiff and sore from a night sleeping in a chair beside Daniel's bed. But the moment she opened her eyes to dawn breaking and sending fingers of light into the room and saw Daniel safe and sound in his own bed . . . When she remembered talking with Luke about him, and what she'd said to him . . . Well, it felt like her heart would burst with happiness.

She sat there, remembering. And tried to think of the last time she'd felt this happy. The day Lillian and Amos had given her this *kind*. The day Sam had asked her to marry him. The day she'd come back here and felt she'd truly come home.

Daniel stirred and opened his eyes. "Hi, *Mamm*."

"Hi, Daniel. Did you have a *gut* sleep?"

"*Ya.*" He frowned. "Why aren't you in your bed?"

"I wanted to make *schur* you didn't need

anything. How does your arm feel this morning?"

"Hurts."

"Why don't we go downstairs and I'll fix you breakfast, and you can have one of the pills the doctor gave you?"

"Pancakes?"

"Pancakes."

She held out her arms and lifted him, hugging him tightly before they descended the stairs.

"Careful, *Mamm,*" he said worriedly. "Don't fall."

Some of the happiness she'd felt faded. She hated to think her little boy was afraid. "I won't. *Mamm* and Daniel will go down the stairs slow and not fall." She held the banister with one hand as she stepped slowly. "Look, Luke fixed the stairs, so now you will hold it and walk slow, right?"

He nodded. "I will, *Mamm.*"

"Did I hear my name?"

Luke stood at the kitchen counter drinking a cup of coffee.

"Look who's here, Daniel!"

"Luke!" Daniel held out his arms and Luke took him from her.

"Guder mariye," he said, looking at Rose over Daniel's head.

"Guder mariye," she responded, feeling

strangely shy.

"We're having pancakes," Daniel told him. "Want pancakes?"

"I *schur* do." He hugged Daniel and then set him carefully in his chair. "I put the teakettle on for you. In case you didn't want coffee."

"Danki." She turned the flame off under it as it began to hiss. "You're here early."

"Had trouble sleeping," he told her, looking at her with eyes filled with love.

"*Mamm* slept in my room," Daniel told him. "But I didn't need her."

"I do," Luke said softly. "I do."

Rose felt her cheeks warm. "Sit so I can get breakfast started for my men."

"I like the sound of that." He took a seat next to Daniel and sipped his coffee as she pulled a big pottery bowl from the cupboard and began assembling ingredients. Soon she was flipping pancakes onto a plate for Daniel and watching Luke pour syrup onto them and cut them up for him.

Two big pancakes went on a plate for Luke and after she set it before him she sat down with a cup of tea.

"Why aren't you eating?"

"I'll eat in a minute." She didn't know how to tell him all she wanted was to sit here and watch the two of them. She'd thought she'd learned how to appreciate each day after Sam had gotten sick. That was the gift that cancer gave, she'd heard so often in the counseling sessions she'd attended — sometimes with Sam, sometimes without him. You learned to appreciate life each day even when those days were difficult. Sometimes because they were difficult. Because each day should be appreciated.

Too often those days were numbered. Too often a person you expected to live with until you were old left.

Daniel ate all his pancakes and looked at her expectantly. "More, *Mamm*?"

Before she could get up Luke was on his feet and tossing his napkin down on the table. "I'm finished. I'll make him some more."

"You?" She stared at him.

"I can handle making a few pancakes," he said a little defensively. "I can cook a little."

He turned the flame back on under the skillet, dropped a couple of pats of butter into it, then poured pancake batter in with a competence that surprised her. She watched him pick up the spatula and after several minutes flip the pancakes onto Daniel's plate.

"Now for some for your *mudder*," he told Daniel.

"*Nee*, I —" she began.

He gave Rose a look that had her subsiding. So she sat in the kitchen of the home she'd grown up in and watched while the man she loved made her breakfast as the sun rose and filled the room with light.

Daniel's pancakes smelled so *gut*, warm and slathered with maple syrup. She hoped Luke didn't hear when her stomach growled. When he set a plate before her with perfectly browned pancakes she found she was actually hungry. How different this morning was from yesterday when she'd woken from snatches of sleep in a chair beside Daniel's hospital bed. She savored each bite as her *sohn* finished his breakfast and chattered away at Luke.

A rap sounded on the door and Lillian sailed in carrying a basket. John followed her with a tote bag.

"We came to see how you're doing, Daniel!" Lillian said as she set the basket down on the counter. She walked over to hug Daniel and stroked his hair as he showed her his "boo-boo" on his arm.

"Daniel slept all night and he's had two helpings of pancakes this morning," Rose told her.

"Lillian, can I fix you a cup of tea?" Luke asked.

"Nee, danki."

"I'll let you two talk, then. I'll be out in the barn doing chores if you need me." He grabbed his hat and left them.

"I told John we could come visit if he promised to play quietly with Daniel." Lillian straightened and put her hand on her back as if it ached.

"Let's go in the living room. You'll be more comfortable there."

They settled the boys down with John's tote bag of books and puzzles.

"You're looking happy," Lillian said quietly as they sat down on the sofa.

"It shows?" But she couldn't help smiling.

"*Ya.* Tell me."

Engagements weren't often shared here even with family. But this was Lillian. There was little they hadn't shared in their lives.

"I told Luke I'd marry him."

Lillian burst into tears.

"Mamm?" John looked up with alarm.

"Happy tears," she quickly assured him as she dug into her apron pocket for a tissue. She hugged Rose.

"We haven't told Daniel yet," Rose said quietly. "I just said yes last night. After Daniel went to bed."

"He loves Luke."

"I know. We'll probably tell him together later today."

"I'm so happy." Lillian wiped at her tears. "I knew the minute I met Luke the two of you would be perfect for each other."

Rose smiled. "And you're always right."

"You know I am."

She laughed. "Amos and I just let you think so."

But Lillian usually was *right,* she thought. And she was definitely right about Luke.

Luke found himself distracted as he worked on his morning chores. He fed Daisy twice and forgot Star. It was only when Star butted his arm with her nose and snorted her disgust that he realized what he'd done.

"Sorry," he told her and corrected his mistake. He was glad he'd tucked an apple into his pocket as he left the kitchen. Star seemed to forgive him after he offered her half.

He shook his head, thinking he was behaving like a lovestruck young boy.

He wondered if Rose would tell Lillian that they were engaged. The two were so close. He wasn't worried that Lillian wouldn't approve. She'd recommended him for the job here and always acted friendly.

But he'd feel better if he knew she approved. Lillian meant a lot to Rose.

Lucky for him he didn't have long to wait. Lillian came in wearing a big smile. "Rose told me the *gut* news. I'm so happy for both of you!"

Relieved, he grinned. *"Danki."*

"Rose told me how you looked after her and Daniel after he got hurt."

He shrugged. "Why wouldn't I?" he asked simply. "I love them both. I just wish it was harvest time."

"I know. Amos and I were engaged for a long time." She covered a yawn. "Sorry, I'm so tired these days. I think I'll see if I can persuade John to go home now and take a nap so I can."

"I'll get him for you."

After they headed home he went inside for a drink. Rose and Daniel weren't in the kitchen or the living room. He decided that Rose had talked Daniel into a nap so he went back outside and worked in their kitchen garden for a while. Rose would be too busy for the next few days tending to Daniel so he figured he'd weed and water before going to the fields for his own work with the crops.

He remembered what he'd learned — that it was a tradition in these parts to plant celery when a wedding was to take place. Maybe he'd pick up some celery seeds next time he was in town and stopped at the feed store.

Restless, he went back outside to work. It would be months before he and Rose could marry. It was the one time he envied those in the *Englisch* world. He'd heard that the rule about weddings not taking place until after harvest was changing in some Amish communities, but it hadn't here yet. He knew there was a *gut* reason for the rule. A farm took a lot of time and attention and matters such as marriage and the resulting full-day celebration had to come second. But a man needed a partner in life, didn't he?

He shook his head. Such thoughts were a waste of time. Church policy took a long time to change and he wasn't the type to argue for it.

That reminded him of how the bishop had encouraged him to pursue courting Rose. He was going to be happy when Luke approached him to tell him they wished to marry.

Well, that was months from now.

He worked off his restlessness in the fields until it was finally time for lunch. When he went inside the two he loved most were in the kitchen waiting for him.

"You *schur* left quickly when Lillian got here," Rose told him as she set a plate with a sandwich and chips before him.

"I thought the two of you would want to talk."

"She was very happy to hear the news."

He grinned. "She came out to the barn to tell me."

"I think my *schweschder* enjoyed playing matchmaker." She glanced at Daniel and smiled when she saw him eagerly eating the sandwich she'd cut into small squares for him. "Maybe it's time to tell someone else," she said, indicating her *sohn* with a tilt of her head.

"Look, *Mamm*!" He held up a chip that was folded over. Luke knew it was his favorite kind. He popped it into his mouth.

"I see. Luke and I have something to tell you. We're going to get married."

"We are?" He stared at her, puzzled.

Luke chuckled. How did you tell a five-year-old such things? "You remember going to weddings last year? When Miriam and Mark got married? And lots of other people from church?"

Daniel scrunched up his face as he thought about that. "We had cake and John

378

and Annie and Barbie and Eli played games."

"That's right." Luke winked at Rose. "We'll have cake and all the *kinner* can play games."

"It won't be until fall," Rose warned him. "You know, after we bring in the harvest and the trees all have gold and red leaves on them."

"I love you and your *mudder,* Daniel," Luke explained as Daniel stared at him with such a serious expression. It was important to him that this little boy understood. "I want to marry your *mudder* and be your *dat.*"

"You'll be my *dat* like John has a *dat*?"

"That's right. I'll come to live here with you."

"And read me stories?"

"And read you stories."

Daniel beamed. "That's *gut.* I love you, Luke."

"I love you, too, Daniel."

"And *Mamm,*" he said.

"And your *mamm.*"

It was just that simple. He looked at Rose and saw that tears had filled her eyes.

"We'll be a family," Rose told him.

"Family," Daniel said thoughtfully. Then he looked at his *mudder.* "Can I have a cookie?"

She laughed. *"Schur."*

Daniel ate his cookie and then got down from the table to go into the living room to read a book John had brought him. Once he was out of earshot Luke turned to Rose. "Do you think he understood what we were telling him?"

"I'm not *schur.* I guess time will tell."

He pushed his empty plate aside. "I didn't expect you to tell him today."

She shrugged. "I wondered if I should wait. If the excitement would be too much. After the accident, I mean. But it's like the doctor and nurses said. Kids bounce back quickly. He seems to be doing well and I think he took to you from the time he met you."

"I think I fell for him before I fell for his *mudder,*" he said and reached for her hand. "Rose, I want to be his *dat* but it doesn't mean he shouldn't be told about Sam as he grows up. He was part of both your lives. Even if Daniel doesn't remember him as much as you do."

He fell silent for a long moment. "Will you ever tell him about what Lillian and Amos did?"

Rose bit her lip. "I'm not *schur.* Lillian and I talked about it once, not long after

Daniel came to us. I guess we'll have a talk about it again sometime in the future."

He stroked her fingers. "Speaking of the future . . ." He lifted his gaze to hers. "I was thinking earlier that I wish we didn't have to wait until after the harvest."

"It's not that far away."

"It feels like it."

"Spring is short here. Then we have summer which is so busy. Before you know it — why, it'll be fall."

"If you say so. I thought I might go into town, to the feed store. Get some celery seeds for you to plant."

"Celery?"

"I remember someone telling me that was a tradition here," he teased. She smiled.

"Knowing Lillian I have a feeling she's home right now planting some in her kitchen garden."

He grinned. "Well, I guess we'll have to look next time we visit."

"*Ya*," she said, meeting his gaze. "I guess we will."

TWENTY-EIGHT

The Amish grapevine worked better than ever. Everyone had heard about Daniel's accident and hospitalization and return, and they began stopping by the next day. Daniel was in heaven. He loved visitors and held court in the living room.

Rose kept an eye on him to make sure he stayed quiet and enjoyed a bit of a break herself as she supplied visitors with cups of tea for the adults and juice and cookies for the *kinner.*

Sarah stopped by with her *sohn* and her *bruder* Naiman. She didn't say anything about the man she'd mentioned dating when she'd visited sometime back but the glow on her face told Rose that things were coming along quite nicely in that department.

Naiman still looked at Rose with such intense interest she didn't know how to deal with it. But it turned out she didn't have to.

Luke didn't come inside once during any of the visits from their community . . .

Until Sarah and Naiman visited.

Then Luke was in the house five minutes later claiming he needed a cool drink because the day was heating up. He wandered into the living room and joined in the visit and Rose thought he seemed to stand in a proprietary way behind her chair.

Daniel showed off his boo-boo to Sarah's *sohn*, who was properly impressed. "I gotta be careful not to run on the stairs no more," Daniel said solemnly.

"Anymore," Rose corrected.

"Anymore."

He went to the basket of books and puzzles in the corner of the room and pulled out the seed catalog Luke had brought him. "Luke read?" he asked hopefully.

"Later. I need to get back to work."

"Allrecht." Daniel sat on the rag rug and "read" the catalog to his friend.

Rose noticed that Luke didn't immediately leave the room. Finally, he cast Rose a frustrated look and left, saying he had work to do.

"Would you like some coffee?" she asked Sarah and Naiman. "I started a fresh pot just before you came."

"Danki, that would be nice." Sarah stood.

"I'll help you."

"*Onkel* Naiman, read to us?"

Naiman gave Rose a disappointed look then turned back to the *kinner*. "But can we read something more interesting than that seed catalog? Maybe the book about Jack and the Beanstalk?"

Daniel set aside the catalog and handed the other book to him. The two boys gathered around Naiman's chair. Rose thought about how Naiman didn't look quite as comfortable with *kinner* as Luke had the day he read to Daniel and Lillian's *kinner*.

Rose and Sarah went into the kitchen and Rose got down three mugs. She found a half dozen cookies in the cookie jar and put them on a plate.

"I'm hoping to do some baking tomorrow," she said. "There hasn't been time running after Daniel these past few days."

"I should have thought to bring something."

"You did. You brought a ray of sunshine over."

When Sarah stared at her, Rose laughed. "You look even happier than you did the last time I saw you."

Sarah smiled. "You can guess why."

Rose set the mugs on a tray and poured the coffee. "*Ya.*"

"And I noticed the way Luke hung around so my *bruder* would get the idea about you two also."

Rose felt herself blush. She went to the refrigerator for juice for the boys and set cups of juice on the tray with the mugs.

"I'm not the only one who noticed that, am I?" Sarah asked.

"I noticed." But she wasn't going to say more. She'd shared the news of being engaged with Lillian but she wasn't going to do so with anyone else.

Naiman gave the book back to Daniel as soon as he saw Rose enter the room with the tray. He took the tray and placed it on the coffee table while Rose gave the boys their cups of juice and a cookie each. Sarah caught her up on the latest goings-on in the community, telling her about who'd just had a *boppli* and how Ruth Ann's *schweschder* was in town visiting. Rose listened and sipped her coffee and felt herself restless to do something other than sit on the sofa and visit. Naiman must have felt the same because he finished his coffee quickly and said he was going outside to see what Luke was doing in the fields.

Rose shifted as she turned back to listening to Sarah. She felt behind in her chores and wanted to be outside on such a pretty

day and weeding in her garden. She knew
Luke had taken care of it the last two days
but it was her responsibility and she enjoyed
having her hands in the dirt tending her
plants.

"It's time we went home for Isaac's nap,"
Sarah said at last. She set down her cup.
"It's been so nice to visit and see Daniel
doing well. And you too," she said, turning
to smile slyly at Rose.

"It was so nice of you to stop by," Rose
said as she stood. "Daniel, say thank you to
everyone."

"*Danki* for coming." He turned to Rose.
"Can Isaac come again tomorrow?"

"Maybe Thursday," Sarah said.

"See you Thursday," Daniel told his
friend.

Outside, they saw Naiman talking with
Luke in the fields. Sarah waved to him but
Naiman was standing too close to Luke to
notice her. Naiman's hands were clenched
in fists at his sides.

"Naiman!" Sarah called and he turned
slowly and looked at them.

"*Ya?*"

"We're ready to go home."

Naiman turned back, said something to
Luke, and then walked over to his buggy.
Rose wondered if it was her imagination

that neither of the men looked happy. They hadn't gotten along so well the last time they'd seen each other, she remembered.

Her three guests piled into the buggy and left. Rose turned to Daniel. "Do you want to work in our garden for a little while and then take your nap?"

"Garden. No nap."

"Garden and then nap," she said firmly. "But first we have to put something on your bandage so you don't get it dirty."

They went into the house, and Rose wrapped a plastic bag around his arm and taped it securely. "There. Now promise you won't get it dirty. *Allrecht?*"

He nodded and bounced up and down. "Outside, *Mamm!*"

They'd both been trapped inside. She wanted to be out there just as much as he did.

He took the stairs down to the backyard slowly, making her proud he was remembering her caution. Once in the yard, though, he ran to the garden to his little plot. Soon he was happily watering and talking to her about how his plants were growing.

Rose put her hands in the warm earth and yanked weeds and checked her vegetables and fruit. It seemed they'd all grown so much since she'd last been out here. The past days of stress faded away as she worked. Seeing how well everything was thriving from seeds she'd planted revitalized her spirit. Things were truly back to normal.

She looked over at Daniel working happily and felt all was well in her world.

Luke tried to work off his feelings but — well, it wasn't working.

The minute Naiman had pulled up in the buggy with his *schweschder* and her *sohn* he'd felt his earlier *gut* spirits fading. The man just did that to him.

It was too bad for Naiman that Rose preferred him. Naiman had known her for many years and lost her to Sam and now to him. He just needed to go off and find his own woman. There were others in the community — attractive *maedels* who were of marriageable age. He'd seen them in church, had seen them look his way until they'd realized he looked in Rose's direction.

Naiman hadn't been friendly from the first time they'd met and he *schur* had made it clear that he didn't like him when he'd brought Sarah over to visit Rose. Today, the third time he'd visited, he'd been even clearer that he thought Luke was an intruder. He'd come out to the fields after

Luke had returned to his work and just stood there on the edge of them and glared at him. Sensing the other man wanted to say something to him Luke had walked over to him, and they'd stood there for a long moment. He'd never know what Naiman wanted to say because the women had walked out then. Sarah had wanted to go home and put her *kind* down for a nap.

Well, he wasn't going anywhere.

He stood there, brooding. He'd thought about going into town earlier. *Allrecht,* it had been just a casual thought about getting some celery seeds. But he hadn't taken much time off since he'd started working for Rose, and the last few days had been stressful not just for Rose. He'd worried himself sick and barely been able to sleep thinking Daniel might not come home.

He turned on his heel and headed for the farmhouse. An hour going into town might be just what he needed.

"Hi, Luke!" Daniel piped up when he stopped at the kitchen garden. "I'm watering my carrots."

"I see. *Gut* job." He turned to Rose. "You need any supplies? I'm going into town," he said in a low voice so Daniel wouldn't hear.

Rose looked up at him, shading her eyes from the sun. "Are you *allrecht*?"

"*Ya.*"

"You're *schur*?"

"Why wouldn't I be?"

She lifted her shoulders, let them fall. "I saw Naiman out here talking to you. Did he say something to you?"

He shrugged. "He didn't really have a chance to say anything. The two of you came out right after he did."

"I'm sorry the two of you don't get along."

"I'll live."

Her mouth quirked in a smile. "*Ya,* I expect you will. Sam got the same treatment after we got engaged."

"So, you need anything in town while I'm there?"

"Maybe some coffee. Nothing urgent if it's out of your way."

"Make a list. I'll stay out here with Daniel."

She got to her feet, brushed the dirt from her apron, and hurried into the house. Luke turned his attention back to Daniel. He'd used the lack of attention from his *mudder* to make some mud, and now he happily splashed in it.

"Oh, my," Luke said and sighed. "Wait until your *mudder* sees you."

Daniel giggled. "Mud pies." He held one out to Luke.

"*Danki* but *nee,* young man. *Kumm,* you need a bath."

Daniel pouted. "No bath."

"*Allrecht,* we'll just let you go around being Mud Boy. But you'll have to stay out in the pen with the pigs."

"Piggies!" Daniel snorted like one and splashed in the mud some more.

"Daniel!" Rose shrieked behind him. "Luke! How could you let him play in mud?"

"He was doing it when I turned to him. I'll take him in and give him a bath."

"*Nee,* you're on your way into town. I'll do it. *Kumm,* young man."

Luke watched them go into the house, a slender young woman holding the hand of a dirty little boy who acted like he was being led to a terrible fate.

Feeling a little lighter in mood, he hitched up the buggy and started for town. It was a lovely spring day, the breeze warm but not too warm. Rose had warned him that spring was a short season here in Lancaster and he knew from a year here that she was right. Soon summer would blast hotter than blazes as men and sometimes their *fraas* worked to bring in the harvest.

So he enjoyed the ride and waved to the men he saw working in the fields he passed.

Traffic was light this time of year, but occasionally cars passed him. Luke could tell those that contained tourists because they leaned out of the windows of their automobiles and snapped photos with their cell phones and cameras. He kept a wary eye on them when they veered too close to the wheels of the buggy. When a car and a buggy collided, the buggy didn't come out the winner.

Vernon, the bishop, was sitting on the porch with his *fraa* as Luke passed. He waved and then impulsively pulled over into their drive.

"How are you this fine afternoon, Luke?" Vernon asked him as he climbed the steps up to the porch.

"*Gut.* I was going into town for some supplies."

"I'm ready for something cool to drink," Mary said as she got to her feet. "Luke?"

"Don't go to any trouble," he said quickly.

"No trouble at all. Vernon here was just saying he'd like a glass of iced tea before you stopped."

She went in and the men rocked as silence stretched between them.

"Heard Daniel had an accident the other day. How is he doing?"

"He's doing fine. Rose was letting him

work in his little piece of her kitchen garden when I left."

"Fine *mudder*," Vernon said as he rocked in his chair. "Fine boy."

"*Ya.*"

Vernon's eyes were shrewd behind his wire-rimmed glasses. "She'll make someone a fine *fraa* one day."

Luke knew he was being pumped. "*Ya*, I remember you telling me such not long ago."

"It'll be summer soon. Harvest. I've had a look at the crops you planted as I drove past your fields."

"Rose's fields," Luke pointed out.

"Maybe she'll share them soon?"

"Maybe so." Luke kept his tongue tucked firmly in his cheek.

"I perform a lot of weddings after harvest. Best to get on the list early so you get a spot."

"I'll keep that in mind."

Mary came out with the glasses of tea and a couple of her famous sugar cookies. She plied him with questions as skillfully as her *mann* had done but they were about Daniel and how he was doing.

"We talked about visiting tomorrow," she said.

"I'm *schur* Rose and Daniel would love a

visit." He set his empty glass on the table beside his chair and stood. "Well, *danki* for the tea and cookies. I'm going to get on my way to town. Do you need anything?"

"*Nee.* We went yesterday. But *danki.*"

He nodded and left them. Feeling cheered, he clucked his tongue at Daisy and set them off in the direction of town. While he'd been in the hot seat with the bishop's questions, he couldn't help feeling *gut* that the man had given a silent approval of his relationship with Rose.

Take that, Naiman, he thought, then chastised himself for such uncharitable thoughts. Surely he could feel more generous when he was getting the woman he loved.

He smiled as he leaned back comfortably in the buggy and rode to town. For perhaps the hundredth time since he'd arrived to help his cousin Abraham after his accident, he thanked God for setting him on the path here to Lancaster County. He'd pick up supplies they needed, some celery seeds at the feed store, and maybe a bunch of flowers for Rose. It had been a while since he'd made a romantic gesture. Seemed like it was time.

TWENTY-NINE

Luke brought Rose flowers the next day. And celery seeds for the kitchen garden. And Daniel got a new coloring book and crayons.

Rose hadn't had any trouble deciding which of her gifts touched her most. It was hands down the celery seeds. This man wanted her, wanted to marry her. How lucky was she that two men loved her in her lifetime? And why had she hesitated to accept his proposal? Hadn't Sam's death taught her that each day was to be cherished and lived to its fullest?

So today she planted her celery seeds and worked in her garden and daydreamed a little as the day warmed and made her a little drowsy. But not so drowsy that she didn't keep an eye on Daniel as he watered his plot. She wasn't going to have him get all muddy the way he'd done the other day when she'd let Luke watch him.

"Mamm?"

She looked up as she knelt to weed. *"Ya?"*

"I wanna see Daisy and Star."

Rose leaned back on her heels. "You do? Why?"

"Miss Daisy and Star," he said and she understood. They hadn't been in the barn or the buggy since before his accident.

"Allrecht, we can go see them. Want to give them a carrot?"

"Ya!"

So they pulled two carrots from the garden, brushed the dirt from them, and walked over to the barn.

Daisy was the first to put her head over her stall door. She greeted them with a neigh and then Star did the same. Rose lifted Daniel so he could stroke their noses and offer them a carrot.

"They like carrots."

"They do."

"I like carrots."

"We'll pick some for us and have them for lunch." She bounced him on her hip. "You're getting heavy."

"I'm a big boy," he told her seriously.

"I know." She set him on his feet and glanced around. Luke kept the barn spotless.

"Mamm, Luke has more books."

396

She should have known Daniel would spot the seed catalogs on the small desk shoved in the corner.

"Can I have one?"

"May I?" she said automatically as she walked over to where he was flipping pages in one. "And *nee,* you have to ask Luke."

He turned from looking at them and as he did his elbow hit one and it fell into the wastepaper basket by the desk. Rose bent to pick it up and as she did she saw a small business card lying on top of some balled-up paper. Curious, she picked it up. She frowned. It was a business card for a realtor.

The barn door opened. "I found you!" Luke called in.

"We brought Daisy and Star a carrot," Daniel told him. "I missed them."

"I'm *schur* they missed you."

Puzzled, Rose stared at the card in her hand.

"What have you got there?" Luke asked her.

She handed it him. "This. How did this get in here?" Her confusion deepened as he reddened.

"Must have been there for some time."

She shook her head. "I emptied the basket last time I was out here."

He shrugged. "Say, are we having lunch soon? I'm *hungerich.*"

Daniel tugged on her apron. "Me, too, *Mamm.*"

"In a minute." She looked at Luke. He was avoiding her gaze.

Rose felt a trickle of unease. Daniel did that when he didn't want to tell the truth. Luke had never avoided looking at her when she asked him something.

"*Mamm?* Lunch?"

Distracted, she turned to Daniel. "*Allrecht,* we'll get lunch." She handed Luke the card and watched him throw it back into the waste-paper basket before she turned to go.

She fixed lunch and got Daniel into his chair. Luke came in, washed up, and took his seat. He thanked her as she placed a plate with a sandwich before him, but she couldn't help noticing that he didn't say much and once again avoided her gaze. He ate quickly and said he had to go back to work.

Rose ate her sandwich and drank a large glass of iced tea. The sun had been hotter today. Spring — always brief — was passing and summer would be here in no time. The heat had tired Daniel so it wasn't hard to nudge him along for a rest in his bed. She'd decided a few days ago not to use the word *nap.* So far, a *rest* had gotten better results. He went quietly and read and ended up falling asleep because he still needed a nap.

She washed the lunch dishes, cleaned up the kitchen, and all the while she did the chores she found her thoughts returning to the card. Was it her imagination that Luke seemed uncomfortable about it? The thought niggled at her.

Unbidden, the memory of how he'd talked with the woman outside the house came to her. It had seemed to her that he knew the woman. She remembered that there had been some sort of sign on the side of the car she hadn't been able to read when she looked out the window. Luke had said she was asking directions . . .

The card had been in the wastepaper basket. That was that. Right? So why did she feel that it wasn't?

Because he hadn't met her eyes, she answered herself.

She sighed and forced herself to concentrate on scrubbing the kitchen floor. When she finished she went out to sit on the back porch while it dried. She propped her elbow on the arm of the rocking chair, put her chin in her hand, and watched Luke working in the fields.

The farm was coming back to life. It no longer looked sad and neglected as it had when she'd returned. She and Luke had fixed it up so much. And crops were thriving in the fields. She was glad Lillian had talked her into returning. This would be Daniel's one day.

Daniel's.

Something niggled at the back of her mind. Something Sarah had said to her one day when she visited came back to her. Sarah had apologized for Naiman's behavior toward Luke that day and had told Rose that her *bruder* worried that Luke was interested in her for her farm.

Had she trusted too quickly? Too easily?

Nee, she wouldn't think like that. Lillian had called her in Ohio and been so enthusiastic about Luke, had gone on and on about how he'd come here to help his cousin Abraham after his accident. How he was interested in helping her run the farm if she came back to Lancaster County.

And Lillian was always right about things. She often told Rose that, didn't she? Rose smiled and pushed aside her doubt.

The screen door squeaked. "*Mamm?* I want a drink."

"Did you have a nice rest?"

He nodded and rubbed his eyes.

Rose took a last look at Luke working in the fields and went inside. She poured Daniel a small cup of juice and sat with him at the table while he drank it.

The other day Luke had seemed restless and said he was going to town. Well, both she and Daniel had been housebound for a while. Maybe they should do the same. Soon they'd all be so busy harvesting and canning there wouldn't be an opportunity to take a little time off. Daniel needed some new clothes for when he started *schul* in the fall. They could go to the fabric store, get him some new shoes, and just enjoy themselves for a few hours.

"How would you like to go for a ride?"

"Ya!"

She hadn't even said where. Chuckling, she led Daniel upstairs and helped him put on clean clothes and shoes. "Sit on your bed and stay clean," she warned him. "I want to put on a different dress."

"Allrecht."

After they were both presentable they went out to hitch up the buggy. Luke appeared at her side. "Let me help."

"Danki, I can manage." She didn't look at him as she led Daisy to the buggy.

"We're going for a ride!" Daniel announced.

"I see. If you need supplies I can get them for you, Rose."

"Nee, danki." She looked at Daniel and saw him stomping in the dirt. "If you get dirty we won't go."

She helped Daniel up and into the buggy. "Can Luke go?"

"Nee." She took a deep breath when she saw Daniel's mouth tremble. "We're going just the two of us. Luke has to work." Rose gave Luke a quick glance. "I'm not sure we'll be back for supper. I'm going to stop by Lillian's after we go to town."

She marched around to her side of the buggy, got in, and guided the buggy down the drive and toward town.

Luke stood with his hands on his hips staring after the buggy.

He knew seeing the business card had upset her and wasn't proud of himself for what he had said about it. But it had been such a surprise.

Still, it wasn't like Rose to snap at him or Daniel or go off for a ride like that.

He pulled off his straw hat and ran a hand through his hair. He hadn't ever told her that he'd wanted the farm before she'd come back for it — had wanted it before he met her. He hadn't thought it mattered.

Well, that wasn't really true. But how was he to tell her now? Wouldn't she think it too convenient that he'd started working for her and then fallen in love with her?

Frustrated, he went back to work and wondered how he was going to fix this.

Hours passed and she didn't return. He did the evening chores and walked to Abraham and Lovina's and shared supper with them, explaining that Rose had gone into town on errands with Daniel.

"We don't mind being second best," Lovina teased as she handed him a platter of sliced roast chicken. Then she frowned. "Are you *allrecht*?"

"*Schur.* This looks *gut.*" He put two slices on his plate.

"That's not enough. Take more."

"I had a big lunch," he said. But he'd eaten only half a sandwich, hiding the other half under his napkin and discarding it when Rose wasn't looking. Now he felt guilty for not telling the truth as well as for wasting food.

As soon as supper was over he went into the barn with Abraham to help him with his evening chores. Abraham glanced at him curiously a couple of times but didn't ask questions like his *fraa.* That was what Luke liked about men, he thought. They didn't ask a lot of questions.

The two of them worked companionably and then headed inside the house. Lovina asked him if he wanted something to drink, but he told her he was tired and going to go to bed early. Another untruth, he chided himself. He went up to his room but he wasn't tired and even when he tried, he couldn't fall asleep.

With a sigh he punched his pillow, turned on his side, and watched the moon rise through his window. Rose would be herself tomorrow, he told himself. She wasn't the type to be cross and act like she had today.

He hoped.

He was wrong. Rose barely spoke to him and avoided him as much as she could. It might have been warm and sunny outside but here in the kitchen the air was a little chilly.

She even used Daniel rather than talk to him directly.

"Daniel, ask Luke if he wants iced tea or coffee with lunch." Or "Daniel, tell Luke what we did in town" when Luke asked if they'd enjoyed the day before.

Bless the little boy. He chattered away about how they'd visited shops and *Mamm* had bought "faberk" to make him clothes for *schul.* He'd gotten new shoes and he wasn't to wear them until *schul* started. Oh, and his favorite part of the day had been eating at McDonald's.

"I had a Happy Meal!" he told Luke.

Lunch at this house not only wasn't happy, it was tense and something Luke wished he could avoid. Supper wasn't any easier. By then Luke had had enough. He didn't make an excuse to go back to work as he'd done at lunch and this time lingered at the table. But instead of doing the dishes Rose went upstairs to bathe Daniel and put him to bed.

The kitchen clock ticked loudly as he waited for her to return. Finally, he washed the dishes, went out to feed and water the horses, then went back to the house.

Rose had turned off the kitchen light. The downstairs was dark.

Frustrated, he stood there in the yard. Who knew the woman would shut him out this way? How was he to explain anything if she wouldn't talk to him?

He left, refusing to glance up at her window to see if the light was on in her room. Well, he didn't glance up more than twice as he left the driveway and walked to his cousin's house, where he spent a nearly sleepless night.

The sun hadn't come up yet the next

morning when he let himself back into the house. They were going to talk. He filled the percolator, set it on the stove, and started breakfast. The scrambled eggs turned out a little overcooked and he almost burned the cinnamon rolls he found in the bread box and tried to warm in the oven. But it was the thought that counted, right?

He looked up when he heard a creak on the stairs.

"I thought I smelled coffee," Rose said as she walked slowly into the room. "What are you doing here so early?" Her gaze slid past him. "And cooking?"

"I wanted to talk to you."

She poured a cup of coffee and sat at the table. Her cheeks were pale and Luke saw lavender shadows beneath her eyes. He wondered if she'd had as much trouble sleeping as he had.

He sat at the table and took a deep breath. "I didn't tell you the truth when you asked about that business card yesterday."

"I know. You're just like Daniel. Neither of you can look me in the eye when you're not telling the truth."

He winced. "Then you should know that's the first time I haven't been truthful with you."

She shrugged. "I wouldn't say that. There

may have been times I just didn't notice."

"Well, I haven't told you any lies before now but by not telling you something it's kind of telling a lie." He took a sip of his coffee to ease a suddenly dry mouth. "You know I came here to help Abraham and Lovina after their accident. I decided I liked Lancaster County and wanted to stay. So I started looking around for a farm."

"And saw mine."

He nodded. "When I first came here to help Abraham there weren't any Amish farms on the market. So I went to see a realtor — the one you saw stop here — thinking I could buy an *Englisch* one near the community. The realtor said she'd talked to Lillian about listing yours and Lillian said no. Then one day at church Lillian and I got to talking. She wanted you to come back and had the idea I could help you. I hadn't found a farm to buy and needed work if I was going to stay in the county. It seemed like a *gut* idea."

"And you just happened to fall in love with me."

His heart sank. He prayed she hadn't hardened her heart against him. "I did," he said. "I did," he repeated firmly when tears filled her eyes and she shook her head. "I remember you once told me it took Sam just one look to know you were the one —"

She stood so suddenly her chair fell backward. "Don't you dare talk about Sam!"

"*Allrecht,* I'm sorry. But it's true. I knew you were the one God set aside for me. And I loved that funny little *sohn* of yours at the same time."

He stood and picked up her chair. "Please, Rose, sit."

"I can't." She shook her head and paced the room. "I don't feel like I know you. I can't trust you."

He stood there, suddenly feeling as drained as an old man. "Don't say such things, Rose. You don't really believe them."

She twisted her hands. "I don't know what to believe." She closed her eyes, then opened them. "I feel like I don't know you. How am I supposed to trust you when you haven't been honest with me?"

"I have been. About everything important. This doesn't have to change anything."

"It does," she said slowly. "How can I think about marrying you when I'll always wonder if you just wanted me so you could have the farm?"

She threw out her hands to ward him off when he stepped toward her. "I don't want to talk to you. I need to think. We'll just —

you do your work and — and we'll go back to the way it was before you asked me to marry you."

Turning, she ran from him up the stairs. Defeated, he sank into a chair.

THIRTY

Lillian showed up just before lunch. Rose wasn't surprised. It was "that twin thing" as Sam had always called it.

"You look awful," she told Rose as they settled in rocking chairs on the back porch and watched their *sohns* play in the back-yard.

"Gee, *danki.*" She studied her *schwesch-der.* Each time she saw Lillian it became more evident that there were *zwillingbopplin* growing under her apron. The pallor and exhaustion that had concerned Rose in the early months of Lillian's pregnancy had faded. Now she glowed and looked like the strong *mudder* she had always been.

Luke came in from the fields and stepped onto the porch. He said hello to Lillian and asked if he could get the two of them something to drink while he got one.

"A glass of tea would be nice," Lillian said. "It's warm out here today even with the breeze."

"Rose?"

She shook her head and kept her eyes on the *kinner*. "Nothing for me, *danki*."

He came out a few minutes later with two tall plastic glasses filled with ice and tea and two cups of Kool-Aid for Daniel and John. Lillian invited him to sit but he shook his head.

"Storm's coming in this afternoon," he told her and took his glass with him back to the fields.

"So that's what's wrong," Lillian said as she sipped her tea.

"What else would it be when a man is around," Rose muttered darkly.

"It's not like you to talk that way." Now Lillian studied her.

"You were so wrong about him."

"Luke? I don't see how. Look how hard he's working out there."

"Well, he fooled both of us." She bit her lip and forced back tears as she remembered how it had felt to find out he wasn't the man she'd thought he was. "Luke just wanted me so he could get the farm."

Lillian practically goggled at her. "Where on earth did you get an idea like that?"

Rose told her the whole sorry story. Lillian listened intently but when Rose finished she was surprised to see that her *schwesch-der* didn't look angry. Instead she looked thoughtful.

"So what you're saying is you think that he looked at the farm and wanted it before he came to work for you."

"Ya."

"He did ask me about the farm. But that's not why he asked you to marry him," Lillian told her firmly. "Anyone with eyes can see how he feels about you. How you feel about him."

"You see what you want to see. You've always been the one with the romantic heart. Not everyone's as lucky as you to get a man like Amos."

"You did with Sam," Lillian pointed out.

Rose sighed. "*Ya.* So I've had the man God set aside for me."

"So now you think He only had one? You don't believe you get a second chance at love?" Lillian shook her head. "How do you explain the women who've found a second *mann*? I could name a dozen. Like —"

"Don't!" Rose held up her hand. "I know their names. But that doesn't mean everyone gets a second *mann*. And it doesn't mean that Luke is right for me. He wasn't truthful with me."

She got up to pace. "Now what do I do? I

can't run the farm myself. I have to see him every day, work with him."

"Ya."

Rose spun around. Lillian wore a thoughtful expression.

"What? You thought of a way I won't have to?"

"Nee. I'm thinking this means you have to work it out. Isn't that what this community is all about? We work things out. Think about why we use buggies."

"Buggies?" She stared at her *schweschder.* "What have buggies got to do with this?"

Lillian smiled. "You know every so often an Amish community considers allowing cars. But the best reason for not doing that isn't just that it keeps us from falling into the trap of coveting what our neighbor has — what the *Englisch* call 'keeping up with the Joneses.' It's that it keeps us closer to home. A horse can only travel so far."

Rose rolled her eyes.

"We don't have church in each others' homes just because of persecution back in our home country," Lillian went on. "If we do something as sacred as worship together in our own homes, how can we fight with one another?" Lillian held out her glass. "May I have more tea?"

"Getting a little dry from the sermon?"

Rose teased. But she nodded. *"Schur."* She went inside, filled the glass with ice and tea, and brought it out to her.

"I wonder if you're not trying to come up with reasons to keep yourself apart from Luke because you feel you don't deserve happiness," Lillian said quietly.

"That's absurd."

"Is it? You didn't think Luke would want you because you couldn't have *kinner*. But it didn't matter to him. Are you now finding some other reason to hold yourself back from him? It's easier, isn't it, not to risk your heart again?"

"It hurt so much when Sam died," Rose whispered. She wrapped her arms around her body. "I'm not *schur* I could have gotten through it without Daniel. I had to get up every day, had to drag myself out of bed and try to keep things normal as much as I could for him. And one day I realized that it's impossible to be around Daniel and not be happy."

Lillian nodded and smiled. "That's why *kinner* are such a gift from God." She sighed. "Well, I'm not *schur* I'm going to be able to get myself out of this chair since I've sat so long. But these two gifts" — she patted her belly — "and two glasses of tea are making a trip to the bathroom necessary before I go home."

Rose stood and held out her hands. "Let me help haul you up."

"Maybe I need more help than that." Lillian's glance slid to Luke in the fields.

"I can get you up." Rose tugged and Lillian groaned but they got her out of the chair. They stood there, laughing like *kinner.*

"*Mamm,* what's so funny?" John wanted to know.

"Your *Aenti* Rose had to help me out of the chair," Lillian told him as she wiped a tear from her eye. "I'm getting so fat."

"I thought you were having *zwilling*—" Daniel stumbled over the word. "You know, two *boppli.*"

"She is," Rose said with a chuckle. "*Aenti* Lillian's not fat."

"She's both," Lillian muttered.

Rose wasn't about to tell her that she waddled a bit as she walked into the house to use the bathroom.

When she returned she had her purse in hand and a mischievous glint in her eyes. "Daniel, would you like to come have lunch with John at our house?"

Rose opened her mouth but Daniel was already jumping up and down and shouting *"Ya!"*

"Lillian!" she hissed. They'd always quietly

asked each other if something was *allrecht* first. Now if she said *nee,* it would just result in a very unhappy Daniel.

"*Gut.* Then we'll bring him back later," Lillian said cheerfully. "Daniel, say goodbye to your *mamm.*"

"I know what you're doing," she told her *schweschder* as the boys raced away.

Lillian just grinned. "Have a nice lunch. The two of you."

Rose went into the house and looked into the refrigerator as she thought about what she'd fix for lunch. Maybe if she was lucky Luke wouldn't come inside.

The back door opened minutes later. Luke walked in bold as day.

"Would you mind if I borrowed the buggy and went into town on an errand?"

She stood there, a plate of sliced ham in her hand. "Er, *nee.*"

"*Gut.* I'll be on my way then." He went out and shut the door, leaving Rose to stare after him.

Well, she thought, *so much for worrying that I'll have to sit here having lunch with him.*

She'd enjoy telling her matchmaking *schweschder* her plan to throw them together hadn't worked.

Luke almost let the door slam. But he

wasn't going to let her know that she'd hurt his feelings when she'd looked relieved he said he was going to town. It almost made him turn back around and say, "Oh, after I have lunch."

Well, if she thought he was giving up she'd soon find out otherwise. He hitched Star to the buggy and set off. Rose had been upset at finding out that he'd wanted to buy the farm. He didn't think she'd be upset when she found out the other thing he hadn't told her.

Rose was upset with him but she hadn't told him to get lost. Maybe it was unfair of him but she needed him on the farm. She couldn't ask family or friends to help — there was too much work, and everyone would be helping anyway at some point when they harvested. She could hire someone else but so far she hadn't thought of that. And he wasn't going to offer to leave. So his job was safe at least until harvest and that was still months away. His future as her *mann* might be in question but he wasn't giving up yet.

Lillian had been at the house today and treated him with her usual courtesy so she hadn't sided with Rose. He'd glanced over more than a few times from the fields and noticed the two of them sitting on the back porch having quite an intense discussion while their *kinner* played in the backyard. He had no idea what they discussed, of course, but his glance had met Lillian's and she hadn't been unfriendly when he'd walked over to get a drink and offered to get her one. When she took Daniel home with her, he wondered if she was giving him the opportunity to have time alone with Rose. He had fond memories of the first time Lillian had done that and he'd taken Rose out for supper to a nice restaurant. That had been a wonderful evening.

He sighed loudly enough to have Star turn her head and glance at him.

"I changed her mind about me once," he told Star. "I can do it again."

Star turned her attention back to the road and Luke used the time to think about how to win Rose back. His *mudder* had often commented on his determination — well, she'd called it stubbornness — but he considered it a positive character trait. Farmers had to have a lot of determination, and if he wanted Rose to be his life partner, he was going to have to find a way to convince her again he was the *mann* for her.

He passed by the bishop's house on the way to town and was grateful the man and his *fraa* weren't sitting on the porch because he didn't want to feel compelled to stop to chat like he had the other day.

A glance at the next farm had Luke frowning. Naiman was working out in the fields. That was one person who would be very happy to hear he and Rose were not getting along right now. Well, Luke was determined Naiman was never going to get a chance with Rose.

The roads in town were busy today. The nice weather had brought out the tourists and they clogged the sidewalks as they went into shops and restaurants. Luke remembered how the last time he'd been in town he'd bought Rose flowers and Daniel a present.

And he'd bought celery seeds for Rose to plant in her kitchen garden for their wedding. Yet there'd been trouble springing up between them before those seeds even had a chance to sprout.

He forced the thought away and looked for parking in the bank lot. Inside, the customer-service representative frowned over his transaction and called the manager, who came out to have a quiet but worried discussion with him. Did he really want a cashier's check withdrawing all his savings? The manager said it wasn't his business but he wanted to make sure that Luke wasn't being taken advantage of the way some of his other Amish customers had been.

Luke told the man he appreciated his concern but all was well and soon had the check in hand. He thought about again picking up some flowers for Rose at the nearby florist and decided she'd think he was trying to cozy up to her. Well, he could buy Daniel a book from the bookstore. He wasn't about to let the temporary tension between Rose and himself keep him from his relationship with the boy. He spent a long time in the shop looking for just the right book that would interest Daniel.

And then his stomach reminded him he hadn't had lunch. He pulled into the McDonald's Rose had taken Daniel to and thought it was too bad that buying a Happy Meal wouldn't brighten his mood as well as it had Daniel's. The boy had been positively giddy telling him about it that evening.

He ordered his food and ate it on the way home. Star knew the route well and needed little direction as Luke munched on his burger and french fries.

As he neared Lillian's house he wondered if she'd taken Daniel home yet. He decided to stop and see if he could save her a trip. *Allrecht,* so he had an ulterior motive. It wouldn't hurt to see if she could give him some help figuring out how to make Rose forgive him. Or maybe he was assuming too much — that because she hadn't been unfriendly to him earlier she was on his side. After all, Rose was her *schweschder* and as a twin, closer than most.

Lillian smiled at him when he knocked at the back door and walked into the kitchen. She was alone and sitting at the table chopping vegetables.

"Can we talk?"

"*Schur.* Have a seat. Want something to drink?"

"*Nee.* Just had lunch." He glanced around. "Did you take Daniel home already?"

"*Nee,* he's upstairs playing with John. So, what's on your mind? As if I didn't know." Her mouth quirked up in a smile.

"Rose told you." It wasn't a question — it was a statement of fact. He knew they told each other just about everything.

She nodded. "Why didn't you tell her?"

He swallowed hard. "I thought about it but when I realized how I felt about her it got tricky for me. I guess I thought she might think I was interested in her because of what she had. I got the impression pretty quickly that Naiman thought so when I met him."

"Oh, Naiman." Lillian shook her head as she slid chopped carrots into a bowl. "He's always wanted Rose. But once she met Sam he had no chance. And when she came back . . . well, she still had no interest in him." She looked at him directly. "I could see her looking in your direction before she even realized it. I'll tell you right now that after I met you when you came here to help Abraham and I got to know you, I started wondering if you could help her out with the farm. Maybe be more than a help."

She set her knife down on the cutting board, and her eyes were cool. "If I'd had a drop of concern that you weren't *gut* for her, you wouldn't have stepped onto the farm."

Luke had heard of *mudders* being tigers when they needed to protect their young. And Rose had told him Lillian always thought of herself as not just the oldest and in charge but a little bit of a *mudder* as well, especially since Sam had died.

"I love Rose and I'd never do anything to hurt her or Daniel," he said quietly.

She sighed. "Well, she has been hurt, but I don't think it's all your fault. Some widows need more time to heal, and I think — *nee,* I know — that she felt she needed more time before she married again. And she hasn't known you all that long."

"She said she didn't know Sam all that long —" he began.

"True. But she was a *maedel* then. Love and life are so much simpler when we're young, aren't they? But she's lost a *mann* and has a *sohn* to think about now. She has to protect him and the farm. It's Daniel's legacy."

She looked up as she heard something fall on the floor over their head. Getting to her feet, she walked over to the stairs. "Do I need to come up there?" she called up.

Luke grinned. He could remember his own *mudder* saying much the same when he and his *bruders* played in their room.

"Nee, Mamm!" John called down. "We're being *gut.*"

"Do you want me to go up?"

She shook her head and sat. "That sounded like a book." She resumed chopping. "So how are you going to fix this?"

He knew she meant his dilemma with Rose. "I think I know how to show her I want her for herself and not the farm. Rose has told me the two of you have a special communication as twins. So I'm not *schur* if I should tell you before I have a chance to talk to her."

She laughed. *"Allrecht."*

He rose. "I thought I'd stop and save you a trip taking Daniel home. But if you don't mind, I'll come back for him later after I talk to Rose."

"Knowing Rose that might take a while." She smiled. "Tell her he's welcome to spend the night."

Luke left her and drove home. As he pulled into the driveway he saw a bright red cardinal sitting on the fence post. Funny, he hadn't seen it for a while.

When he walked into the kitchen, he found Rose sitting at the table writing a letter. She stopped and looked at him coolly as he entered. He ignored the look and held out his hand. "We need to talk. Come outside with me."

She ignored his hand but walked out onto the back porch with him and sat in one of the rocking chairs.

Luke took a moment and looked out at the fields. "I'm sorry that my not telling you I was interested in the farm caused a misunderstanding between us. But I have something for you."

He pulled out the cashier's check and handed it to her. "I didn't tell you about this when I asked you to marry me. Maybe I was holding back a little because someone I dated in Ohio was a little too interested in what I had — just as you think I was about this farm. When we marry this is going into a joint account with both of our names. Think of what we can do here with it."

She took the check from him and her eyes widened as she stared at it. "Where did you get —"

"If we'd grown up in the same community, you would know that my family has a very big farm and several successful businesses," he told her. "Since only one *sohn* or *dochder* would take over the farm, my parents have been generous with each of us. And I've worked since I was out of *schul.*"

He paused. "So, Rose, *lieb,* will you forgive me and marry me and let me give you myself and all that I have? I can give you all that, but please don't tell me you need more time. Please tell me we'll get married after the coming harvest and not the next one."

"Ya," she said and tears ran down her cheeks. "We'll be married after the coming harvest."

He smiled as he leaned over and kissed her.

A fluttering noise made them pull apart. A cardinal winged away from them. They watched it as it flew out of sight.

GLOSSARY

ab im kop — off in the head; crazy
ach — oh
allrecht — all right
boppli — baby
bruder — brother
daed — dad
danki — thank you
dat — father
dawdi haus — a small home added to or near the main house into which the farmer moves after passing the farm and main house to one of his children
Der hochmut kummt vor dem fall. — "Pride goeth before the fall."
Deitsch — Pennsylvania German
dippy eggs — over-easy eggs
dochder —daughter
eck — the corner of the wedding table where the newly married couple sits
eldres —parents
Englisch — what the Amish call a non-

427

Amish person

fraa — wife

grossdaadi —grandfather

grossdochder —granddaughter

grosseldres —grandparents

grosskinner — grandchildren

grossmudder —grandmother

grosssohn — grandson

guder mariye — good morning

gut — good

gut-n-owed — good evening

haus — house

hochmut — pride

hungerich — hungry

kapp — prayer covering or cap worn by girls and women

kind, kinner — child, children

kumm — come

lieb — love; term of endearment

liebschen — dearest or dear one

maedel — young single woman

mamm — mom

mann — husband

mudder — mother

nacht — night

nee — no

newehocker — wedding attendant

onkel — uncle

Ordnung — The rules of the Amish, both written and unwritten. Certain behaviors have been expected within the Amish community for many, many years. These rules vary from community to community, but the most common are to have no electricity in the home, to not own or drive an automobile, and to dress a certain way.

Redding up — cleaning up

roasht — a stuffing or dressing side dish

rumschpringe — time period when teen-agers are allowed to experience the *Englisch* world while deciding if they should join the church

schul — school

schur — sure

schweschder — sister

sohn — son

verboten — forbidden; not done

wilkumm — welcome

wunderbaar — wonderful

ya — yes

zwillingbopplin — twins

DISCUSSION QUESTIONS

Spoiler alert: Please don't read before completing the book as the questions contain spoilers!

1. What does *home* mean to you? Is there one place that means home the most to you?

2. Rose and Lillian are twins and share a special bond. Are you a twin or know someone who is? Has that person told you that she shares a special bond with her twin?

3. The Amish believe God sets aside marriage partners for them. Do you believe this? Rose's husband died, and she is doubtful that God has a second one set aside for her. What do you think? Do you believe in love at first sight?

4. Luke and Rose both have secrets. What

are they? Which secret did you think was going to cause the biggest problem for their relationship?

5. Who shares the secret first?

6. Do you think Rose overreacted when she heard Luke's secret? Why or why not?

7. Rose will pass the farm on to Daniel one day. What material thing or spiritual quality do you hope to pass on to your children, if you have them?

8. Many people idealize the Amish way of life — particularly living on/owning a farm. Would you want to try the Amish life? Why or why not?

9. A cardinal appears in many scenes in the book. What do you think he represents? Why?

10. Have you ever felt comforted by something you felt is a symbol of someone you loved who passed on?

11. It's hard for Rose to move on to a new stage in her life. If you've known someone

who was a widow or widower, what words did you use to offer comfort?

12. Do you believe in happy endings? Why or why not?

ABOUT THE AUTHOR

Barbara Cameron is a gifted storyteller and the author of many bestselling Amish novels.

Twice Blessed, Barbara's two-novella collection, won the 2016 Christian Retailing's Best award in the Amish Fiction category. Two of her other novellas were finalists for the American Christian Fiction Writers (ACFW) awards. She is the first winner of the Romance Writers of America (RWA) Golden Heart Award. Three of her fiction stories were made into HBO/Cinemax movies.

Although Barbara is best known for her romantic and Amish fiction titles, she is also a prolific nonfiction author of titles including *101 Ways to Save Money on Your Wedding* and two editions of *The Everything Wedding Budget Book.*

Barbara is a former high school teacher and has also taught workshops and creative writing classes at national writing conferences, as well as locally. She currently teaches English and business communication classes as an adjunct instructor for the online campus of a major university.

Barbara enjoys spending time with her family and her three "nutty" Chihuahuas. She lives in Jacksonville, Florida. Visit her website at barbaracameron.com.

The employees of Thorndike Press hope you have enjoyed this Large Print book. All our Thorndike, Wheeler, and Kennebec Large Print titles are designed for easy reading, and all our books are made to last. Other Thorndike Press Large Print books are available at your library, through selected bookstores, or directly from us.

For information about titles, please call:
(800) 223-1244

or visit our website at:
gale.com/thorndike

To share your comments, please write:
Publisher
Thorndike Press
10 Water St., Suite 310
Waterville, ME 04901